Mrs. D

Foxcroft Davis

Alpha Editions

This edition published in 2023

ISBN : 9789357953030

Design and Setting By
Alpha Editions
www.alphaedis.com
Email - info@alphaedis.com

Contents

Chapter One

Time was, not so long ago, when Washington had some primitive aspects. This was when the city was merely a political capital and society was made up of the high government officials, the diplomatic corps, the army and navy, and senators were very great personages and even the now despised members of the House of Representatives had a place on the social chess-board. This was before the influx of recently acquired wealth and the building of splendid mansions wherein to house the retired trade. There were few private ball-rooms, and certain subscription dances were reckoned to be very smart. To these dances young ladies were not ashamed to wear muslin gowns, nor to go in the tram, carrying with them a contrivance known as a "party-bag," which held their white slippers, fans, and gloves.

The young ladies were just as beautiful then as now, as certainly Captain Reginald Darrell and Captain Hugh Pelham, officers of the 178th Foot Regiment, then stationed in India, thought one night as they watched from the street those charming Washington girls thronging to the big Charity Ball of the season. It was a cold, clear January night, and the two young officers, cousins and chums, who had wandered idly from their hotel, watched with profound interest this phase of an American ball.

The event being a great Charity Ball, tickets were on sale at all the hotels. Pelham and Darrell had invested in a couple of tickets, and were now standing outside the building, doubting whether after all they should go in or not. They had heard and read much of American splendor, and this had come nearly deterring them from coming to America at all, considering their small allowance and modest pay in a foot regiment. Both of them, it was true, were the grandsons of a peer, but a peer almost as poor as Lazarus. Each had the enormous advantage of good birth, good breeding, and the urgent necessity of making his own way in the world. There was, it is true, some shadowy expectation of a fortune which Darrell might inherit as heir-at-law, and Pelham was next heir after Darrell. But the chance was so remote that the only present benefit they had out of it was mess-table joking, and a declaration on Darrell's part that his love-affairs were always cruelly interfered with by Pelham. In fact, Pelham's interference—that is to say, influence—with Darrell in every way was complete, Darrell being simple, brave, polite, handsome, and commonplace, while Pelham was short, dark, rather homely, of uncommon powers of mind and character. Pelham was much favored by women, whom he treated with remarkable gentleness and courtesy, but for whom he had felt a secret indifference.

Darrell, on the contrary, was devoted to the whole sex, their petted and curled darling. He thought a woman the object of the highest consequence,—that is to say, next to sport, which he regarded as something sacred, ranking with Church and State. He always had a dozen love-affairs on hand, and like the man in the old song, "He loved the ladies, every one." In Darrell's eyes, Pelham's only fault was that he considered these love-affairs legitimate subjects of chaffing and laughing, while Darrell took them all with perfect seriousness.

It was Pelham who, in his desire to see the world, so far as his narrow purse would permit, had induced Darrell to plunge, so to speak, to the extent of going to India by way of the United States and spending three weeks in Washington, relying upon economy for the next five years when they would be with their regiment in India in the Punjaub.

They were somewhat surprised, however, to find that in the capital of the richest country in the world there was no great amount of splendor in those days, but rather a modest standard of living for a capital. In particular it appeared to them this evening that the splendor of the ball was conspicuous by its absence. It must be premised, however, that they had not then seen the supper, which was truly regal. Exteriorly, they could not but compare the scene with the real magnificence of such an occasion in London during the season, with the superb coaches magnificently horsed, the gorgeous-liveried footmen, the army of servants lining the stairways and the approaches, and the universal elegance which pervades these balls of the summer nights given under the sky of London. At the Washington ball, however, they saw only a moderate number of private carriages, ordinary in every way, a vast number of shabby old cabs,—known then as "hacks,"—gentlemen arriving on foot, and even young ladies, their ball-dresses discreetly covered with large cloaks, tripping along the streets, with their escorts of father or brother carrying a party-bag. This, remember, was before the Deluge, that is to say at least fifteen years ago.

The building in which the ball was held was large and plain, both inside and out, but blazing with lights. The street itself had long since been deserted by fashion. The negroes, never absent from a spectacle in Washington, with their white teeth shining in the wintry moonlight lined the sidewalk. A few white persons loitered under the gas-lamp, watching the long line of carriages discharging their inmates at the big, wide-open door, from whence the strains of the Marine Band floated out into the cold, still night.

The two young Englishmen entered the street and stood watching the scene with interest, leaning against the tall iron railings of the old-fashioned quarter. Pelham and Darrell noticed near them, also leaning against the iron railings, a man of about middle age, with a sort of leonine beauty and handsomely dressed, though far too showily. His fur-lined greatcoat brought out the clean-cut outlines of his clean-shaven face, his iron-gray hair, and straight, narrow brows over eyes of singular eloquence. Both young officers observed him, for it was difficult at any time to look once at James Clavering without looking at him twice.

In the circle of light made by two flashing gas-lamps in the front entrance, suddenly appeared a young girl leaning on the arm of an elderly gentleman. At the same instant the eyes of Pelham and Darrell and Clavering fell upon her, and each thought her the most beautiful woman that he had ever seen— which was, however, a very great mistake. Elizabeth Brandon had, it is true, hair of satin blackness and skin of milky whiteness, and eyes that reminded one of a summer night, so soft, so dark with occasional flashes of starlike brilliancy, and a figure as slight and graceful as a lily-stalk. Other women have as much beauty of feature as Elizabeth Brandon, but she had that which is beauty itself, the power to charm at a glance. She was not really as handsome as her father, General Brandon, on whose arm she leaned, and who carried her party-bag.

ill6

"'OH, PAPA!' SHE SAID, 'SAVE MY LITTLE PEARL HEART.'"

Both Pelham and Darrell saw at a glance that General Brandon was a military man. And Clavering recognized him as the Captain Brandon he had known twenty-five years before at a post in Texas, where Clavering was at the time a sutler. He had heard that, at the breaking out of the Civil War, Captain Brandon, who was a Southern man, had resigned and had become a brigadier-general in the Confederate Army. Since the war, Brandon had disappeared in the great, black gulf that opened where once stood a government which called itself the Confederate States of America. But Clavering gave no thought to this, as under the cover of darkness he surveyed the charming girl who clung to General Brandon's arm. The two stood directly in front of Pelham and Darrell, who bestowed upon Elizabeth those glances of respectful admiration which is the homage due to beauty.

"My dear," said General Brandon, in a peculiarly musical voice, to his daughter, "I think we had better wait here until Mrs. Luttrell's carriage arrives. It is in line down the street, but will not be here for five minutes or more."

Darrell and Pelham moved a little aside so that the young lady and her father might be somewhat out of the way of the passing throng. General Brandon recognized this civility by lifting his hat punctiliously to each, which courtesy both of them returned. At the same moment, Elizabeth lifting her hand to her white throat, her sleeve caught in a slender gold chain around her neck and a sudden movement broke it.

"Oh, papa!" she said, "save my little pearl heart. I would not lose it for the world."

General Brandon immediately looked down on the wet sidewalk for the trinket, a search in which he was joined by both Pelham and Darrell. Clavering, who was in the shadow, did not move, but his eyes followed every movement of the group. Elizabeth unconsciously brushed against him. There was some mud on his boots, and it became transferred to her white muslin skirts, which she let fall in the anxiety of her loss. The trinket, it would seem, had fallen at their very feet, but it was not to be found. Elizabeth's eyes filled with tears, and she mourned for her little pearl heart as if it had been a lost child.

"It is of no real value," she said to Pelham, raising her soft, dark eyes to his, "but I would not have lost it for anything."

Both Pelham and Darrell were keen-eyed and searched diligently for the lost trinket, but unavailingly. Pelham, usually the most unimpressed of men where women and their fallals were concerned, felt that he would have given a month's pay to have found the little ornament and thereby dry the tears that glistened on Elizabeth's long, black lashes; but it was soon obvious that there was no finding her lost treasure. Its disappearance, though mysterious, was instant and complete.

General Brandon said in his slow, suave voice: "My dear child, all our efforts are vain. I think your little treasure must have been stolen by an unseen hand at the instant you dropped it; but you, gentlemen," he said, turning to Pelham and Darrell, "have been most kind, and I beg to introduce myself to you. I am General Brandon of Virginia, formerly of the United States Army and lately of the Confederate Army. Here is my card, and I shall be most pleased to see you at my house."

Pelham and Darrell were nearly knocked down by this unexpected invitation. They did not know that a Virginian never loses the habit of asking Thomas, Richard, and Henry to call upon him, on the slightest provocation and often without any provocation at all. But they recognized in a moment that this handsome and courtly person who went around recklessly inviting street acquaintances to visit his house, was a gentleman of purest rays serene, and being of the same caste themselves, and thereby made free, both of them promptly accepted. Pelham, who was quick of wit where Darrell was slow, introduced himself and his friend, each handing his card.

"Ah!" cried General Brandon, "so you are officers of the British Army. I am more than pleased to meet you. I am, like most persons in my native state, of unmixed English descent, my family being a younger branch of the Suffolk-Brandons; and I also am of the profession of arms. I was in the old army, where I held the rank of major, and afterward, when I followed my state out of the Union, I had the honor of being brigadier-general in the army of the Southern Confederacy. Permit me to introduce you to my daughter." And this General Brandon proceeded to do. Elizabeth bowed and smiled and was not at all taken aback by the suddenness of the acquaintance. Virginians think that all well-bred persons constitute a sort of national and international oligarchy, whereof every member is or ought to be known to every other member.

Pelham and Darrell were perfectly delighted, Darrell at the chance of meeting so beautiful a girl as Elizabeth, and Pelham charmed with the courtesy and innocent simplicity of General Brandon, who, while a man of the world in its best sense, was yet unworldly.

"And may I ask," said the General, "if you are attending the ball to-night?"

"Yes," said Pelham, "we understood it was a Charity Ball, and bought tickets at the hotel; but as we are entire strangers, we were doubtful whether after all it would be judicious for us to show our faces in the ball-room."

"My dear sir," replied General Brandon, earnestly, "do not give yourself the least uneasiness, I beg of you. I myself am not going, and a friend Mrs. Luttrell will chaperon my daughter; but Mrs. Luttrell will likewise chaperon you, and I shall have pleasure in introducing you to any one whom you may desire to meet. My daughter also will do the same."

"With pleasure," said Elizabeth, quickly and sweetly.

"If you will do me the honor to dance with me," said Darrell to Elizabeth, thinking to cut Pelham out.

"I can't compete with Captain Darrell on that ground," said Pelham, quickly, with a certain grimness in his smile, "but if Miss Brandon will only condescend to notice me in the ball-room, I shall feel that I am well established."

Elizabeth looked at Pelham closely. He was not at all handsome, but he was far from insignificant, and he had one of those beautifully modulated English voices and a look and a smile which were extremely winning to women, children, and lost dogs. Darrell on the contrary was as handsome as a dream, with the unmistakable blond, clean, Anglo-Saxon beauty.

By this time, among the slow procession of carriages, ever moving, a big, old-fashioned landeau, with a pair of long-tailed horses to it and a colored coachman and footman, halted directly in front of them. A lady with very dark eyes and very white hair and a voice sweet, but with a singular carrying quality which could make itself heard over all the clatter of the street, called out:—

"My dear General Brandon, I am mortified to death almost. I meant to bring Elizabeth to the ball with me, but I declare I forgot all about it until it was too late, and my nephew has been scolding me about it ever since I left home. Richard, go and fetch Elizabeth now."

The carriage door opened, and Richard Baskerville got out. He was a little better looking than Pelham, though not half so good looking as Darrell; but he belonged in the category of Pelham,—that class of men who can attract notice and admiration without the aid of good looks. He advanced and, bowing to General Brandon, offered his arm to Elizabeth, saying with the air of old acquaintanceship, "My aunt has really behaved shockingly to you, and I am ashamed of her."

"Stop, Richard," said General Brandon, detaining him. "I wish to present to you two friends of mine." General Brandon had never laid eyes on Darrell or Pelham in his life until five minutes before; but Richard Baskerville, who understood General Brandon thoroughly, would not have been the least surprised if he had introduced a bootblack who had obliged him and was therefore a valued friend. "May I introduce you to Captain Pelham of the 178th Foot, and Captain Darrell of the same regiment,—British officers? I need say no more."

Baskerville politely shook hands with both Pelham and Darrell, who discerned in him one of the most agreeable traits of American character, cordiality to strangers—a cordiality which prevails in all American society among the retired tradespeople, the newly rich.

"And," continued General Brandon, "they are both going to the ball. I intrust them to Mrs. Luttrell to make acquaintances among the young ladies, and to you for the same duties among the gentlemen."

Then Mrs. Luttrell's penetrating voice was heard calling to General Brandon, "Come here this minute, General Brandon." And when he was about halfway across the muddy street to her carriage, she inquired, in a tone perfectly audible to both Pelham and Darrell, "Who are those two nice-looking men standing with Elizabeth?"

"English officers," replied General Brandon. "I hope you find yourself very well this evening."

"Bring them here this instant. I shall take them to the ball with me!" was Mrs. Luttrell's reply to this information—Mrs. Luttrell being a pirate and freebooter of the worst description whenever desirable men were discerned.

"Just what I was about to ask you, but as usual you anticipate everything."

Pelham, Darrell, and Baskerville, who were looking gravely at each other, exchanged glances, which were equivalent to winks, and Baskerville said:—

"You might as well give in to my aunt. She is a very determined woman, but she will do a good part by you with the young ladies. I need not say I shall be most happy to introduce you to any one of my acquaintances you may wish to know. Come, Miss Brandon." He gave Elizabeth his arm and escorted her, with Pelham and Darrell following, across the street to where Mrs. Luttrell's big coach, with the lamps flowing out in the darkness, had its place in the line of carriages.

Elizabeth had felt from the beginning the strange influence of the unknown man in the shadow, whose eyes had been fixed upon her from the moment of their arrival. She had glanced back half a dozen times at his tall and imposing figure and had been acutely conscious of his keen observation. She felt it still as she walked away from him.

Elizabeth felt as if in a dream. She was distressed and even superstitious about the loss of her little ornament. It not only distressed her, but had given her a presentiment of evil, and she was vaguely conscious of some malign influence near her and likewise of the admiration and incipient tenderness which Darrell and Pelham felt towards her, of her father's deep and protecting love, of being the object of solicitude to Mrs. Luttrell and Baskerville. She was at that moment surrounded by admiration and love and care, but she was haunted by a sudden sense of evil close to her. She stepped silently into the carriage, and took her seat by Mrs. Luttrell's side. General Brandon then presented the two young British officers as if they were his long-lost brothers. Mrs. Luttrell received them, not as if they were her long-lost brothers, but like a perfect woman of the world, born to command, and who, seeing what she wanted, took her own, wherever she found it, as Molière says. And now she said to them: "Please get into the carriage. It holds four very comfortably. I do not care for these miniature broughams and coupés, meant to hold a woman and a poodle. I like a good big carriage, the sort our great-grandfathers had when everybody had fourteen children and generally took seven with them when they went visiting. My carriage holds four, and I could pack six away in it if I chose. I can take you in, General Brandon," she said.

"A thousand thanks, my dear Mrs. Luttrell," replied General Brandon, who did not have at that moment the price of a ticket either at home or in his pocket. "I have no intention of going to the ball since you are so kind as to chaperon my child. Good night."

"Good night."

Baskerville then shut the door. "You needn't ask me to get in. I shall walk down. It is only a step anyhow, but I know your propensities for packing your carriage as full as an omnibus, and I don't believe in encouraging you in your vices."

"The way my nephew talks to me is perfectly shocking," said Mrs. Luttrell, resignedly, to her new-found guests; "but he is the best and dearest fellow in the world."

Pelham and Darrell were more and more delighted at every turn in their adventure. Darrell recognized by instinct and Pelham by his naturally thorough reasoning powers that here they had come across an American lady—no sham Englishwoman, with the sham English manner, sham affectation of speech, and with all the defects of an exact imitation. And each of them felt a strange joy at being so close to Elizabeth Brandon. She sat back in the carriage, and they could see her white breast rising and falling as she threw back her large gray cloak; and the soft beauty of her eyes was visible in the half darkness of the carriage. Elizabeth, who, like most Southern women, was naturally talkative, kept singularly quiet. Her gaze was turned towards the spot where they had just been standing, and she was conscious rather than actually saw the dark brown eyes of the man who had stood just behind her and whose presence near her she had felt without seeing him. But she recovered herself and began to talk with a graceful ease and familiarity at once charming and flattering to the two young Englishmen. Mrs. Luttrell, however, held the centre of the stage, according to her invariable custom, and gave Pelham and Darrell a pretty fair idea of what they would meet at the Charity Ball.

In a few minutes more the carriage reached the door of the hall, where Baskerville was awaiting them, and he escorted them up the stairs. He utilized the time when Mrs. Luttrell and Elizabeth were in the dressing-room, to introduce the two young officers to several of the men best worth knowing in Washington.

As for the ladies, Elizabeth, on removing her cloak, was dismayed to find that her fresh white muslin gown had more than one spot of mud on it, and it took ten minutes of diligent rubbing, washing, and pressing to get it out. She realized that she must have got it from the boots of the man who stood behind her, whose dark and striking face had fixed her attention at first and in whose neighborhood she had felt strangely influenced. And then the loss of her little pearl heart—But the Marine Band was playing loudly a rhythmic waltz, there were partners at the door waiting for her. She had two desirable men, both strangers, whom she might consider her property for that evening. She was young and beautiful, and in a little while all of her unpleasant sensations passed away. She found herself whirling around the room in Darrell's arms. For a wonder, although an Englishman, he knew how to dance, and Elizabeth was intensely susceptible to rhythm and music. She felt when she began to waltz with Darrell, as if she would like to waltz forever with him. He was so strong, so supple, so graceful,—so susceptible, like herself, to that charm of dance music in which two people dancing together are conscious of that sensuous counterpart of real love which makes a man and a woman feel as if they constituted one being with a single heart and a single soul.

Darrell realized the first moment that he held Elizabeth in his arms and floated with her to the languorous waltz music, that he had never really been in love at all before; but, as he frankly confessed to himself, it was all up with him now. He knew not who or what she was, but it could make but little difference to him. He loved her and he knew it. He would have liked not to leave her side once during the evening, and in fact he was near her most of the time and danced with her six times.

Pelham, on the contrary, only sat out a single dance with her, as he was not a dancing man. He too felt a charm about her which he had never known in any other woman. Sitting out dances with young ladies had been a species of torment to him, but not so this time. He thought the charm that Elizabeth exercised over him was that she was the first of all unmarried English-speaking women that he had known who was perfectly and entirely at her ease with an unmarried man. She assumed an attitude openly and yet most delicately flattering towards him. He had known Englishwomen of fascination who were entirely at ease with men, but never flattering; and he had known other women who were very flattering to men, but never at ease with them. Here was a woman who treated him with the frankness she would have shown towards a younger brother, with the confidence she would have shown a respected elder brother, and with the deference she would have shown the greatest Duke in England. Pelham rightly judged that here he had met the true American type. A woman with an ancestry of gentle people, dating back two or three hundred years, and developed in a country where respect for women is so insisted upon as to be professed by those who neither believe in it nor practise it,—as such Elizabeth was to him the most interesting woman he had ever met. He was himself a reading man, and Elizabeth Brandon at twenty had read only a few books, but these were the English classics and they had given her the capacity to talk to a reading man like Pelham. He foresaw that at thirty Elizabeth would have read a great many books, and with the untrammelled association with men of all ages and in the free American atmosphere, her mind, naturally good, would have developed admirably.

As Pelham and Elizabeth sat at the foot of the stairs, a cabinet officer passed them slowly, as they sat under a bower of great palms, with the throbbing music far enough away not to interrupt their talk; and Elizabeth spoke to the cabinet officer. He was an elderly man from the West, manly and even gentlemanly, though not polished. Pelham noticed with what ease Elizabeth spoke to this type of man, the smiling, tactful answers she gave to his pleasant but rather blunt questions. She introduced Pelham promptly to him, accompanying the introduction with a request that he would be very nice to Captain Pelham while he was in Washington; and when the cabinet officer asked her what she wanted him to do for Captain Pelham, she replied promptly:—

"Send him a card to the club."

Pelham was aghast at the boldness of this, and tried to imagine the daughter of a half-pay officer in England asking a cabinet minister to send a card to White's and Brooke's to a chance acquaintance she had just picked up.

Elizabeth continued placidly: "Of course I could get a card through papa. He does not belong to the club,—it is too expensive,—but he knows a great many men in the club. You know he can't afford anything except me; and there are plenty of other men who would send Captain Pelham a card if I asked them, but you happen to be the biggest man I know and that is why I am asking you."

At which the cabinet officer, laughing, said, "Will you be kind enough, Captain Pelham, to give me the name of your hotel?—and I will have a card sent to you to-morrow morning."

"And he has a cousin, Captain Darrell," added Elizabeth, promptly, "and he must have a card, too."

"Certainly," replied the cabinet officer, taking out his note-book and writing down the two names. "His brothers, cousins, and his uncles and all his relations, if you like," and after taking the names down the cabinet officer walked away, laughing. This was an experience that Pelham thought his comrades would doubt when he told it at the mess-table of the 178th Foot.

Pelham spent much more time with Mrs. Luttrell than with Elizabeth, and the two were mutually charmed. Mrs. Luttrell's daring and positive language and her air of command were accompanied with a fascination of smile and voice which was effective even with her snow-white hair and crow's feet around her eyes, still full of light and life. Pelham noticed that she was always surrounded by men, young and old. She treated the young men like patriarchs and the patriarchs like boys.

Baskerville, quiet, rather sedate, and seeking the middle-aged rather than the young, struck Pelham as one of the pleasantest fellows he had ever met. It looked as if this chance incursion of the Charity Ball would reveal more of the real American life to Pelham and Darrell than they might have met in a month of ordinary traveller's advantages. Mrs. Luttrell had already engaged them for a couple of dinners and Baskerville for a club breakfast. Most of the people they met were agreeable, and they noticed that buoyancy of spirit and gayety of heart which a great writer on America, and another writer who was the most patronizing literary snob ever seen in North America, mutually agreed to be characteristic of American society. The ball itself, which was described by the society correspondents as of surpassing brilliancy, hardly reached that mark; but to three persons, Elizabeth Brandon, Pelham, and Darrell, it was an evening of delight, never to be forgotten.

Meanwhile, James Clavering still stood outside in the sharp, starlit night, listening to the bursts of music which came at intervals from the ball-room and watching the great lighted windows. He saw Elizabeth Brandon float past in Darrell's arms, and watched them enviously. His exterior showed that the price of a ball-ticket was nothing to him, but he knew that he had no place then in a ball-room. He had taken no part in searching for the trinket which Elizabeth had dropped, but presently, moving a little, he saw under his heel the crushed fragments of pearls. He had unconsciously ground the little heart under his foot. It gave him a spasm of regret and even of sentiment, and he thought to himself, with an odd smile flitting across his well-cut features, "Suppose some day I should give that girl a diamond heart, five times as big and a thousand times as costly as this. It wouldn't be so strange, after all."

He had stood watching the last stragglers to the ball and searching the windows for a passing glimpse of the beautiful Elizabeth. Meanwhile, outside, General Brandon had returned to the sidewalk. He would have dearly liked to go, himself; but it had been all that he could do to buy a ticket for Elizabeth,—a ticket and seventeen yards of white muslin, which she herself had fashioned with her own fingers into a beautiful gown and had trimmed with her grandmother's old lace.

As General Brandon was moving off, a hand touched his elbow, and James Clavering, who had been standing a little in the background, spoke to him.

"This is General Brandon?" he said.

"Yes," replied General Brandon, looking into the clear-cut face of the man before him, who towered a head above him. "And you, I cannot at this moment call your name."

"It's Clavering. Don't you remember me when I was a sutler at Fort Worth in Texas, and you were a captain of cavalry at the same post?"

A light dawned upon General Brandon. He grasped the ex-sutler's hand as cordially as if he had been an officer of the British Army. "Certainly I do. You knew me before the war." All Virginians divide time into three epochs, before the war, during the war, and after the war. "And a very excellent sutler you were. I recall that you had a good, industrious wife and several promising children. You look prosperous. The world seems to have gone well with you."

"Pretty well," replied Clavering, ignoring the mention of his wife and children. He had a voice of music which added to his other personal advantages. "I hope the same is the case with you?"

The General smiled placidly. "I resigned from the army when my state seceded, and went through four years on the battlefields of Virginia, and I attained the rank of brigadier-general. Then I entered the service of the Khedive of Egypt and served in Egypt for eight years, but you know what has fallen out there. So I have returned to Washington, and through the influence of old army friends I have secured a clerkship in the War Department."

"Pretty hard lines, isn't it?" asked Clavering, looking at General Brandon's seedy greatcoat, and knowing what stupendous changes were involved in the story told so smilingly by the time-worn veteran.

"Scarcely that," answered General Brandon, with the same gentleness of tone and smile. "I have a small house here in rather a good part of the town, and my salary is sufficient for my simple wants and those of my daughter, who has no extravagant tastes. Thanks to my old army friends I am here, and they have met me with extraordinary kindness and good-will and shown me much hospitality. On the whole I think myself decidedly well off, all things considered."

Clavering looked at General Brandon with pity and good-natured contempt. He seemed to Clavering about as guileless and innocent as a boarding-school miss or a college sophomore; and yet he had commanded three thousand fighting men, during four fierce years of a bloody war, and had been relied upon by no less a man than Stonewall Jackson himself. All this Clavering knew, as he knew most of the contemporary history of his own country.

"And that charming young lady," he asked after a moment, "was your daughter?"

"Yes, my only child and as good as she is beautiful. May I ask if Mrs. Clavering is alive? I remember her as a most worthy woman."

"Yes," answered Clavering, shortly. "Now will you come with me to one of the up-town hotels and have a smoke and a drink? In the old days when I was a sutler and you were a captain, I should have known better than to ask you; but I never expected to remain a sutler always. I have made money in the West, and I have ambitions of various sorts. Some day you will hear of me."

"Nothing," said General Brandon, impressively, "should be or is, in this country, out of reach of any man with brains and solid worth." The General himself was an aristocrat from the crown of his head to the sole of his feet, but he never dreamed of it.

"And some education," added Clavering. He knew his man thoroughly. "Brains are the first requisite, and solid worth is all very well. But a man must have some other qualifications. A man must know something beyond the common school of his youth and the bigger common school of his manhood, in order to make a lasting impression on his time. Of course I don't include geniuses in this category, but men of talent only. I have not what I call education, but I have the next best thing to it. I know my own limitations. I have a boy on whom I shall put a twenty-thousand-dollar education, but I am very much afraid that he is a twenty-dollar boy."

General Brandon did not exactly understand this, and Clavering said no more about his boy. They walked off together, and in a little while they were seated in the lobby of an up-town hotel and Clavering was telling the story of his life—or what he chose to tell of it—to General Brandon. It was not an instinctive outpouring of the truth, but as a matter of fact Clavering was rehearsing for the rôle he intended to play in a few years' time,—that of the rich man who has hewn his way through a great forest of difficulties and has triumphed in the end. He was astute enough not to despise men of General Brandon's stamp, simple, quiet, brave, having little knowledge of affairs but perfectly versed in ethics. Clavering in short knew the full value of a gentleman, although he was not one himself.

They sat late, and when the General reached his own door in a tall old house far up town, Elizabeth was just descending from Mrs. Luttrell's carriage, escorted by Richard Baskerville.

"Oh, papa," she said, running up the steps, her white muslin skirts floating behind her, "I have had the most glorious evening." She was quite unaware that the hour of fate had struck for her, and that she had entered the portals of destiny—a new and strange destiny.

Chapter Two

Pelham and Darrell had reckoned upon spending three weeks in Washington, but it became a full month. They were practically adopted by Mrs. Luttrell, and found her large, handsome, old-fashioned house a centre of the best society, where they saw all that was worth seeing in Washington. At their own Embassy they soon became favorites, and it was after a ball there that a revelation came to Pelham. He had seen Elizabeth Brandon every day of their stay in Washington, and every day she had absorbed a little more of his strong, reserved, and silently controlled nature and had gained an inch or two in his reserved, tender, but devoted heart. He discovered that Elizabeth had both goodness and intelligence as well as charm and beauty. She was very young to him,—that is, in his own thirty years he had seen and known, realized and suffered, ten times more than Elizabeth during her twenty years of life. He recognized in her a naturally fine mind and taste for reading, a delightful and subtle power of accommodating herself to the mode and manner of any man she wished to please. How attractive this would make her to the man she loved and married! The thought almost dazzled Pelham's strong and sober brain. He saw that she was a little intoxicated with the new wine of life, her beauty, her grace and popularity; she was quite unburdened with the cares and anxieties of richer girls who wore finer gowns and sighed for the partners who crowded around Elizabeth.

Pelham was not in the least disturbed by the fact that Darrell had fallen violently in love with Elizabeth and proclaimed it to him a dozen times a day. It was Darrell's normal condition to be violently in love with some pretty girl; but frankly admitting that his pay and allowance were not enough for one, much less for two, there was small danger of his actually committing himself, so Pelham thought. Nor did he observe any difference in Elizabeth's acceptance of Darrell's attentions from those of any other man whom she liked—her manner was uniformly flattering and complaisant; in truth, he had very little conception of Elizabeth's feminine power of concealment.

On the night of the ball at the British Embassy, Pelham, on his return to his hotel, sat in his own room, smoking and turning over an important question in his mind, which was "when should he ask Elizabeth Brandon to marry him." He had not much to offer her in a worldly point of view. His own position was good, but no better than hers, and he discovered that General Brandon, who had been to England once or twice, had hobnobbed with persons of higher rank even than the peer of the realm who was grandfather to both Darrell and himself; but Pelham realized with an admiration as deep as his love that Elizabeth was not the woman to marry for either money or position. He was reflecting on what he should say to General Brandon next day, before speaking to Elizabeth, for he had old-fashioned notions as to the rights of fathers. He was wondering, in case Elizabeth accepted him, how General Brandon would take the proposition that she should come out to India and marry him there after the English fashion, and was in doubt whether General Brandon would fall on his neck and embrace him or kick him downstairs.

While he was considering these things, the door opened and Darrell walked in. He threw himself in a chair close to Pelham and, closing his eyes, went into a revery. Pelham looked at him goodhumoredly. No doubt he was dreaming about Elizabeth. He was a handsome fellow, no denying that, and candor, courage, and honesty were writ large all over him. Presently he roused himself, and leaning over towards Pelham, and blushing like a girl, for the first time in his life, he said in a whisper, "She loves me."

Pelham received a shock such as he had never known before. He knew Darrell's sincerity and real modesty too well to doubt him, and his mind took in immediately and quietly the calamity to himself which Darrell's words implied. He sat still, so still that Darrell shook him. "Do you hear, old man? It was all settled to-night at the ball, not two hours ago, behind a big hydrangea in a flower-pot, and you've got to help me out. I am to see the Ambassador to-morrow and ask him to cable for two weeks' additional leave, so we can be married before sailing."

Yes, with Pelham the dream was over, the fairy palace had crumbled. The heavenly music had dissolved in air. The world had suddenly grown bleak and cold and commonplace, but pride and common sense still remained.

"It seems to me," said Pelham, in a quiet voice, after a pause, "that there isn't much left for me to do. You and—Miss Brandon have agreed, and the Ambassador can no doubt get you two weeks more leave—" Pelham stopped with a choking in his throat which he had never felt before in all his life.

"But why don't you congratulate me?" cried Darrell. They had been like brothers all their lives, and Pelham was to Darrell his other self; while Darrell was to Pelham a younger brother whose excellence of heart and delicacy of soul made up for a very meagre understanding.

"I do congratulate you," said Pelham, grasping Darrell's hand, the old habit of love and brotherly kindness overwhelming him. "I think Miss Brandon the most charming girl I ever knew. Any man is fortunate to get her. But I don't think you are half good enough for her, Jack."

"That is just what I think," answered Darrell, with perfect sincerity. "But no man is good enough for her as far as that goes, and I am not the man to be running away from an angel; but there are lots of things to be attended to. I must give my whole time to Elizabeth, and I cannot ask the Ambassador to see about transportation, tickets, and transferring luggage. You must do that, and pay for it all; and I will pay you back when we get our respected aunt's fortune—fifty years or more from to-day."

"Of course I shall do all that is necessary," replied Pelham, "and there will be plenty to do. Getting married is heavy business, and taking a girl away to India at a fortnight's notice—How did you have the courage to ask so much of such a woman?"

"I don't know. It happened, that's all, and I was in heaven. I shall be there again to-morrow morning at eleven o'clock, when I shall see Elizabeth." He spoke her name as if it were a saint's name.

The two men sat talking for an hour or two. Darrell's manner in speaking of his acceptance by Elizabeth was not gushing, but expressed a deep and sincere passion, which he told Pelham, with perfect simplicity, was the first and only love of his life; and Pelham believed him. After parting from Darrell, Pelham sat up until dawn, wrestling with his own heart; but when the day broke he had conquered his anguish. He saw that Elizabeth had possibly entered upon a thorny path by marrying Darrell. He saw all the pitfalls which awaited a young and beautiful woman, the wife of a subaltern in a foot regiment in India. He foresaw that Elizabeth's charming freedom of manner, her flattering attitude towards men of all sorts and conditions, which might answer well enough in America, would probably be misunderstood by others more or less strict than herself, and he determined to be her friend, and felt sure that she would soon need one. Darrell was the best fellow alive, but he was not the man to manage that complicated problem, a pretty, vivacious, innocent, intelligent, admiration-loving American girl, without family or friends, cast loose at an Indian station.

In the afternoon of that day, Pelham paid his first call on Elizabeth as the prospective bride of Darrell. He thought her more love-compelling in her new relation of a promised bride than he had ever seen her before; her shyness, her pallor, her tears, her deep feeling, her constant remembrance of what her father would suffer, endeared her to Pelham, and yet her willingness, like the Sabine women of old, to go with the man she loved was deeply touching. It was a deliciously old-fashioned love match, both Elizabeth and Darrell looking forward to an uninterrupted honeymoon for the rest of their lives—Elizabeth quite as much so as Darrell. Pelham at this interview was kindness and sympathy itself, and even in the midst of her dream of love Elizabeth felt the serious value of such a friendship as this quiet, silent, rather ugly young officer, sparing of words, but full of tact, was offering her.

When Pelham came out of the shabby old house which was Elizabeth's home, he met General Brandon face to face on the steps. Pelham grasped his hand cordially. He felt acutely for the poor father who had to give up such a daughter, to go upon such a lifelong journey. Something prompted Pelham to say, "I congratulate my friend and cousin Darrell with all my heart, but for you who are to give up your daughter, I can only say that I feel for you more than I can express."

"You should congratulate me, too," replied General Brandon, gently. "It was written that I should have to give up my child, and since it had to be, I am glad to give her to a man as admirable in every way as Captain Darrell." General Brandon would have said this about any son-in-law not an absolute blackguard. But accidentally he happened to be right, for Darrell was indeed admirable in many ways. "She will go far from me," said the General, with a sudden break in his voice, "but that a father must be prepared for. May she be happy,—that is all I ask. Captain Darrell came to see me this morning and mentioned settlements. At the words I was somewhat offended, not being used to having such matters mentioned in connection with marriage; but I speedily found that his intentions were most generous, he merely wanted to give my daughter everything he had. On my part I endowed my daughter with all I had, seven bonds of the Egyptian government, for which I paid a thousand pounds in English money, the best part of what I received during my service with the Khedive Ismail. I believe they would now bring very little in the market, but no doubt in the course of time the Egyptian government will meet all of its obligations in full. We must not lose our faith, my dear Pelham, in human nature. I also wished to make over to my daughter the equity in my house, for I have never been able to pay off the mortgage which I acquired when I bought it; but this Captain Darrell most generously refused to accept. And when he told me that his pay and allowances would amount to something like five hundred pounds a year, I felt that it should be quite enough to support a young couple in India, at least for the present."

Pelham had to look away and laugh, at the bare idea of two such innocents as General Brandon and Jack Darrell attempting to transact business, and the gravity with which General Brandon mentioned the Egyptian bonds would have provoked a laugh from a dead horse. But there was so little money concerned in the transaction that it really did not make much difference.

In the course of twenty-four hours, through the good offices of the British Ambassador at the Washington office with the War Office in London, a cablegram arrived, granting an extension of leave for fourteen days to both Pelham and Darrell. Their prolonged stay in Washington had already made it necessary for them to return to India by way of Suez, and to give up their transcontinental trip. The additional two weeks gave time for the wedding preparations, which were necessarily simple for a wedding tour of two days and the sailing from New York in time to catch the next steamer of the Messageries Maritimes at Marseilles.

Pelham saw Elizabeth nearly every day during the two weeks preceding the marriage, and every time he saw her the melancholy conviction came over him that she was the woman he was never to forget and never to cease to love.

Mrs. Luttrell took charge of affairs, as much as Pelham would let her. She gave the newly engaged pair a large and splendid dinner in honor of their engagement, and there were other festivities of the same nature given by other persons on a smaller scale. All of Elizabeth's former admirers, and they were legion, sent her wedding presents, and the shabby house was nearly swamped with them.

Richard Baskerville was of great assistance to Pelham in putting things through, for it was Pelham who made the marriage possible. Darrell could do nothing but gaze into Elizabeth's beautiful black eyes, and if Pelham would have let him, would have spent all the money necessary for their first-class passage to India in buying bouquets for Elizabeth. Between Richard Baskerville, already known as one of the cleverest young lawyers in Washington, and Pelham a sincere friendship sprang up, as the two men were alike in many respects.

On a bright, sunny day in February, Elizabeth Brandon became the wife of Jack Darrell. The wedding took place at a little suburban church where the seats were cheap enough for General Brandon, who was a strong churchman, to afford seats for two. There were neither bridesmaids nor groomsmen, nor any of the showy paraphernalia of a smart wedding. Elizabeth, as much in love as she was, yet felt too much the coming parting from her father to make her wedding a merry one; it was, rather, sad, as are many of the sweetest things in life. Pelham was best man, and the Ambassador, who had good-naturedly helped the matter along, was present. Also there were half a dozen fossils, old comrades and Virginia relations of the Brandons. Richard Baskerville and Mrs. Luttrell were there, and the society newspapers described Mrs. Luttrell as wearing a superb black-velvet gown and a magnificent ermine cape. Mrs. Luttrell's black-velvet gown and ermine cape were a uniform which she had worn for the last forty years, replacing each velvet gown and ermine cape, as fast as they wore out, with new ones.

Her carriage took the bride and her father to the church, the bridegroom and his best man having preceded them in a cab. Elizabeth, in her simple white wedding gown, with magnificent old lace and her grandmother's pearls, made an exquisite bride, and Darrell looked every inch a soldier in his scarlet tunic. It was a wedding where love and honor presided, yet Pelham's heart was heavy at what might be the outcome.

There was a simple wedding breakfast at Elizabeth's home, where were assembled a few persons, some of them, like the Ambassador and a couple of cabinet officers, sufficiently important to have delighted the newly rich to have secured as guests, and others, like the old comrades and the decayed Virginia relatives, so unimportant that the newly rich would not have touched them with a ten-foot pole. The bride's health was drunk in cheap champagne. When she departed in her travelling gown for her two days' wedding trip before sailing on that other tremendous journey to India, tears were in the eyes of most present, but General Brandon was dry-eyed and smiling. When he had bidden the last guest farewell and turned into his lonely home, which had that strange look of emptiness that follows a wedding or a funeral, Pelham returned with him.

General Brandon, seeing the sympathy in the eyes of Pelham, who had his own heartache, laid both hands on his shoulders and said, "My dear sir, believe me, I am at this moment a perfectly happy and delighted man," and then suddenly wept like a child.

Pelham spent the next two days comforting and uplifting General Brandon, and felt himself comforted and uplifted by association with such a man. He said earnestly, at parting with the General: "Believe me, your daughter has the best of friends as well as husbands in Darrell, but she shall never want a friend as long as I live. India is a treacherous place to men who are out in the hot sun, and life is held there by a very uncertain tenure. So your daughter may survive us both; but as long as either one of us is alive, she shall be as well protected as if she were in your house."

Two days after the wedding Pelham saw Elizabeth on the deck of the steamer which was to carry them to Havre. Her first words were, "How is my father?" and despite the deep glow of happiness which radiated from her soul through her eyes, she could not speak of him without tears. Nor did she at any time show any forgetfulness of him. She wrote him every day, and posted her letters at every stopping-place on that long journey to India.

Travelling makes people as well acquainted as marriage does, and by the time Captain and Mrs. Darrell and Pelham reached Marseilles, Pelham knew Elizabeth quite as well as Darrell did, and understood her far better. It was a delightful but saddening joy to Pelham when he found Elizabeth soon turning to him, rather than to Darrell, to answer her intelligent questions. In fact, Darrell himself, when she asked him, would say, "Pelham will tell you; he knows a lot more about those old classic beggars and Greek cads and ruffians than I do." Elizabeth still found Darrell the most charming man in the world.

It was at Marseilles on a late afternoon in early March that Darrell said this to Elizabeth. The three were sitting at a table on the terrace of a café overlooking the old harbor, with its crumbling Vauban forts. The ships' lights were twinkling against the dark blue of the water and the darker blue of the sky, while afar off they could see faintly the outline of the Château d'If, where Monte Cristo learned his language of the Abbé. Pelham had been telling Elizabeth the story of the city. The ancient Massilia, inhabited by a people whose talk was not, as the old Greek wrote, of seed-time or ploughing or harvest, but of

"Mast and helm and oar-bench,
And the stately ships wherein
They have all joy and pleasure
O'er the wet sea way to win."

Elizabeth, with the keen delight of a mind newly awakened to books and travel, was capable of enjoying both. Her childhood and first girlhood had been spent in a secluded country house, where the books were few and old and of little value. The two or three years she had spent in Washington since her father's return from Egypt, enriched only by his Egyptian bonds, had not been of a sort to develop her mind. They had chiefly been spent in dancing and flirting; but Elizabeth, with the Southern girl's inevitable tendency both to dance and flirt, had that which often goes with it, a depth of intelligence and a serious understanding. It was a like seriousness of understanding in Pelham which attracted her so powerfully. Darrell, whom she still thought, and was to think for some time to come, the most charming man in the world, was never serious about anything except dogs and horses and Elizabeth. He took everything easily, especially life and death, and would have ridden up to a roaring battery or into any other of the many mouths of hell with a smile upon his lips. He did not quite understand why Elizabeth, in the midst of her bridal joy, often shed tears for her father, and although never showing the least impatience at it, or aught but the tenderest kindness, wondered why she should want anybody but him, as he wanted no one but her.

He was, like many men of his kind, perfectly modest, too high-minded if not too large-minded for jealousy, and thought it the most natural thing in the world that Elizabeth should turn to Pelham for sympathy and information, as Darrell himself had always done. At this moment he was very much interested in Pelham's account of the ancient tunny fisheries, as they had just had among their *hors-d'œuvres* dried tunny fish, as well as their bouillabaisse. Elizabeth knew something of the man of yesterday who had made bouillabaisse immortal, but Darrell was surprised to hear that Thackeray had ever written verse. Pelham, sitting next Elizabeth and, although habitually a silent man, doing most of the talking, began to wonder sadly how long it would be before Elizabeth became desperately bored by her lover husband. No such thought entered Elizabeth's mind; she only deemed herself twice fortunate in having the companionship of such a friend as Pelham as well as the love of her hero husband Darrell.

Next morning they sailed through Suez for Bombay. Elizabeth proved a good sailor and spent most of her waking hours on deck. Darrell lay back in his steamer chair and smoked, being quite satisfied with the spectacle of his charming Elizabeth tripping up and down the deck and talking with Pelham. The other passengers were not quite certain at first whose wife she was.

As they sailed over the blue Mediterranean, it was Pelham who told Elizabeth when they would come in sight of Stromboli; and it was on his arm that she watched before daybreak a great, pallid moon sinking into the black world of waters on the west, while on the east the dun sky, across which fled great ragged masses of dark clouds, was lighted by the vast torches of Stromboli waving like a blazing head of Medusa. Meanwhile Darrell was sound asleep in his berth. It would have taken more than ten Strombolis to have gotten him up on deck at that hour. But a gun, a dog, or a fishing-rod would have kept him up all night and made him as alert and watchful as if his life depended upon the issue. It was Pelham who showed to Elizabeth the sickle-shaped port of Messina, and told her of the ancient coins of the city, which bore a sickle upon them. And together, as they sailed along the desolate shores of Crete, they followed the itinerary of Paul of Tarsus.

When the ship made its slow way through the Canal to Suez, Darrell was roused to study it from the aspect of a military man. But it was Pelham, who had more military science in his ugly head than Darrell had in his whole handsome young body, who watched with Elizabeth the red flamingoes rising from amid the tamarisk trees. Once out of the Canal, Darrell again resumed his life of smoking, sleeping, eating, and adoring Elizabeth; but Elizabeth, who was being educated by Pelham, listened with the eagerness of an intelligent child to Pelham's stories of those historic lands whose bleak, black-scarred, and rocky shores border the Red Sea. He told her of those strange Mohammedan people who inhabit this country, where nature is as fierce as man, and where "Allah is God of the great deserts," as Pierre Loti says,—those people in whom Islam is incarnate. Together Elizabeth and Pelham watched the passage around Bab-el-Mandeb, the "Gate of tears."

At last, on a hot, bright morning, they landed at Bombay, the great busy, dirty city, and after a week's travel by night and day they finished their journey at Embira, in one of the remotest depths of the Punjab. Elizabeth had travelled far and fast, since that January night when both Pelham and Darrell had searched for the little pearl heart, dropped from around her milk-white throat; but she had travelled farther and faster than she knew.

Chapter Three

Embira was like most second and third rate Indian stations, neither better or worse. There were a dirty native city, where plague and famine alternated; a river that was either a rushing torrent or as dry as a bone; and cantonments which had seen little change since the Mutiny. A battalion of Pelham and Darrell's regiment was stationed there, with large detachments of artillery and cavalry.

The only remarkable thing about the station was that, although it was very far from being garrisoned by any part of a crack regiment, the social status of the officers and their wives appeared to be almost on a level with that of the household troops. The wife of the Colonel commanding was the niece of an Earl besides being the commanding officer of the C. O. There were a couple of titled women among the officers' wives, and no less than two subalterns would inherit baronetcies. Neither Pelham nor Darrell stood any chance of inheriting his grandfather's title, nor did there seem much more possibility of Darrell's inheriting the problematical fortune which was the staple joke between Pelham and himself.

Darrell, who would have been classed as a detrimental in London, was of the sort to be adored by the young ladies of the post; and his appearance with a bride, and that with scarcely a day's warning, was both a slight and a grievance to the ladies of Embira. And an American wife, too! It was the aim and object of the ladies to maintain the social tone of the regiment, of which they were enormously proud, and here was Darrell, the grandson of a peer, introducing a person among them whom it was taken for granted he had met in the wilds of the Rocky Mountains near Philadelphia, or who was perhaps a miner's daughter in the vicinity of Boston.

It was in this critical and even hostile circle that Elizabeth made her first appearance, three days after her arrival at Embira. It was on the occasion of the regimental sports, which were rendered brilliant by the presence of a large party of visitors from England, including the noble Earl who was uncle to the C. O.'s wife, a commissioner who had brought his own new wife on purpose to eclipse the pretty wife of the deputy-commissioner, and a vice-regal aide-de-camp,—all together a brilliant party for a remote Indian station.

The afternoon was hot and bright, but the gardens which were reserved for tea and flirtations were still unparched and the white polo grounds adjoining were not as yet dust blinded. When Elizabeth, at five o'clock in the afternoon, appeared dressed for the occasion, on the veranda of their quarters, Darrell surveyed her with pride and pleasure, not unmixed with apprehension. She looked, it is true, exquisitely charming in her pale green muslin, her rose-crowned hat, her white parasol, and with her little, black, silver-buckled shoes, a model of daintiness to the eyes of the Englishmen. But Darrell also felt some anxiety; he suspected that she would be coldly received by the unkind women and patronized by the kind ones, and he feared that Elizabeth might be as crushed by both as an English girl might have been. Pelham, on the contrary, who understood Elizabeth far better than her husband did and felt even a deeper pride in her as his silent adoration for her had grown deep and strong, felt not the slightest fear. Elizabeth was in manner and bearing, as well as in beauty, far above the most patrician woman at the station. Every other woman except herself realized and recognized that there was some one above her in station, she was of necessity the social inferior of somebody. Not so with Elizabeth. As an American woman of good birth, she had never seen or heard of any one who was above her, and would have been perfectly at her ease with royalty itself. The admiring glances and compliments of Pelham and Darrell flattered Elizabeth and brought the wild-rose color to her creamy cheeks; and with the consciousness of looking her best, she entered the gardens with her husband walking on one side of her and Pelham on the other, and was duly presented to the Colonel's lady.

There is perhaps nowhere in the world that the inability of Englishwomen to dress well and their total subjection to their dressmakers are so obvious as in India. There the woollen gowns which look well on an autumn day among the Scotch hills, and the tailor-made dresses which are suited for Regent Street on a dull morning, the elaborate silks and laces which are fit for London drawing-rooms and theatres, are worn with a serene unconsciousness of unfitness. On this hot afternoon the ladies of Embira had put on their best,—that is to say, their worst clothes as far as unsuitability went. Hats bristling with feathers, large white boas, rustling silks, and gorgeous parasols made the gardens bright, but made the wearers look half-baked. Among these came Elizabeth's delicate green muslin and airy lightness of attire. The men, on looking at her, felt as if they had just had an iced drink. The ladies saw that she had accomplished something quite beyond them in the way of dress, which, as Darrell half feared, made the unkind determine to be more icy to her and the kind even more patronizing.

The Colonel's lady, a vast person in purple silk and a collection of diamond ornaments which made her appear as if covered with a breastplate of jewels, was one of the latter kind. She greeted Elizabeth as if she were a fifteen-year-old schoolgirl who must needs be awed by all she saw around her. Elizabeth, who knew well the cosmopolitan society of Washington and was accustomed to see power and importance classed together, was in no way terrified; nor was she even astonished when the Earl, a shabby person who had a turbulent wife whom he was very glad to leave at home, asked to be introduced to Mrs. Darrell.

The Colonel's wife, who had spent the whole time of her uncle's visit trying to induce him to be introduced to people against his will, was staggered, but promptly agreed to his proposition. She whispered his name and rank in Elizabeth's ear and advanced a step or two towards the Earl, but Elizabeth quite unconsciously stood perfectly still and had the Earl brought to her to be introduced, receiving him exactly as she would have done some of the numerous pleasant elderly gentlemen whom she had met in Washington. The Earl, who was not without humor, saw the look of amazement on the face of the Colonel's lady at Elizabeth's calm attitude and secretly enjoyed the situation. He was an easy-going person who had but one requirement on the face of the earth, and that was to be perpetually amused and entertained. And this one requirement of his soul was amply satisfied by the charming young American girl. She was not in the least like most of the American girls he had known and met in England, who were usually the daughters of retired tradesmen and rather poor imitations of Lady Clara Vere de Vere. The Earl, however, much to his chagrin was not allowed to have Elizabeth all to himself and was compelled to share her society with a couple of impudent subalterns, who in the pursuit of a pretty face and a dainty foot feared neither man nor devil.

This was only the beginning of an afternoon of triumph for Elizabeth, a triumph which she enjoyed without appreciating its true significance. She had the enormous advantage of being distinctly different from the women around her, and of having the perfect ease which comes from the feeling of perfect equality. She was perhaps the best-born woman of all those present, reckoning good birth to mean many generations of people at the top of the ladder. Ever since the first Brandon, a decayed gentleman, had set foot on American soil in the days of Charles I., the Brandons had been in the front rank, with none better than themselves. The Earl himself had a great-grandmother who began life as a milliner's apprentice and thence progressed to the London stage. But Elizabeth's great-grandmothers were all of the Brahmin caste in her own country. The ancestry of the titles in the regiment went back only as far as the early part of the eighteenth century, while Elizabeth's ancestors had behind them already some hundreds of years as gentle people, before their advent into the new country. It was that perhaps which gave Elizabeth the patrician nose and her delicate hands and feet, and it certainly gave her that perfect composure of manner which, unlike Lady Clara Vere de Vere's icy stateliness, could not be successfully imitated by any parvenu who ever walked the earth.

Darrell was secretly delighted at the admiration which Elizabeth excited. He had not felt so great a sensation of triumph since he had introduced into the regimental mess a certain Irish setter with a pedigree which could be proved back to the time of Queen Elizabeth. Pelham, who would have been a favorite among the ladies had he allowed it, saw everything out of the tail of his eye and was rather sorry when he saw the drift of men towards Elizabeth. When the trio returned to Darrell's quarters through the soft Indian twilight, Darrell was openly elated and Elizabeth secretly so, but Pelham felt that Elizabeth's course lay in dangerous waters.

And Pelham was right. Englishwomen have their charms and their virtues, both of which are great and admirable, but they have no sense of comradeship. Elizabeth was to them an alien, but instead of appealing to their sympathies, they saw her without effort easily become the acknowledged belle of the regiment. There was little in common beyond the mere formal exchange of courtesies between herself and even those women and girls at the station who wished to be kind to her. She had no accomplishments in the usual sense. She neither played, nor sang, nor drew, nor painted, either on china, fans, screens, or picture frames, nor could she do anything in water colors. She had no taste for games, and would not take the trouble even to play tennis. She disliked cards and would not play bridge, nor was she in any sense the athletic woman and had no tales of prowess to tell of tremendous mountain walks or long excursions on horseback. She rode well in a graceful, untaught manner which improved distinctly under Darrell's masterly coaching, but she did not give up her days to it as did some of the girls with statuesque figures who looked their best on horseback.

The ladies wondered how Mrs. Darrell disposed of her time. If they could have taken a look into Elizabeth's own sitting room, they would have seen a big sewing-table; and the beautiful and dainty gowns which from time to time Mrs. Darrell appeared in, and the immense variety of hats which caused the other women to think that she was squandering her husband's substance, came forth from that sewing room. Instead of drawing trashy pictures and embroidering mats and picture frames, Elizabeth with an artist's eye designed and made beautiful little costumes which looked as if they came from Regent Street or the Rue de la Paix. Her housekeeping, too, was well attended to, and the little dinners which she occasionally gave were remarkably good. Her mind had not been much cultivated, but under Pelham's direction she learned with avidity—much to the amusement of Darrell, who protested against a learned wife and predicted that Elizabeth would soon be writing a novel or doing some other unholy thing likely to result from women who meddled with books.

Meanwhile Elizabeth's belle-ship in the regiment became firmly established. Her charming appearance and her graceful and affable manners with men, the subtle way she had of making every man believe that he was her favorite, went farther with the officers of the 178th Foot than the sketching, painting, playing, and singing of the other women. Her manners had that fascinating combination known only to American women, and possibly the secret of their ascendency over men, of something between an appeal and a command; it was like the rule of a favorite and delightful child in a household. It may be imagined that this did not enhance Elizabeth's popularity with her own sex.

Elizabeth wondered and was piqued at the coldness of the women towards her. She made faint, ineffectual attempts at intimacy with the Colonel's daughters and the wives of various subalterns, but it was of no avail. She was the daughter of the regiment as far as the officers were concerned, but by no means a sister of the regiment to the ladies. Pelham was surprised that the tongue of scandal passed her by, but with innocence on Elizabeth's part, and a couple of able-bodied men like Pelham and Darrell to stand by her, the gossips found it safe to let Mrs. Darrell alone.

Elizabeth was for a time quite happy in her new life, her only sorrow being the separation from her father. She wrote him passionate letters imploring him to come to see her; but it costs money to get from Washington to Embira in the Punjaub, and General Brandon was chronically hard up. And so her life moved on, almost as closely linked with Pelham's as with Darrell's, for two years. It was, however, moving in a direction which Elizabeth only dimly foresaw and understood. By Pelham's tact and judgment rather than her own there never was a breath of scandal concerning their deep and obvious intimacy. Pelham was a man to be feared as well as respected, and such people are tolerably safe from criticism.

Every day of these two years found Pelham more and more deeply and hopelessly in love with Elizabeth, with the knightly love which would guard her not only against the whole world but against himself and herself; for in those two years Elizabeth's mind, ripening and developing, perceived that she had married a man with every grace and virtue joined to a tiresome and amiable commonplaceness. It frightened her sometimes when she discovered how bored she grew by her husband's conversation, and she was still more frightened at the prospect which sometimes occurred to her of being separated from Pelham, on whom she had learned to depend as other women depend upon a brother or a father or even a husband. But she was not unhappy, although she gradually found her way out of the lover's paradise into which she had embarked with Darrell.

For Darrell himself she never lost the slightest respect. He was as truthful and honorable and truly unselfish as Pelham himself was. Nevertheless, at the end of two years came the beginning of a crisis. A beautiful boy was born to Elizabeth, a child of fairness and of delightful temper. "The jolliest little chap I ever saw," swore Darrell at the club, when the baby was less than a week old.

Elizabeth was a devoted mother, but Darrell was the most passionately fond father imaginable. The child merely as a pet was worth to him more than all the dogs and horses in existence, including the Irish setter. In him there was a deep well-spring of fatherhood. He had thought himself perfectly happy before the boy was born, but afterwards he felt he had never known what true happiness was until then; and when the child was a year old Darrell, proudly calling him "my soldier," used to put his own cap on the baby's pretty head and his sword in its little hand, and throw his military cloak around it and sit and gaze in rapture at the child as it laughed and crowed, delighted with its trappings.

At the end of a year, like a judgment from heaven, the child died, after a day's illness. In general it is the father who consoles the heart-broken mother, but in this case it was Elizabeth who kept Darrell sane in the midst of his terrible grief, who sat by him day and night, who checked by her own tears his strange cries of grief, and who upheld him when he passed through the deep waters. She herself was stricken in heart as only mothers can be, and she had a presentiment that she would never again have a child.

Pelham, who would cheerfully have borne all of Elizabeth's sorrow at the boy's death, was amazed and even indignant that Darrell should not have sustained her in this dreadful hour. Silently and with a sleepless vigilance and constancy Pelham supported and comforted Elizabeth.

Chapter Four

There was no one else to sustain Elizabeth. Darrell needed comforting even more than herself. She had formed no intimacies with any of the ladies of the station. There were among them many kind and tender-hearted women, but a barrier had grown up between them and the stranger from America.

Gradually the truth was beginning to dawn upon Elizabeth, that she depended more upon Pelham than upon Darrell; that is to say, she had married the wrong man, and the full revelation of this terrible truth came to her within two months of the time that she was left childless. It was in the heat of summer, and Elizabeth was one of those two or three of the officers' wives, who braved the terrors of the hot season away from the hills in order to be with their husbands.

One stifling August evening, about ten o'clock, as Elizabeth was walking in the small grounds around their bungalow, the moon shining upon the tops of the great cypress trees which skirted the grounds, Pelham came down the steps of the veranda at the back of the house and joined her. The night was hot, as only Indian nights can be, but Elizabeth in her filmy white gown looked cool. She was as graceful and charming as ever, for the touch of sorrow, the knowledge of disappointment, and the necessity of keeping ceaseless watch and ward upon her own heart had added a deeper interest to her beauty while robbing her of some of her girlish fairness. Pelham, who was in mufti, wore a suit of white linen, and the two white figures could be seen for half a mile. They had not met since morning, a long time for them to be apart, because Pelham, who had lived with Darrell after the manner of a brother before his marriage, had continued it ever since. As he came up, holding his straw hat in his hand, Elizabeth said to him:—

"Where have you been all day? We waited dinner for you until at last we could wait no longer, as I wanted my poor Jack to go to the club. It doesn't do for him to stay in this house too much."

ill64

"...SHE CAUGHT HIM BY THE ARM AND WHISPERED, 'AND COULD YOU LEAVE ME?'"

"I have been hard at work all day," replied Pelham, in a tired voice. "I got a letter at noon to-day, offering me a staff appointment. It would be a very good thing, a great thing, and I have been studying it over and looking things up concerning it all the afternoon and evening. It would take me away from the regiment for a good many years, but still—"

Elizabeth's face was quite plain to him in the white moonlight. She was already pale from the heat and from her months of suffering, but he saw a total change of expression, a look of terror, come into her eyes. It was unmistakable. Pelham himself had long known how things were with him, and it was chiefly from despair that he had seriously considered that day tearing himself from Elizabeth. He thought she would miss him as a woman misses a friend and brother, but something in her sad and lovely eyes suddenly revealed to him that it was not as a friend and brother she would miss him, but as the being dearest to her on earth; and Pelham, being then tempted of the devil, asked in a low voice:—

"Elizabeth, would it be painful to you if we parted?"

Elizabeth, staggered at the quick blow which had been dealt her, made full revelation of all she felt; she caught him by the arm and whispered: "And could you leave me? What would become of me? I think it would half kill me. First my child was taken, and now you—"

She paused, recalled to herself by the sound of her own words. She dropped Pelham's arm as quickly as she had taken it and withdrew from him a step. They looked away from each other, alarmed and ashamed that they had drawn so near the brink of the gulf. But the winged word had been spoken; it was now gone, never to be recalled. Neither one of them could move or speak for a time. Pelham was a strong man and Elizabeth was a strong woman, and they loved not as weaklings love; their hearts were not to be conquered in an instant. They remained thus for what seemed to them an interminable time. It was really not five minutes. Then Pelham said quietly:—

"I shall remain with the regiment."

And Elizabeth, without in the least knowing what she was saying, replied, "Thank God!"

Then, involuntarily and unable to bear longer the stress of the situation, they both turned back to the house. The scene had lasted all told five minutes; it was in full sight of many eyes if any had cared to look; but for both of them it had changed the face of creation itself. It had not, however, changed their natures, which were singularly delicate and high-minded; nor had it involved them in any dishonor.

As they entered the bungalow together, they met Darrell, who had noticed them walking through the shrubbery. Elizabeth went up to him, and placing her hand on his shoulder, a familiarity she had never used before in the presence of Pelham or any other human being, said: "I am so glad you have come back; I was beginning to feel so lonely without you. After this you must stay with me more than you have done, because I am never really happy away from you."

This was one of the most stupendous lies ever uttered by a woman's lips; but the recording angel had no occasion to shed a tear over it, as he inscribed it on the records of high heaven. A look of pleasure came into Darrell's honest, sombre eyes. It was not often that love like this survived the honeymoon, and Elizabeth must indeed be deeply in love with him, if she used such language before Pelham. He put his arm around her slender waist, and spoke to Pelham instead of her.

"You miserable dog," he said, "why don't you get a wife like mine?"

Pelham, with a smile upon his dark, expressive, and somewhat homely face, answered quite naturally, "Because I can't find a wife like yours."

From that day, in spite of the fact that Elizabeth was a true wife of an honorable man, her whole life was irradiated by the joy of knowing that she was loved by Pelham and even that she loved him in return. It made them both careful in a thousand ways where heretofore they had been without thought. It made Elizabeth the sweetest as well as the most dutiful wife imaginable to Darrell. Her constant ministrations to him, her untiring efforts to please him, did more than he thought possible to soothe his grief over the dead child.

Elizabeth had always been kind and flattering to Darrell's friends, not only out of respect for him, but from the pleasure which every woman takes in exercising the conscious power to please. But now she was if anything more attractive to them than ever, and Darrell enjoyed a delight most gratifying to his pride in finding himself the preferred admirer of a charming wife who was admired by every man who knew her. Elizabeth felt, without one word being spoken, that her conduct was approved by Pelham. She sometimes suspected what Pelham never did, that he, rather than she, deserved credit for the lofty purity of their relations, and doubted whether after all Pelham were not stronger in a sense of honor and rectitude even than herself, so great was his mastery over her. For, after all, the greatest power which one human being can exercise over another is the power of uplifting and making better; and such Elizabeth felt was Pelham's influence over her, just as Pelham felt that Elizabeth was his guardian angel.

The Darrells and Pelham spent all together four years at Embira. Every year Elizabeth thought she would be able to return to America to see her father, if for only a few weeks, but every year the Darrell exchequer showed the impossibility of this. Their narrow means did not permit them to travel, or even to entertain except in the simplest manner, and Elizabeth only remained well dressed from the fact that she knew how to make her own gowns better than most Regent Street dressmakers. They often joked and laughed about their old relative Lady Pelham's fortune, which was to come first to Darrell, and, failing a son and heir, to Pelham. Darrell dolefully related how Lady Pelham's mother had lived to be ninety-six, and her father to be ninety-seven, and not one of her uncles or aunts had died under ninety years of age, while the lady herself was not more than fifty years of age and reckoned the most robust woman in England. They built castles in the air, of what they would do when they got the Pelham fortune, and Darrell tried to induce Pelham to agree to a division of the spoils in advance. It was a great joke; but one day, nearly nine years after Elizabeth's marriage, death came to the three lives which stood between Darrell and Lady Pelham's money, and Darrell came into the life estate of a fortune of forty thousand pounds.

Chapter Five

After nine years in India one is glad to get back to England, particularly as Darrell, in spite of the large stock of health and spirits which he took from England with him, had found as most men do in India that he had a liver. Elizabeth had remained perfectly well during all the nine years of her life under the hard blue Indian skies. She was now in her thirtieth year, and Darrell was nearly forty. Their attachment had assumed the fixed and settled form which nine years of constant association and respect must inevitably produce in every marriage. There were no jars or disagreements between them, and except for the absence of children Darrell reckoned his domestic life absolutely perfect.

Pelham, who like Darrell was now a major with a lieutenant-colonelcy in sight, knew that the time had come, if he was ever to see anything of the world beyond India, England, and his flying trip to the United States, for him to start upon his travels. In one way he was no longer necessary to Elizabeth, as she was now a trained and experienced woman,—the least likely, he thought, of any woman in the world, to make a false step of any kind. Elizabeth herself, although she had never ceased to depend on Pelham, had developed under his tutelage, so that she was in many ways able to stand without him; and, not being a woman to keep a man at her side without cause, she encouraged Pelham in his desire to travel.

The three returned to England together. After being established in the fine London house which was a part of their inheritance, Elizabeth's first thought was for her father. It was in the spring-time that the Darrells arrived in Europe, and a delightful plan was arranged by which Elizabeth was to send for General Brandon, and he with the Darrells and Pelham were to begin in August a three months' journey on the Continent. Elizabeth, whose mind was now well formed and furnished, looked forward with eagerness to seeing the brilliant capitals of Continental Europe,—those spots of romantic beauty and poetic sights, of which she had first read and dreamed in the old country house in Virginia and afterwards under the solemn deodars and in the shady bungalows of the Punjaub.

Darrell's health improved wonderfully from the day he arrived in England, and it was thought that this Continental tour would restore him to the physical perfection which he originally possessed. They found London delightful, as London is apt to be with youth, good looks, beauty, and forty thousand pounds. Pelham had his own lodgings near them, but Darrell's house was home to him. He saw almost as much of Elizabeth as in the years when they lived in cantonments together, but both Elizabeth and Darrell were fonder of society than Pelham. After they had breakfasted, Darrell and

Elizabeth went together shopping, a novel and delightful experience to both of them; and they generally carried Pelham along with them, much to his disgust. They always referred things to him and never took his advice.

Darrell loved to adorn Elizabeth's beauty, and one of the things which gave him the most pleasure was the making of a fine diamond and pearl necklace for his wife's white throat. He had inherited a diamond necklace along with the Pelham properties. To these he added other stones and some fine pearls. Elizabeth insisted that the pretty pearl brooch which had been her wedding gift from Darrell should be included in the necklace, and they spent hours together at the jeweller's planning the making of the necklace. Pelham stood by listening good-naturedly, and never suggesting any reduction in expense where Elizabeth's wishes were concerned.

When August came, however, Darrell was not so well, but he was eager for the Continental tour, upon which Elizabeth had set her heart. Elizabeth, however, would not hear of his going, and as Pelham's leave was limited he would be forced to go without the Darrells. The doctors had not absolutely said that Darrell should not go, but considered it best that he remain in England; it was Elizabeth's over-solicitude for Darrell which really induced her to give up a plan so dear not only to her, but, as she well knew, to Pelham also. It cost her far more to deny Pelham than to deny herself, and this he well understood; for by that time they read each other like an open book, although no word of love had been spoken between them after that sudden out-break of their hearts on that night now eight years past when, standing in the solemn gloom of the cypress trees in the sultry Indian night, they had uttered unforgetable words. Pelham never felt prouder of Elizabeth and her forgetfulness of self than on the day she told him of her decision about the Continental tour, in her pretty London drawing-room, in which she fitted beautifully. It was so, as Pelham thought, that she fitted every place in which he had seen her.

"You know how delightful it would be for us to go,"—she always spoke of "us," Darrell and herself being in fact never separated,—"but the doctor says it wouldn't be the best thing for Jack; he would be sure to overdo it, and that is what I don't intend to let him do."

"Elizabeth," said Pelham, after a pause, "I think you are all in all the best wife I ever knew."

"Why shouldn't I be a good wife—haven't I the best husband in the world? Jack often reminds me of my father, who has just such an open, frank, simple nature as Jack's,—one of those natures which nobody fears and yet of which everybody is a little afraid."

"That is true," replied Pelham. "Jack as a little fellow was the straightest lad I ever knew. If your boy had lived, I think he would have been as straight a little fellow as Jack."

Elizabeth's eyes filled. She had not yet learned to bear unmoved any mention of the child, who was quite forgotten by all except Darrell, Pelham, and herself. Just then Darrell entered from riding. He was neither as handsome nor as young-looking as he had been ten years before; and Pelham, who never had been handsome or particularly good-looking, was now quite gray and looked as if he had been baked in an oven, but he had the clearest, kindest eye and the firmest thin-lipped, sensible mouth, which redeemed his face from positive ugliness. Elizabeth was no longer a girl, but with the same striking and touching beauty of her girlhood.

"So," said Darrell, after kissing Elizabeth's hand, "you are leaving us next week. By gad, I wish I were going with you, but Elizabeth won't hear of it. Now if I had married an English wife instead of an American, she would have let me do as I please."

"And make yourself ill," replied Elizabeth. "But if you will take care of yourself and do all I tell you, perhaps in the autumn I may take you to the Continent."

"But Pelham won't be with us."

"You're very complimentary," replied Elizabeth, with a cheering air of coquetry. "Ten years ago you could get along with only me. Now you must have Pelham and I don't know how many other men to keep you from being bored to death." Such speeches are common when husband and wife are sure of each other.

It was the next evening at dinner time that around the table Darrell began to tell of an expedition into West Africa which he had heard talked of at the club. It would be partly private and partly governmental, and would require more than a year's absence from England. Pelham's grave eyes lighted up as the story went on. He had an indestructible love of bold adventure, and he had no more been able to indulge his fondness and taste than he had been able to indulge his fondness for intelligent travel. Elizabeth, with prophetic intuition, saw that the idea had taken hold of Pelham's imagination. She felt assured that if she were to make the same appeal that she had done unconsciously in the garden that night at Embira, Pelham would not resist it, and would remain in England with her; but she was of too generous a nature to wish to hold him back from what would be an advantage as well as a strong man's delight to him. She was not surprised, therefore, when Pelham turned up next day, to hear that he had been to the War Office and had been looking into the West African expedition.

Pelham spent a fortnight making inquiries, and then one night, as he and Darrell, with Elizabeth sitting by them, sat over their cigars on the balcony of the morning-room, he told the story of what he had heard of the expedition. The command of the expedition had practically been offered him, and it was a tremendous opportunity and one not likely to occur again to a man of his age, for his fortieth birthday was upon him. It would mean much to him in the way of his profession, upon which he was entirely dependent,—that is, unless Darrell should die without an heir. Its opportunities in every way were such, and the offer made him so flattering, that it was out of the question that he should decline them unless there were some specific reason. Darrell told him so.

There were steps from the balcony leading down into a little lawn with a bench at the farther end. Elizabeth quietly rose and, walking down the steps, passed to the farther end of the gravelled path and back again. It was a June night, warm for London, but cool compared with that other sultry night when the question had first been raised of Pelham's departure from her for a long time. After a while Pelham rose and said to Darrell, "I will go and ask Elizabeth what she thinks of it."

"Do," said Darrell. "I bet you five to one she will tell you, just as I have done, that it is the greatest chance you ever had in your life."

Pelham followed Elizabeth down the gravelled path to the little iron bench under an odorous hedge of rose trees, where she sat. There was no moon, but the starlight made a softened radiance around them. He sat down by her and said in his usual quiet voice and laconic manner, "Elizabeth, what do you think of my accepting the West African offer?"

"I think you ought to accept it," replied Elizabeth, in a soft voice.

Not another word was spoken for five minutes, and then they rose and walked back to the balcony, where Darrell's cigar still glowed. Each understood the other perfectly. That day fortnight Pelham started for West Africa, giving up his Continental tour. The London season was in full swing, and Darrell, who was naturally fond of society, liked to go out; nor was this prohibited, in moderation, by the medical men. Elizabeth, too, liked society; and besides, now that Pelham was gone, she felt the need of contact with other minds and natures.

Chapter Six

Elizabeth was under no uneasiness concerning Pelham. The West African expedition was one of great responsibility, but of trifling danger, and Elizabeth had the highest respect for Pelham's ability to take care of himself. The thought had been in her mind, as it was in Pelham's, that she was far better prepared to do without him then than in those earlier days when she had been a stranger in a strange land. Such indeed was the case, but ten years of close companionship and reliance on Pelham's judgment and kindness for almost every act of her life had bred in Elizabeth a dependence which she did not fully realize until he was gone. It was as if the sun had dropped out of the heavens when he was away. In Darrell she had the companionship of a husband who adored her, but who except for his love could not give her the least assistance in any other way; while with Pelham it was, besides the intimacy of a great, unspoken love, the ever present aid of sound sense, good judgment, and a cultivated mind.

Elizabeth, with her youth and beauty and her natural taste for gayety and admiration, could not but find the London season charming; and as for Darrell, it seemed the very wine of life to him to be once more in England. They were invited everywhere, and had pleasure in returning the hospitality offered them. As regarded their income the Darrells, it is true, had a large one, as the late Lady Pelham was supposed to have left about forty thousand pounds; but it was hampered in many ways, as the late Lady Pelham was one of those persons who try to transact business after they are dead and buried.

Darrell knew nothing of business, and seemed incapable of learning. He spent money liberally for himself and more liberally still for Elizabeth. She had only to express a wish for it to be gratified. Darrell desired to cover her with jewels, but Elizabeth with better taste preferred to wear only one ornament, the handsome diamond and pearl necklace which seemed so peculiarly hers. Of the new gems in it, she and Darrell and Pelham had spent hours examining and deciding; and the idea of inserting in it her wedding gift of a pearl brooch, was Elizabeth's entirely and she was proud of it. Darrell, who grew more in love with his wife each day, was charmed at this bit of sentiment, on which they had united in defeating the jeweller.

On the night before the Goodwood races, there was a great ball at Marlborough House, to which Elizabeth and Darrell were commanded. Never had Elizabeth looked handsomer. A black evening gown showed off the perfections, the exquisite beauty, of her white shoulders and slender arms. The necklace around her milky white throat looked like moonlight and starlight combined.

"You will make a sensation to-night, my girl," said Darrell, kissing her.

"If you like my looks, that is the main point," replied Elizabeth. She habitually made him these pretty speeches, which was gratifying to Darrell, as the husband of a beauty.

They went to the ball, which had a gayety unsurpassed in balls. It established Elizabeth's place in society as one of the beauties of the season. She received vast attention from those London exquisites who claim to fix a woman's place in beauty's calendar. She was noticed, admired, and conversed with by royalty itself, and the Prince having thus set his mark of approval on her, Elizabeth's title as a London beauty was settled beyond cavil. She enjoyed it thoroughly, of course; but the image of Pelham did not leave her mind. She would turn her head in the midst of the splendor and magnificence of the ball, wishing to herself, "Could I but see him now!"

The ball lasted late, and it was not over until night had flown and the rosy dawn had come. Elizabeth was one of the few women sufficiently natural to look well after a night of dancing, and she looked as fresh as the dawn itself when she stepped into her carriage. Not so Darrell, who appeared so wearied that Elizabeth reproached herself at not having left earlier.

"I didn't wish to bring you away," he said with his usual kindness of tone. "Nine years in the Punjaub entitles you to some indulgences, and besides I was proud of you. I like to see you happy and admired."

Elizabeth laid her head on his shoulder in the seclusion of the brougham, and Darrell, after a pause, said in a low voice: "This is the anniversary of the boy's death. I wouldn't speak of it before, Elizabeth, but I hadn't forgotten it."

"And I," said Elizabeth, her heart suddenly turning to the dead child, sleeping under the cypress trees in the military cemetery at Embira, "had not forgotten it, but I hoped that you had, dearest."

They talked together for a little while of their lost darling, as the parents of dead children do, and then Darrell suddenly grew quiet. Elizabeth thought he was asleep, and would not move for fear she might disturb him. When she reached their own door, she raised her head from his shoulder. Darrell was dead.

Of all that happened in the succeeding weeks, Elizabeth had afterward but a confused recollection. She was stunned by the blow and deeply grieved. Although she had long ceased to return Darrell's affection in kind, yet she had a deep love for him. It was so deep, so sincere, so unselfish, that his death could not fail to be a heavy grief to her,—the heaviest but one that she could know: that other was Pelham's. Her sorrow was not joined with remorse. She had honestly and earnestly devoted her life to Darrell, and felt sure that she had made him happy; but nevertheless it was a deep and sincere sorrow.

Her first thought had been naturally and inevitably for Pelham. She was so ignorant of business, so absolutely untrained in affairs, and so much a stranger in England, that she scarcely knew where to turn. Darrell had plenty of relatives, but Elizabeth had never known them, except during her few short months in England, and none of them were particularly near Darrell either in blood or friendship. His grandfather was long since dead, and the cousin who inherited the title was in West Africa. From the beginning Elizabeth seemed overwhelmed with difficulties, with annoying details which she was called upon to decide without having the slightest experience in them. She knew nothing of the value of money, having had but little until she came into what seemed to both Darrell and herself an enormous fortune. She knew not what she had spent nor what she was spending. Thus, as in everything else, could she have only turned to Pelham and asked him what to do, everything would have gone right. But Pelham was in West Africa; it would possibly take anywhere from four to five months to communicate with him, nor was it possible for him to return for at least a year from the time he had started.

It was Pelham, however, who inherited everything that came from Lady Pelham. The sole provision for Elizabeth was about one hundred pounds a year, which was Darrell's own small inheritance. But the fact that Pelham was the sole heir relieved Elizabeth's mind when it was brought home to her that she would be obliged to account for everything Darrell and she had received,—every chair and table in Lady Pelham's house, and every jewel, however trifling. Elizabeth, who was as high-minded as she was inexperienced, desired to hand over everything to Pelham direct, but she knew him, or thought she knew him, too well to suppose it possible that he should make her position the least painful or embarrassing to her. In the first weeks of her widowhood, when she had wished to remain alone in her London house, entirely secluded from the world and its affairs, she was forced to see solicitors, attorneys, business men, and persons of all sorts. Some of these presented unpaid bills for large amounts, and foremost among the intruders was one Andrew McBean, a Scotch attorney who was Pelham's agent.

This man, with his persistence and insistence, annoyed Elizabeth almost beyond endurance; but the thing which troubled her most was the continual presenting of unpaid bills. She gave up her carriage and sold it with the horses, imagining in her simplicity that she could use this money for the payment of the accounts which rained upon her every day; and she actually did so use this money until informed by McBean that she had sold Pelham's property and misused the proceeds. This McBean said to her one day in her own drawing-room, or what she supposed was her own drawing-room. Elizabeth's heart fluttered with terror as McBean warned her that she would be required to account for every penny of this money—in fact of all the money that she was spending.

She had that morning, in despair, taken her diamond and pearl necklace to a jeweller's agent, who really acted as an amateur pawn-broker, and who had advanced her five hundred pounds on it. Had McBean asked her then about the necklace, she would have fainted on the floor; but he did not. As soon as he had gone, Elizabeth, in her widow's dress, flew pale and panting to the agent to whom she had intrusted the necklace, and told him what McBean had said to her. The agent, who saw that he had a frightened woman in his power and a valuable piece of property worth four times what he had advanced on it, soothed Elizabeth by telling her that McBean had no right to demand the necklace from her, as it was hers, being partly her husband's wedding gift to her. Elizabeth returned home, in that hour of darkness, with but one thought uppermost in her mind. Could she but see Pelham, he would not suffer her thus to be persecuted. She knew quite well how he would wish her to act,—to pay off the pressing debts which humiliated her, and to take the small balance of money left and remain in England until he should return. This she determined to do.

She had not heard from him either by cable or by letter since Darrell's death, but that was nothing. Communication with him would be necessarily slow. It might be weeks or even months before she should hear, but she was certain of what the purport of his letter would be, and of what his wishes already were. So, dismissing her servants and turning the house over to McBean, she went to live in a small lodging-house, there to await Pelham's return. She put away from her all the thoughts about him as a lover,—thoughts which would occasionally force themselves upon her, but from which she turned steadfastly,—and thought of him only as a brother and friend, the man most anxious to help her in the world, not even excepting her own father. General Brandon had written to her urgent and affectionate letters, telling her that his heart and hand and home were open to her as the best of daughters; and Elizabeth, whose heart yearned unceasingly for her father, found in the thought of once more being held in her father's arms the heartiest consolation she could have at that moment. But she knew it was useless to tell General Brandon any of her money difficulties. She understood his straitened circumstances, his mortgaged house, and the story of his Egyptian bonds. The only thing to do was to write Pelham frankly and fully every circumstance of her affairs, and to await his reply in England. She did this, and set herself to the task of waiting.

It was now autumn, a dull London autumn, and it seemed to Elizabeth as if she were living in a bad dream. Only the other day she had a devoted husband in Darrell, a friend in Pelham who was all that a friend could be to a woman, a home, servants, carriages, jewels, everything that the heart of woman could ask, with the prospect of having her father as an honored guest; and now she was widowed, alone, and in deep poverty. She had brought her expenses down to the lowest possible penny. Friendless, overwhelmed with debts of which she understood nothing, and in the clutches of a Scotch attorney and a jeweller's agent, she felt a certainty of relief when Pelham should write and then should come.

Every time the lodging-house bell rang, she thought it was Pelham's letter, but it did not come. Instead came McBean, first hinting and then threatening legal proceedings, especially in regard to the necklace. This seemed to Elizabeth an undeserved outrage and, reënforced by the counsel of the jeweller's agent, she said firmly, her dark eyes flashing: "That necklace was my husband's gift to me, his last gift to me, and part of it was his wedding gift. It is to me the most valuable thing on earth apart from what it cost, and it is mine and I shall not give it up. When Major Pelham returns, I promise you he will see the matter as I do."

This conversation occurred in Elizabeth's dingy room at the lodging-house, in an unfashionable part of Bayswater. "I judge Major Pelham will take the same view as I do, the only possible view," replied McBean, a wizened, fox-eyed man, who loved a five-pound note better than his own soul. "I am following out Major Pelham's exact directions when I demand of you the return of the necklace." At these words Elizabeth felt as if a knife had been thrust into her heart. She understood McBean to mean that he had received from Pelham explicit instructions in the matter of the necklace, while as a matter of fact he had heard nothing from Pelham any more than Elizabeth had. McBean had honestly thought that he was acting exactly in Pelham's interests and as Pelham would have wished him to do, who had in general terms authorized him to collect all debts due Pelham and pay all authorized bills.

McBean noticed Elizabeth's pallor and shock at his words, and rightly judged that he had hit upon the means of alarming her. He continued to talk as if repeating Pelham's words. Elizabeth listened with horror. Was there then no such thing as love and faith in the world? Could she have known Pelham for all these years, have felt the assurance of his devotion, and yet after all not known him? No word of McBean's was lost upon her, dazed as she was; but, feeling that she was unable to bear the scene longer, she got up and walked out of the room like an insulted queen, leaving McBean still talking. Not by one Scotch attorney, nor in one hour, could Elizabeth's belief in Pelham be shattered; and after the first horror caused by McBean's words, Elizabeth experienced a revulsion of feeling. She reproached herself for believing that Pelham could, for the sake of a few hundred pounds, so persecute and humiliate her. If she lost faith in Pelham, she would lose faith in humanity, even in her own father. McBean must be lying. What he had said to her was incredible. It stiffened her resolution to remain in England at any cost until she could hear from Pelham, and of eventually hearing she could have no doubt. She wrote him a few lines, simply asking if he had received her letter and recounting the circumstances under which she remained in England after Darrell's death. This letter she forwarded to the War Office, and then set herself to the task of waiting three months, or perhaps five, until she could get a reply. Meanwhile she continued to receive tender and affectionate letters from her father, imploring her to return to him. Elizabeth replied, saying that she would come to him as soon as the condition of her affairs permitted, and merely adding that there were certain things to be settled up in connection with the estate which required her presence in England.

The dull autumn deepened into a winter of fierce cold, with scarcely a ray of sunshine. Elizabeth suffered from this as only one can suffer who has spent many winters under an Indian sun. Even if her pride had permitted her to call for assistance from their former friends, of whom she had scarcely one among the women, but many among the men, she dared not; she was afraid that McBean's story had gone far and wide and that every action of hers might be under suspicion. And then came the crowning blow. The time passed when she might have returned the five hundred pounds advanced on the necklace. She could not pay it, having barely enough out of the one hundred pounds left her by Darrell to keep body and soul together. And no word came from Pelham.

The spring advanced, and the trees in the Bayswater district grew green. The time returned when only a year before she had been adored by her husband and loved and revered by the man who was now treating her with insulting neglect,—for to this belief Elizabeth had at last been forced. She spent many nights walking up and down her narrow room wringing her hands at the thought of the last letter she had written Pelham. The first she had no regrets for. It had been sent under the impression that Pelham was not only a sincere man but a gentleman; for certainly, knowing as he did every circumstance of Elizabeth's life and condition, it was ungentlemanlike of him to seize everything on which the law permitted him to lay his hands and to leave her destitute, alone, and a stranger. She felt that she could no longer doubt McBean's word, of which nothing could have convinced her short of Pelham's own conduct. Hope died hard within her, and she lingered in London during the spring and late summer; but as autumn came on she realized there was but one refuge left her, her father's roof in Washington.

She dared not let her intention of leaving London be known, for fear she might be stopped and a scandal might ensue. She raised money enough to take a second-class passage on a cheap steamer, and on a gloomy day in the last part of September she started upon her homeward journey. She had endured grief, anxiety, and privations, and especially that last overwhelming blow, the admission of Pelham's faithlessness. It had transformed her delicate and seductive beauty, but strangely enough it had not rendered her less delicately seductive. The pathos of her eyes, the sadness of her smile, the droop of her beautiful mouth, her mourning attire, refined and even elegant, in spite of her poverty, marked her out. She was not less beautiful than in her days of joy, and was far more interesting.

Chapter Seven

The return of a woman once married to a home under her father's roof is always a tragic episode. It implies death or disaster, and means the giving up of the prestige and independence a woman is supposed to attain by marriage. It may be the most sordid or the most dignified of tragedies that brings her back. Nevertheless it is a tragedy, and almost invariably has its sordid aspects, because it is oftenest poverty, to the accompaniment of divorce or death, which leads her, wounded and smarting and hungering, to that last remaining refuge, her father's house.

To Elizabeth Darrell, on the gloomy October day when she reached Washington from England, it seemed as if all the cruel reasons which ever brought a woman to such a pass existed in her case. She pondered over all the sources of her unhappiness with that curious passion for the analysis of their own misfortunes which is peculiar to women and poets. Her general and specific quarrel against fate had not been absent for a moment from her memory since she first undertook that long journey overseas. As every hour brought her nearer to her old home, the pain and the apprehension of pain increased. One mitigation she had hoped for, the sight of her father's kind, handsome old face as soon as she reached Washington; his courtly placing of his hand within her own; his valiant pretence that her home-coming was a happy one. But her despatch on leaving the steamer had not arrived in time, and when she reached the station there was no one to meet her.

It was a cool, damp autumn afternoon; a fine rain was falling and a general air of misery brooded over everything. With that dazed intelligence about places which were once well known but are now half forgotten, Elizabeth watched the streets and squares through which her cab rolled. She was forced to observe that Washington had become a fine city in the ten years since she had seen it. But as she was accustomed to the crowded thoroughfares of foreign cities, the quiet streets seemed to her dreary and deserted beyond expression. Was everybody dead in those silent, handsome houses? The cab stopped at last before the tall, plain house, quite far out in the northwest, in which Elizabeth had passed the beautiful though happy-go-lucky days of her girlhood. The finer residences were crowding the poor house in an unseemly manner. Elizabeth remembered it as surrounded by vacant lots, tenanted only by real estate agents' signs. Now the region was well and handsomely built up. The house, commonplace and shabby, looked still more commonplace and shabby from its fashionable surroundings. It was near the end of the square, where the smaller street debouched into a splendid avenue. On the corner was a fine white stone house, with an entrance on the avenue and a porte-cochère on the side street.

It made Elizabeth Darrell feel more of a forlorn stranger than ever when she saw the new luxury that surrounded her father's poor old house. She descended from the cab and with a faltering hand rang the bell. Her ring was answered by a negro woman, stout, elderly, and decent, but far removed from the smart English maids and native Indian servants to whom Elizabeth had been long accustomed. However, so strong is early habitude that the sight of this honest black face gave Elizabeth the first sentiment of home she had felt since her widowhood. In that black face was a doglike softness and kindness, and in the voice a compassionate yet deprecatory quality, which is not heard often in any but an African voice.

"You is Mis' 'Lisbeth," she said kindly, holding the door wide. "De Gin'l, he ear'n lookin' fer you 'twell to-morrer—but come right in heah."

There were signs of preparation within, but the room designed for Elizabeth—the best bedroom in the house—was not ready. Serena—for so she informed Elizabeth was her name—was full of humble, soft apologies.

"De Gin'l will be mighty worried dat he war'n home when you come; he was countin' on meckin' you mighty comfortable."

To which Elizabeth, her spirit dying within her at the aspect of things, answered: "Is not the front bedroom in the third story furnished? Perhaps I could go there."

Serena eagerly led the way. It was the room which had been Elizabeth's ten years ago. She had chosen it because General Brandon was always entertaining some of his relations, and had the old-time idea that hospitality to a guest meant the upsetting of all family arrangements; so Elizabeth had chosen this upper room for her own, secure in not being turned out of it to accommodate some ex-Confederate general, judge, or other person distinguished in "our great Civil War," as General Brandon always spoke of it. The windows had a good outlook upon the blue Potomac and on the misty line of the Virginia hills far beyond. Otherwise it had not a single recommendation.

Serena, her heart in her beady black eyes, was all sympathy and attention. She brought tea, called Elizabeth "honey," and talked in her slow and soothing voice of "de Gin'l." Evidently General Brandon was a hero to his maid-of-all-work.

At last Serena went out, and Elizabeth was alone. She sat down before the little dressing-table and removed her widow's bonnet and veil. And remembering that when she had last seen herself in that mirror she had been a bride and in the glory of her youth, she could not but study the changes in herself. She had then been beautiful, in a vivid, irregular manner, and ought to have been so still, as she was but little past her thirtieth birthday. But she saw plainly that she was haggard, that she was sallow, that she was painfully thin. She looked at her own reflection with self-pity, thinking, "I should be handsome still if I had but some flesh and color, and if life were not so hard and disappointing." She sat a long while, leaning her head on her hand, and seeing in the mirror, not her own reflection, but the hapless story of her own life passing before her. Then, recalling herself, like a person waking from a dream, she went to the window and looked out upon the quiet street.

It was already dusk, and the mist of the late autumn afternoon made mysterious shadows, through which the houses loomed large and near. Directly before her towered the great stone house, and just above the porte-cochère was a large, square window, with delicate lace draperies. It was quite dark enough for the wood fire, sparkling in the white-tiled fireplace, to show the interior of the room, which was evidently a boudoir of the most beautiful and luxurious character. Elizabeth was keen of sight, and she could not refrain from looking into so charming a room placed under her eyes. The walls were panelled with flowered silk; the furniture was of gold and spindle-legged; there was a delicious little sofa drawn up to the fire; everything spoke of wealth informed by taste.

In a minute more the mistress of this delightful room entered—a graceful, girlish figure, enveloped in a long, full cloak of a shimmering, silvery satin and wearing a flower-decked white hat. She threw aside her cloak and sat down for a moment on the sofa before the fire. Her air was not that of happy abandon, but rather of thoughtfulness, even of sadness. She was not beautiful, but Elizabeth, with a woman's ready appraisement of another woman's charms, saw at a glance that this girl's appearance was interesting. Her features were delicate, but her face was too pale for beauty; her thin-lipped mouth was large, though redeemed by perfect teeth; but her air, her figure, her walk, were full of grace and elegance. She remained only a few minutes in the room, then passed into the inner room and closed the door after her. And in a moment a maid came in and drew the silk curtains, leaving only a rosy glow from the window instead of a captivating picture.

Elizabeth, distracted for only a little while from her own thoughts, went back to the sad employment of casting up her sorrows and disappointments. She remembered her childhood on the old Virginia plantation with her father's mother. The war was not many years past then, and over all her life hung that great black shadow of chaos following defeat, the wreck of fortune, the upheaval of society, the helplessness, the despair of millions of people, with their whole social fabric a wreck, all values destroyed, everything disrupted and out of joint. She had realized later on how General Brandon had stinted himself for the little dark-eyed daughter on the Virginia plantation, and his magnanimous investment of his savings in Egyptian bonds, which made Elizabeth smile faintly in the midst of her wretchedness. In those years of separation and of learning from the great, wide-open book of life, Elizabeth had come to understand her father better than during that part of her life passed with him.

The General was a West Point graduate, and had been the best-loved man in his class, in spite of having been also the handsomest and one of the dullest. So when his old classmates in the army had heard of his straits, they all agreed that "something must be done for Dick Brandon." Although a West Point man, he was not a scientific man; he was too handsome to know much. His old friends did the best they could for him by getting him a clerkship in Washington; and General Brandon, who had commanded a brigade of three thousand fighting men, during four years of unremitting warfare, found himself subject to a chief of division young enough to be his son and as ignorant as men are made.

The old soldier had borne his lot with a fine patience and a sweet calmness that placed him well up in the ranks of unrecorded heroes. He had a superb courage, a charming temper; he remained incurably handsome, and likewise he was and always remained incurably simple in every way. Anybody could hoodwink him, and most people did. When he had come to Washington, bringing with him his daughter Elizabeth, then eighteen, and some remnant of property coming to him, he bought the shabby house. Or, rather, he thought he bought it, for it had a heavy mortgage on it, which General Brandon never had the least expectation of lifting—mortgages being as natural to Virginians as sparks flying upward.

Washington in those days was a simple, merry place, with a delightful and unique society based upon official rank, and a few old resident families, who were in society when Abigail Adams had the clothes dried in the East Room of the White House. Elizabeth remembered that she had been a great belle with gay young army and navy men and sprigs of diplomats and was not unhappy, although she had felt at every turn the prick of poverty. She had been ashamed to complain, however, in the presence of General Brandon's cheerful submission. He had his compensations, though,—chiefly his evening visits to and from other grizzled officers of both sides, when they sat and talked gravely and tensely of issues as dead as Julius Cæsar, and solemnly discussed what might have been, to an accompaniment of whiskey and cigars. General Brandon's whiskey and cigars were poor—he smoked a pipe himself, declaring he preferred it. But no army man of any rank ever animadverted on the General's whiskey or cigars; and, although both were evilly cheap, they drank and smoked cheerfully, with a relish for the man if not for his entertainment.

General Brandon had no knowledge of the words "getting on in society," or anything like them. He belonged to that sturdy oligarchy in Virginia which, whatever might be its shortcomings, knew nothing of snobs or snobbery, because everybody was just as good as everybody else. But his social career had been such that the newly rich might have asked him his patent for knowing everybody worth knowing. He was asked everywhere in those days, which he took as a matter of course, just as, during his occasional brief sojourns in England during his Egyptian days, he was asked everywhere and took it as a matter of course. Your true Virginian has many faults and some vices, but he is socially the wisest person in the world because he is the simplest. Nobody can patronize him, nobody can snub him. He takes the notice of royalty with the same unconscious ease that he does the rapturous salutation of a negro barber who belonged to him "befo' de war, sir,"— always polite, considerate, mindful of the small, sweet courtesies of life.

There is but one section of society with which he cannot get on. This is the newly rich smart set, fresh from the forge, the shop, the mine, the liquor saloon—that rapid fungus which has grown up in America during the last forty years, of which it has been said that no parallel exists to its license and irresponsibility, unless one goes back to the later Roman and Byzantine emperors. This class is free with a freedom that is staggering to contemplate; free from any traditions of the past, any responsibility in the present, any accountability to the future; free to marry, to be divorced, to live where it likes, to change its residence every week in the year; free from the care of the few children they have, free from taxes as far as rank perjury goes, and free to command all the science of the world to keep death at bay as long as possible. The advent of this class anywhere changes the aspect of things, and therefore when it moved in columns upon Washington, the people of General Brandon's class and Elizabeth's time became "Cave-dwellers," and the General was asked "nowhere,"—that is, he was still asked, but it was "nowhere." The General, however, did not know this at the time, or ever afterwards.

Elizabeth sat at the window and, looking out upon the murky evening, continued that sad review of her life.

There is a French school of moralists which says that a man may love two women at once. Elizabeth Darrell had certainly loved two men at once. Pelham was always and forever the man she would have married, but Darrell's honest love was not thrown away on her. She mourned him as she had mourned for her child, neither one infringing in the least on Pelham's place in her heart. She had been a wife and a mother, she had suffered a real and lasting passion for a man not her husband, but she had not transgressed a hair's-breadth; she had experienced both poverty and wealth, she had known and felt more in her thirty years than most women do in a lifetime;

and yet it seemed to her as if she had only turned over, without the opportunity to read and study, those glowing pages in the book of a woman's life—the love of a man, the love of a child, the beauty of the world. Now all was over—even Pelham's love and tender consideration, which had been hers for so long that she scarcely recognized the face of life without them. Nothing was left for her except her father, the best of men and fathers; but this was not enough for a nature like Elizabeth Darrell's.

While these thoughts were passing through Elizabeth's mind, darkness had fallen. Lights were twinkling everywhere. The great house opposite radiated brightness from many windows, and it occurred to Elizabeth, as to every sorrowful and disappointed person, that every one in that luxurious and brilliant home must be happy. Probably the girl of the boudoir, whose attitude had expressed such dejection, was grieving over some trifle like a disappointment in a dance or the failure of some plan of pleasure. Then she heard the street door open and a step which she recognized as her father's, and she had the first sensation of gladness she had felt for so long that she had almost forgotten what gladness was.

General Brandon, standing under the flaring gas-jet in the narrow hall, saw the black figure flying down the stairs towards him. He stopped, trembling with emotion; he who had without a tremor faced death a hundred times was shaken at the sight of his child in her mourning garments. The next minute her head was on his shoulder and he was patting it, saying, "My child,—my ever dear child,—welcome at all times, more welcome in your sorrow."

Elizabeth looked up, smiling and weeping. It was the first time since her husband's death that she had not seemed in everybody's way. General Brandon gazed at her, at the changes that ten years had made, at the marks of the recent shipwreck of her hopes and joys, at the pallor and thinness that brooding over her misfortunes had brought upon her; and then he said, with a tremulous smile and with tears in his honest eyes, "It is doubly sweet to have you back unchanged."

He led her into the dingy, well-remembered drawing-room, and they sat hand in hand on the sofa, talking, Elizabeth dwelling upon her husband's goodness to her, and mentioning none of her woes and perplexities in that first hour of meeting. Then Serena announced dinner, and General Brandon, with the air of escorting a queen regent, placed his daughter at the head of the table. "And never, since the day of your marriage, my love, have I ever sat down to this table without remembering you and wishing that you were seated at this place," he said.

To Elizabeth it seemed that the place she had in that dull dining room was the only spot she had had any right to, except under sufferance, since that June morning, now nearly a year and a half past, when her husband had died. Not only was General Brandon glad to see her, but Serena seemed equally so. Serena was a distinct acquisition to Elizabeth. When the dinner was fairly begun the General produced a bottle of that doubtful champagne which had been served at Elizabeth's wedding. "Saved to celebrate your return, my dearest," he said. Elizabeth could scarcely drink it for the tears that threatened to overflow.

The dining room was just as it had been ten years ago, only duller and dingier; but it was scrupulously neat. General Brandon's joy at seeing her was not troubled by any apprehensions as to the shortcomings of his household. All during dinner his spirits did not flag, and insensibly Elizabeth's turbulent heart grew more composed. Her father asked her minute particulars concerning her married life, and when Elizabeth told of Darrell's unvarying goodness to her, a singular look of relief came into her father's face. He had always had a dim apprehension that Elizabeth was not rightly mated with Darrell—which was true. He delicately refrained from asking any questions about her means, but Elizabeth told him frankly that the sole provision available for her, after Pelham inherited the property, was about one hundred pounds a year, contingent on her remaining a widow.

"Why, that is opulence!" said General Brandon, with the ideas of opulence of an ex-Confederate officer in a government clerkship. "That will suffice amply for your needs; and whatever I can supply, my dear, is yours, and my house and all in it are at your complete disposal."

Elizabeth rose and went over to him and kissed him. After all, there was some goodness left in the world. She did not once mention Pelham's name; but presently her father asked: "And in your trouble, where was Major Pelham, of whom you so often wrote me in years past, as being most kind and brotherly to you? As he was the next heir, he owed you much consideration."

Elizabeth, by an effort, spoke calmly. "He had just started for West Africa when Jack died. I have heard nothing from him, but I know through his solicitor—a very rude person—that Major Pelham has not been to England."

"And Major Pelham has not even written you a letter of condolence?"

"No."

"Most strange. And his solicitor is in communication with him?"

"Yes." Elizabeth was surprised at the steadiness of her voice in answering these questions, but General Brandon noticed for the first time a tremor in her tones.

"I cannot understand such conduct, and particularly as I retain a most agreeable recollection of Major Pelham,—Captain Pelham he was at the time of your marriage."

Then, to Elizabeth's relief, her father left off speaking of Pelham and gave her a minute account of all her Virginia relations and their doings during the last ten years. Elizabeth listened, her head on her hand, the light from the flaring chandelier falling upon her rich hair, one of her beauties left unimpaired. She appeared to be strictly attentive, but in truth she scarcely heard one word of what her father, in his soft, well-bred voice, was saying. Her mind was going over, as it had done many hundreds of times, the strange problem about Pelham. Was it possible that a mere matter of money and an estate had so changed him that he could forget her, after nine years of devotion—silent, it is true, but none the less eloquent? Or was it, after all, mere lip service he had paid her? This she could not quite believe, and so was ever tormented between longing and regret on one hand, and a silent but furious resentment on the other. Pelham at least was a gentleman, and yet he had not observed any sentiment of courtesy or attention to her when he was under every obligation to do so. He must know what sort of man Mr. McBean was, and yet he had left her completely in the solicitor's power. And the remembrance of McBean brought back the recollection of the money she owed on the necklace of which McBean had tried to rob her. She went over the whole weary story again, that strange, contradictory story of Pelham's agent, technically and actually—and she was glad to take refuge from her perplexing and contradictory thoughts by paying more heed to what her father was saying. He had got through with a part of his relations, and with a view to interesting Elizabeth in her future home was telling her something of those friends and acquaintances left in Washington.

"You remember Sara Luttrell, my dear?" asked General Brandon, with a smile. "Well, she is the same Sara Luttrell I danced with forty-five years ago at West Point. Nobody knew her age then and nobody knows it now—and time seems to have passed her by. She still lives in her fine old house, gives two dinners a week herself and goes out to dine the remaining five evenings, and nobody dares cross her except her nephew—her husband's nephew, I should say—Richard Baskerville."

"I remember Mr. Baskerville perfectly. He was always very kind to me, and so was Mrs. Luttrell."

"Richard Baskerville, my dear, is a very remarkable man. He has developed a comfortable fortune of his own, and will inherit every stiver of Sara Luttrell's money. But he works hard at his profession of the law and has made a name for himself. His fortune and position make it possible for him to devote himself to civics, and he is frequently engaged in the investigations of violations of the civil service law and in matters coming before Congress in which there is reason to suspect fraud. Just now he is in the thick of a fight with my neighbor in the fine house across the way, Senator Clavering, who is under fire at the present time before a senatorial committee concerning some alleged gigantic frauds with railway land grants in the Far West. I knew Clavering well before the war, when I was a captain of infantry and he was a sutler,—post-traders they now call themselves, and I understand that at army posts their daughters aspire to be visited by the young officers."

So the big, beautiful house belonged to this man Clavering. Elizabeth felt an immediate and strange interest on hearing about the people who lived in that charming abode. She wondered why she should wish to hear more of these people whose names she had heard only at that moment, but nevertheless she did. Nothing pleased General Brandon so much as to talk of things which happened before the war, except to talk about those which happened during the war.

"Clavering, however, was not the man to remain a sutler very long. He made money at the business—they all do; Napoleon Bonaparte was the only man who knew how to treat a man supplying soldiers. In the days when I knew Clavering, a sutler was a sutler; nevertheless, Clavering was such a remarkable man that no one who knew him could forget him. I used often to talk with him, and he professed to be under some obligations to me for certain small acts of kindness. After giving up the post-tradership for something better, I heard of him at intervals. I even saw him once here in Washington just before your marriage—sometimes he was up and sometimes he was down. Then he went into mining, prospecting, and land buying on a great scale and developed what I had always observed in him, a remarkable capacity for men and affairs. Five years ago he came to the Senate, built this splendid house you saw on the corner, and set up for a statesman and a gentleman. Ha, ha! I must say, however, that he had some qualifications for both. His family are conspicuous socially. He has three daughters and a deadly pious son, a confirmed ritualist like most of those common people. He goes to St. Bartholomew's Chapel, where I attend service still, as I did when I had the joy of having you with me, my child."

The General was a strict churchman, and it was no small recommendation that Clavering had a son who was also a strict churchman.

"And one of Clavering's daughters—Miss Anne Clavering—is very much admired and respected. Another of his daughters has had the misfortune to be divorced. His wife is little seen in society. She was a plain but most excellent woman when I knew her thirty years ago. This investigation of which Richard Baskerville is one of the leading spirits must be extremely painful to the ladies of Clavering's family."

General Brandon prattled on until ten o'clock came, when he always went to his modest club for an hour. He escorted Elizabeth to her door and said good night, giving her a blessing like the patriarchs' of old.

As soon as she was alone Elizabeth put out the gas and, opening the window, looked out upon the night. It was a damp and chilly night, with a few vagrant stars in the sky and a sickly moon setting. The vast mass of foliage which makes Washington a great park still hung upon the trees, but was yellowing and decaying. There were not many lights in the houses round about, except in the Clavering mansion, for it was not yet the full season in Washington. But while Elizabeth was looking a carriage drove under the Clavering porte-cochère, an alert footman opened the huge street door and spread a carpet down the steps. In a moment the girl Elizabeth had seen in the boudoir came out in an evening costume, with a white silk mantle enveloping her. Elizabeth had a perfectly clear view of her as she passed down the steps under a great swinging lantern. She was not beautiful, but interesting, graceful, and with an air of perfect breeding. After her came one of the handsomest men Elizabeth had ever seen. He was well past middle age, but his figure was noble, his features without line or wrinkle, his complexion ruddy with health, and his close-cropped iron-gray hair abundant. Elizabeth divined that it was Clavering, and what was more, the instant her eyes rested upon him she knew that she had seen him before; that she had seen him at some crisis in her life and seen him so as never to have forgotten him. She drew back from the window when the shock of surprise struck her. She could not recall at what particular crisis her eyes and this man's had met, except that it was long ago. She had not once during all those intervening years recalled him, but now his face was as instantly recognized by her as had been her own father's. It was as if, sailing upon the ocean, she had passed a beacon light upon a headland, which she remembered perfectly having seen in a remote past, but of which nothing was known to her except the fact that she had once seen it and the sight of it was at a crucial point in her life. The girl had by no means the beauty of the man, but there was sufficient likeness to indicate that they were father and daughter.

Elizabeth watched them with singular interest as the carriage rolled off. She had never expected to feel an interest in anything again, and that which she felt in these strange people seemed ominous. For Elizabeth, being a woman, was superstitious, and where before had she seen the face and figure of that man?

Chapter Eight

Sara Luttrell, as General Brandon called her, was sitting in her fine, old-fashioned drawing-room, enjoying her invariable Saturday evening gossip with her nephew-in-law, Richard Baskerville, preparatory to her customary Saturday evening dinner. This Saturday dinner was as much of an institution with Mrs. Luttrell as her ermine cape and her black-velvet gown, which were annually renewed, or her free-spoken tongue, all of them being Medic and Persian in nature.

Nobody knew how many decades this Saturday evening dinner had been established, just as nobody knew Mrs. Luttrell's age, except that it was somewhere between sixty and ninety. This dinner, which no more than six persons attended, took place at the unfashionable hour of seven. But seven had been the fashionable hour when Mrs. Luttrell began her Saturday dinners, and although she conceded much to the new fashions introduced by the smart set—more indeed than she ever admitted—and had advanced her formal dinner hour to half-past eight, yet she clung to seven for this Saturday evening institution. No other dinner invitation could lure Mrs. Luttrell from her own table on Saturday evenings, and it was one of the incidents of the warfare which had once raged between her and the then lady of the White House that Mrs. Luttrell should have been asked to dine at the White House on a Saturday evening. Mrs. Luttrell, however, came off triumphant. She could not have her own dinner that night, but in the very nick of time she heard of the death of a seventeenth cousin in Maryland. Mrs. Luttrell immediately asked to be excused from the White House on the ground of the death of a relative, and clapped herself, her coachman, and footman in mourning for a seventeenth cousin she had not seen in thirty years and had always cordially detested.

To be in ignorance of the sacredness of Mrs. Luttrell's Saturday evenings was a crime of grave magnitude in her eyes, and to respect her rights on Saturday was to take a toboggan slide in her favor. It was the law that Richard Baskerville should dine with her on Saturday, and although that young gentleman maintained a perfect independence towards her in every other respect, in spite of the fact that she had made a will giving him every stiver of her fortune, he was careful to reserve his Saturday evenings for her.

The old lady and the young man sat opposite each other before a glowing wood fire in the great drawing-room. Mrs. Luttrell was a small, high-bred, handsome woman, with snow-white hair, perfect teeth, a charming smile, a reckless tongue, and a fixed determination to have her own way twenty-four hours out of the day and three hundred and sixty-five days in the year, with an additional day thrown in at leap-year. Time had left a few external marks upon her, but in essentials she was the same woman General Brandon had danced with forty-five years before. She was in love with the same man, who even then was in his early grave,—Richard Luttrell, the husband of her youth. He had been dead unnumbered years, and only one person on earth—his nephew, Richard Baskerville—suspected that Mrs. Luttrell cherished her husband's memory with a smouldering and silent passion,—the only thing she was ever known to be silent about in her life.

Mrs. Luttrell sat bolt upright, after the ancient fashion, in her carved ebony chair, while Richard Baskerville lounged at his ease on the other side of the marble mantel. He was a well-made man of thirty-five, without any particular merit in the way of beauty; but so clear of eye, so clean cut of feature, so expressive of a man's intelligence and a man's courage, that people forgot to ask whether he was handsome or not. Mrs. Luttrell always maintained that he was very handsome, but found few to agree with her. Her belief came, however, from his resemblance to the miniature of her husband which she kept in her capacious pocket—for she still insisted on pockets in her gowns, and this miniature never left her by day or night.

Mrs. Luttrell's drawing-room was the admiration and the despair of people who knew something about drawing-rooms. It might have been taken bodily from the Second French Embassy, of which Mrs. Luttrell had seen a good deal, for she had known the third Napoleon well at some indefinite period in her history. The room was large and square and high-pitched, and wholly innocent of bay-windows, cosey corners, and such architectural fallals. The ceiling was heavily ornamented with plaster in the Italian style, and the cornice was superb. Over the fireplace was a great white marble mantel with a huge mirror above it, and in one corner of the room a grand piano something under a hundred years old looked like a belle in hoopskirts. There was a wealth of old rosewood furniture, pictures, candelabra, girandoles, Dresden ornaments, and other beautiful old things which would have made a collector turn green with envy.

Mrs. Luttrell was vain about her drawing-room, and with reason. She proudly claimed that there was not a single technical antique in it, and frequently declared she could tell the age of any family by a glance at their drawing-room. The newer the family the more antique the furniture, and when a family was absolutely new their house was furnished with antiques, and nothing but antiques, from top to bottom.

Mrs. Luttrell was gossiping hard as she sat before her drawing-room fire, shading her eyes from the leaping blaze with an old-fashioned lace fan and waiting for her guests to arrive. When Mrs. Luttrell gossiped, she was happy. One of the compensations to her for the new dispensations in Washington society was that it gave her plenty to gossip about. Ever since the advent in

Washington society of pickles, dry-goods, patent medicines, shoes, whiskey, and all the other brands of honest trade, she had been engaged in a hand-to-hand fight to maintain her prestige as a leading hostess of Washington, against the swarms of newcomers, whose vast fortunes made Mrs. Luttrell's hitherto ample income seem like genteel poverty. The rest of the "Cave-dwellers," as the original society of Washington is now called, had never made any fight at all. They regarded the new influx with haughty disdain in the first instance, laughed at their gaucheries, and spoke of them pityingly as, "Poor Mrs. So-and-so," "Those queer persons from nobody knows where." The first accurate knowledge, however, that came to them of the "smart set," as the new people are called, was when the Cave-dwellers were seized by the backs of their necks and were thrown over the ramparts of society, leaving the smart set in possession of the citadel.

Mrs. Luttrell, however, was not so easily disposed of as the rest. She saw that the Chinese policy of ignoring the enemy and representing a total rout as a brilliant victory would never do; so she set about holding her own with intelligence as well as courage. She called upon the new people, invited to her house those she liked, and Baskerville, who was the only living person who dared to contradict her, declared that Mrs. Luttrell never was known to decline an invitation to dine with any form of honest trade, no matter how newly emancipated. Her strongest weapon was, however, the capacity she had always possessed of bringing men about her. She was one of those men's women whom age cannot wither nor custom stale. Her esprit, her knowledge of how to make men comfortable in mind and body when in her house, her insidious flattery, which usually took the form of delicate raillery, had charmed successive generations of men. Her kingdom had been long established, and she knew how to reign.

In her early widowhood she had been much pestered with offers of marriage, but it had not taken many years to convince her world that she would die Sara Luttrell. Every cause except the right one was given for this, for of all women Mrs. Luttrell was the last one to be suspected of a sentiment so profound as the lifelong mourning for a lost love. But it was perhaps just this touch of passionate regret, this fidelity to an ideal, which constituted half her charm to men. At an age when most are content to sink into grandmotherhood, Mrs. Luttrell was surrounded by men of all ages in a manner to make a débutante envious. Other hostesses might have to rack their brains for dinner men; Mrs. Luttrell was always embarrassed with riches in this respect. An afternoon visit at her house meant finding a dozen desirable men whom hospitable hostesses languished for in vain. Even a tea, that function dreaded of women because it means two women to one man, became in Mrs. Luttrell's splendid, old-fashioned drawing-room a company in which the masculine element exactly balanced the feminine. She could have made the fortune of a débutante, and hence ambitious mothers sought her favor. Mrs. Luttrell, however, never had made a débutante's fortune and never intended to, holding that the power to grant a favor is more respected than the favor itself.

Then, too, it was well known that Richard Baskerville, one of the most desirable and agreeable men in Washington, was always to be found at her house, and was certain to inherit her fortune; and he had the ability, the wit, and the grace to be an attraction in himself. The old lady would have liked it well if Baskerville had consented to live in a suite of the big, unused rooms in the house, but this he would not do. He agreed as a compromise, however, to buy a small house back of Mrs. Luttrell's, and by using an entrance in her large, old-fashioned garden, it was almost as if he were in the same house.

Mrs. Luttrell followed the new customs and fashions so far as she thought judicious, and no farther. She knew the power of old customs and fashions when properly used. She held to her big landau, with her long-tailed black horses and her portly negro coachman and footman, because it gave her opportunities to intimidate the newly rich while apparently apologizing for her antique equipage.

"My carriage and horses and servants haven't varied much for forty years, and I can't change now. It's all very well for you people who are accustomed to sudden changes to have your smart broughams and victorias, and your pink-and-white English coachmen and footmen, but it would look perfectly ridiculous in Sara Luttrell, don't you see?" This to some aspiring newcomers whose equipage had been in a steady process of evolution from the time that a Dayton wagon was a luxury until now every season saw a complete revolution in their stables. Or, "I know my ermine cape looks as if it was made in Queen Elizabeth's time, but I can't afford to throw it away; and, Lord bless you, what does it matter whether one is in the fashion or not?" This to a lady who knew that her whole social existence depended upon her being in fashion.

It was insolent, of course, but Mrs. Luttrell meant to be insolent, and was so successfully, smiling meanwhile her youthful smile, showing her perfect teeth and certain of an answering smile from the men who were always at her elbow. Her whole world then thought she defied and laughed at the smart set; but Richard Baskerville saw, and had the assurance to tell her, that she secretly liked them very much and even sought their countenance by unique means.

"Well," said Mrs. Luttrell, settling herself and adjusting the immortal ermine cape around her lace-covered shoulders, "I have a surprise in store for you to-night. Who do you think is to dine here?"

"Myself number one, Senator and Mrs. Thorndyke, and Judge Woodford. I believe you are in love with that man, Sara Luttrell." This calling her by her first name Mrs. Luttrell reckoned a charming piece of impudence on Richard Baskerville's part, and in saying it his smile was so pleasant, his voice so agreeable, his manner so arch, that he conveyed extreme flattery by it. It made her the same age as himself.

"No, my dear boy, you are mistaken in that particular; but I have a surprise in store for you."

A pause.

"Why don't you ask me who it is?"

"Because you'll tell me in two minutes, if I just let you alone. You never could keep anything to yourself."

"It is—Anne Clavering."

Richard Baskerville sat up quickly. Surprise and pleasure shone in his face. "Why, Sara, I didn't think you could do anything as decent as that."

"I don't know why. I've always liked the girl. And I believe you are about half in love with her."

"You are such a suspicious old woman! But considering the share I am taking on the part of the original mortgages in those K.F.R. land grants, which may land Senator Clavering in state's prison, I feel some delicacy in paying any attention to his daughter."

"Naturally, I should think. But you were deep in the land-grant lawsuits before you ever met Anne Clavering."

"Yes, that's true. She once asked me to call but I never felt I could do so under the circumstances, though Clavering himself, who is a pachyderm so far as the ordinary feelings of mankind go, is as chummy as you please with me whenever we meet. And he actually invited me to visit his house! Miss Clavering probably knows nothing of the specific reason that keeps me away, but Clavering does, you may be sure. I have met Miss Clavering everywhere, and every time I see her I am lost in wonder as to how she came to be Senator Clavering's daughter or the sister of Mrs. Denman and that youngest daughter, Lydia."

"A couple of painted Jezebels, that are enough to drag any family to perdition. The old woman, I hear, murders the king's English and eats with her knife, but is a good soul. And if it wasn't for the determined stand Anne Clavering has taken for her mother, I don't imagine there is much doubt that Senator Clavering would have divorced her long ago. But Anne stands up for her mother and makes them all treat her properly, and is assisted by the brother,—a poor rag of a man, but perfectly respectable,—Reginald Clavering. Did you ever notice how common people run to high-flown names? None of our plain Johns and Georges and Marys and Susans and Jameses for them—they get their names, I think, out of Ouida's novels."

Richard Baskerville rose and stood in front of the fire. Mrs. Luttrell could not complain of any want of interest on his part in the subject under discussion. "Miss Clavering, as I told you, invited me to call on her, when I first met her. However, I had scruples about going to the house of a man I was fighting as I am fighting Senator Clavering. So I never went, and she never repeated the invitation. She is a very proud woman."

"Very. And she is the only one of her class I have ever seen who was really a scientific fighter."

"How pitiable it is, though, for a girl to have to fight her way through society."

"Yes—but Anne Clavering does it, and does it gallantly. Nobody can be impertinent to her with impunity. Do you know, the first thing that made me like her was the way that she hit back when I gave her a gentle correction."

"I am delighted to hear it, and I hope she whipped you well."

"Not exactly—but she stood up before me long enough to make me respect her and ask her to come to one of my little Saturday dinners."

"Mrs. Thorndyke is always asking her to dinner, and I know of no woman more discerning than Mrs. Thorndyke."

"Yes, Constance Thorndyke knows a great deal. But you see her husband is in the Senate and so she has to have some sorts of people at her house that I don't have. However, I know she is really a friend of Anne Clavering, and it is perfectly plain that although Miss Clavering is a *nouveau riche* herself, she hasn't any overwhelming respect for her own 'order,' as Ouida would say. She is ten times more flattered to be entertained by people like the Thorndykes and myself than by the richest pork-packing or dry-goods family in Washington."

"Certainly she is, as a woman of sense would be."

"As for that divorcée, Élise Denman, and that younger girl, Lydia, they are the two greatest scamps, as they are the two handsomest women, in this town. They are not deficient in their own peculiar sort of sense and courage, and they have whipped the Brentwood-Baldwins handsomely about that pew in St. John's Church. The religion of these brand-new people is the most diverting thing about them, next to their morals!"

"They also are the sons of God!" replied Baskerville, quoting.

"Don't believe that for a moment! Most of 'em are sons and daughters of Satan and nobody else. If ever the Episcopal Church—the Anglican Church, they call it—comes out squarely against divorce, I don't know where it will land the smart set or what they will do for a religion. They will have to become esoteric Buddhists or something of the sort. At present a pew in a fashionable church is the very first round on the social ladder. I have gone to St. John's all my life, and my father was one of the original pew-holders; but I declare, if I could find a well-warmed Episcopal church in southeast Washington or Anacostia even, I'd go to it."

"No, you wouldn't."

"Yes, I would. I don't know how the dispute with the Brentwood-Baldwins came about, but there was a pew near the President's which both the Claverings and the Brentwood-Baldwins wanted, and those two pagan daughters of Senator Clavering got it. You ought to have seen the Brentwood-Baldwin girl and those other two girls pass each other last Sunday morning coming out of church; they exchanged looks which were equivalent to a slap in the face."

"And you wouldn't have missed seeing it for worlds."

"Why, it's true I like to see a fight."

"For pure love of fighting I never saw your equal, Sara Luttrell."

"I come by it honestly. I am of as good fighting stock as you are, Richard Baskerville. But the Clavering-Brentwood-Baldwin row is not the only religious war in this town. You know Mrs. James Van Cortlandt Skinner—I know her husband was originally Jim Skinner before he went to glory."

"Now who told you that?"

"Oh, nobody; I just felt it in my bones. Well, Mrs. Skinner has a new and original fad—that woman is clever! She has seen the automobile fad, and the fancy-ball fad, and the monkey-dinner fad, and the dining-on-board-the-Emperor's-yacht fad, and the exclusive-school fad, and the exclusive-theatrical-performance fad, and the marrying-of-a-daughter-to-a-belted-earl-like-a-thief-in-the-night fad. She has done horse shows and yacht races and dinners to the Ambassador, and now she has outfooted New York and Newport, and left Chicago at the post. She has a private chapel, and she's going to have a private chaplain!"

"Oh, Lord, you dreamed it!"

"No, I didn't, Richard, my dear. You see, the Jim Skinners"—Mrs. Luttrell pronounced it as if it were "jimskinners"—"were originally honest Methodists; but these people shed their religion along with their old clothes and plated forks. And now Mrs. Jimskinner has become Mrs. James Van Cortlandt Skinner and an ardent Episcopalian, and so has Gladys Jimskinner, and Gwendolyn Jimskinner, and Lionel Jimskinner, and Harold Jimskinner, and I believe that woman has set her heart on having what she calls an Anglican archbishop in these United States."

"If she has, I know it was you who put the microbe in her head."

It was a chance shot, but it hit the white. "I think I did, Richard," meekly replied Mrs. Luttrell. "Mrs. Jimskinner—I mean Mrs. James Van Cortlandt Skinner—was urging me to join the Order of St. Monica; that's an order in which widows pledge themselves not to get married again. I told her there wasn't the least reason for me to join, for, although I've never told my age to any living person, I hardly consider myself on the matrimonial list any longer. And then Mrs. Van Cortlandt Skinner told me of the various beautiful brand-new orders in the Church, and said she thought of getting an order founded for one of her boys; the other would have to marry and perpetuate the family. And I suggested a contemplative order with a nice name, like the Order of St. Werewolf."

"Oh, Sara!"

"Yes, I did. I told her St. Werewolf was much respected in the Middle Ages; one heard a good deal of him; and she swallowed the wolf and the saint at one gulp. She said she rather liked the notion and might build a beautiful monastery on her estate on the Hudson, and whichever one of her boys she decided to indulge in a life of celibacy she would have made the first superior. And then I said—now, Richard, don't be rude—I said how much simpler all these delightful things would be if we only had an archbishop like the Archbishop of Canterbury; and Mrs. Van Cortlandt Skinner said that she had often longed for an archbishop and had always thought that the development of the Church in America required one; and then I caught Senator Thorndyke's eye—we were coming out of church—and I ran away."

"You wicked old woman! What will you do next!"

"I haven't done anything. You see, Mrs. Jimskinner belongs to that class who don't see any reason why they shouldn't have anything they happen to fancy. If they get married and don't like it, they get a divorce and a new husband or a new wife as they get a new butler when they discharge the one they have. If they want a title, they go and buy one. If they want a crest, they simply take one. They can't understand why they shouldn't do anything or have anything they want. I declare, Mrs. Jimskinner was talking to me with the simplicity of a child, and she's as bent on that private chaplain and that archbishop as if each was the latest style of automobile. I don't wonder the London newspapers guy Americans, remembering what kind of Americans find their way into London society."

"That reminds me—I met General Brandon two days ago, and his daughter Mrs. Darrell."

"Yes, Elizabeth Darrell has come back, as poor as a church mouse, and dreadfully changed. I shall call to see her. She will find a very different Washington from the one she left ten years ago."

"Miss Clavering," announced the negro butler.

Anne Clavering, graceful and self-possessed, entered the room. She had not the sumptuous beauty of her sisters, nor remarkable beauty at all; yet, as Elizabeth Darrell had seen in that first accidental view of her, she was more than beautiful—she was interesting. She had no marks of race, but she had every mark of refinement. Her gown was simple, but exquisite, and she wore no jewels. Mrs. Luttrell received her amiably and even affectionately, and her quick eye noted that both Anne and Baskerville blushed at meeting.

"So you are not above coming out to an unfashionable dinner with an old fogy," she said, taking Anne's hand.

"I believe it is considered one of the greatest privileges of Washington to dine with you at one of your 'unfashionable dinners,'" Anne replied, with her pleasant smile. This made Anne's fortune with Mrs. Luttrell.

In a minute or two more Senator and Mrs. Thorndyke were announced, and they were promptly followed by Judge Woodford, a handsome antique gentleman, who had for forty years counted on being one day established as the head of Mrs. Luttrell's fine house. The Thorndykes were not a young couple, although they had not been long married. Their love-affair had covered a long period of separation and estrangement, and at last when fate had relented and had brought them together in their maturity, it gave them by way of recompense a depth of peace, of confidence, of quiet happiness, and a height of thrilling joy at coming into their own inheritance of love, that made for them a heaven on earth. Thorndyke was a high-bred, scholarly man of the best type of New England, who hid under a cool exterior an ardent and devoted nature. Constance Thorndyke was exteriorly the scintillant, magnetic Southern woman, but inwardly she was as strong and as sustaining as Thorndyke himself. Neither of them had a grain of mawkish sentimentality, and they were always differing playfully when they really differed seriously; but they never differed in their love and admiration of what was good.

Baskerville took Anne out to dinner. He had several times had that good fortune, especially in Mrs. Thorndyke's house, and so far as dinner companions went he and Anne were well acquainted. Anne had been deeply mortified at Baskerville's ignoring her invitation to call, and the reason she at once suspected—his knowledge of her father's character and his share in furnishing information to the senatorial committee which was investigating Senator Clavering. She did not for one moment suspect that Baskerville put compulsion on himself to keep away from her house. She was conscious of a keen pleasure in his society, and a part of the gratification she felt at being asked to one of Mrs. Luttrell's intimate dinners was that Baskerville should know how Mrs. Luttrell esteemed her.

ill138

"BASKERVILLE TOOK ANNE OUT TO DINNER."

The dinner fulfilled all of Anne's expectations. The Thorndykes were socially accomplished, and Judge Woodford had been a professional diner-out since the days when President Buchanan had made him a third secretary of legation at Paris. Anne Clavering found herself adopted into the small circle, so different in birth and rearing from her own, by the freemasonry of good sense and good manners—in which she, however, was the equal of anybody.

Mrs. Luttrell shone at her own table, and the restraint she put upon her own tongue revealed her to be, when she chose, a person of perfect tact. And, indeed, her most courageous speeches were matters of calculation, and were in themselves a species of tact. When entertaining guests in her own house, however, she showed only the amiable side of her nature; and she was always amiable to Richard Baskerville, the one human being in the world whom she really loved and feared. Anne was extremely amused at the attitude of Baskerville to Mrs. Luttrell, shown by such things as calling her by her first name and hectoring her affectionately,—all of which Mrs. Luttrell took meekly, only prophesying that if he ever married, he would make an intolerable husband.

Anne Clavering noted that among these people of old and fixed positions there was a great deal of chaff, while among the new people there was always great formality. The manners of the one set were simple, and of the latter elaborate. She also saw, being of a quick eye, that there were many differences in little things between the old and the new. The new had a different and complex fork for every course, but Mrs. Luttrell had, except some very old-fashioned oyster forks, the same handsome, plain old forks which had been in use in her family since silver forks were first adopted. There was no opportunity, if she had wished, to emulate a brand-new Washington hostess, who mentioned to a distinguished guest that he was eating his fish with the wrong fork. And Mrs. Luttrell had the temerity to have on the table her splendid old decanters, in which was served the very last old port in Washington, "laid down by papa in '59."

When the dinner was over they closed around the drawing-room fire and talked cosily, as people can seldom talk in the hurrying, rushing twentieth century; and then Mrs. Thorndyke, at Mrs. Luttrell's request, went to the grand piano and sang sweetly some songs as old-fashioned as the piano. Anne remembered with a blush the professional singers who were considered essential to the Clavering house after one of the large, magnificent, and uncomfortable dinners which were a burden and an anxiety to all of the Clavering family.

When the carriages were announced, everybody was surprised at the lateness of the hour. Anne went up to Mrs. Luttrell and thanked her sincerely and prettily for one of the pleasantest evenings she had ever spent in Washington. Mrs. Luttrell, who declared herself totally indifferent to blame or praise from one of the new people, was hugely flattered by this expression from a Clavering.

Baskerville, having antique manners, put Anne in her carriage, and contrived to express in this small action a part of the admiration and homage he felt for her. Anne, driving home in the November night, experienced a strong and sudden revulsion of feeling from the quiet enjoyment of the evening. Bitterness overwhelmed her. "How much happier and better off are those people than I and all my kind!" she thought. "They have no struggles to make, no slights to swallow or avenge, no social mortifications, nothing to hide, to fear, to be ashamed of, while I—" She buried her face in her hands as she leaned back in the carriage, and wept at the cruel thought that Baskerville would not come to her house because he did not think her father a decent man.

As she entered her own street she caught sight of Count Rosalka, a young attaché, helping Élise Denman out of a cab at the corner. Élise ran along the street and under the porte-cochère as Anne got out of the carriage and walked up the steps. Élise's eyes were dancing, her mouth smiling; she looked like a bacchante.

"Remember," she said, catching Anne by the arm, "I've been out to dinner, too."

The door was opened, not by one of the gorgeous footmen, but by Lydia, handsomer, younger, and wickeder-looking than Élise. "Good for you, Lyd," whispered Élise; "I'll do as well by you sometime." The footman then appeared, and grinned openly when Lydia remarked that as she was passing through the hall she recognized Miss Clavering's ring and opened the door.

Anne went upstairs, her heart sick within her. As she passed her mother's door she stopped, and a tremulous voice within called her. She entered and sat awhile on her mother's elaborate, lace-trimmed bed. Mrs. Clavering, a homely and elderly woman, looked not less homely and elderly because of her surroundings. But not all the splendor of her lace and satin bed could eclipse the genuine goodness, the meekness, the gentleness, in her plain, patient face. She listened eagerly to Anne's description of the dinner, which was cheerful enough, albeit her heart misgave her cruelly about Élise and Lydia.

When she had finished speaking Mrs. Clavering said, patting Anne's head with a kind of furtive affection, "I think you know real nice, well-behaved people, my dear, and I wish the other girls"—"gurls" she called them—"were like you."

At that moment Baskerville and Senator Thorndyke were sitting in Baskerville's library, discussing a bottle of prime old whiskey and looking at some books from a late auction. Mrs. Thorndyke had driven home, and Senator Thorndyke, preferring to walk, was spending an hour meanwhile in masculine talk unrestrained by the presence of the ladies. The two men were intimate, an intimacy which had originated when Baskerville was a college senior and Thorndyke was on the committee of their Greek-letter society. There was a strong sympathy between them, although Thorndyke was a New Englander of New Englanders and Baskerville a Marylander of Marylanders. Both were lawyers of the old-time, legal-politico sort, both of them scholarly men, both of them independent of popular favor; and both of them, while preaching the purest democracy, were natural aristocrats. They belonged to opposite political parties, but that rather added zest to their friendship. The library in Baskerville's home, across the garden from Mrs. Luttrell's, was in the second story and extended the full width of the house. It was essentially a bachelor's working library, plain, comfortable, well warmed and lighted, and with an engaging touch of shabbiness. A big leather-covered table was in the middle of the room, and under the green light from a student lamp were displayed the books, the whiskey, the water, and the glasses. Baskerville's mind was not, however, on the books he was showing, but on Anne Clavering, and incidentally on Senator Clavering.

"How do you account for Miss Clavering being the daughter of Senator Clavering?" he asked Thorndyke, as they pulled at their cigars.

"Those things can't be accounted for, although one sees such strange dissimilarities in families, everywhere and all the time. Miss Clavering is, no doubt, a case of atavism. Somewhere, two or three generations back, there was a strain of refinement and worth in her family, and she inherits from it. But I see something in her of Clavering's good qualities—because he has some good qualities—courage, for example."

"Courage—I should think so. Why, the way that man has fought the courts shows the most amazing courage. He is a born litigant, and it is extraordinary how he has managed to use the law to crush his opponents and has escaped being crushed himself. And in trying to follow his turnings and windings in this K. F. R. swindle it is astounding to see how he has contested every step of an illegal transaction until he has got everybody muddled—lawyers, State and Federal courts, and the whole kit of them. As fast as one injunction was vacated he would sue out another. He seems to have brought a separate and distinct lawsuit for every right in every species of property he ever possessed at any time—of all sorts: lands, mines, railways, and corporations. He has pocketed untold millions and has invoked the law to protect him when ninety-nine men out of the hundred would have been fugitives from justice. He is the most difficult scoundrel to catch I ever met—but we will catch him yet."

"I think you are hot on his trail in the K. F. R. matter," answered Thorndyke. "I believe myself that when the great exposé is made before the investigating committee it will recommend his expulsion from the Senate, and three-fourths of the senators will support the committee. The legislature is safe, so the party won't lose a seat; and in any event I don't believe we can afford to hold on to a man like Clavering after the country knows about him— especially with a presidential campaign coming on within the year. I think, with all his talents, he would not be fitted for public life if he were as honest as he is dishonest. He has no idea, after all his litigation, of sound legal principles, and he is fully persuaded that any man, any court, any legislature, may be bought; and a more dangerous fallacy doesn't exist for a public man than that. He has never submitted to party discipline and has played politics with every party that has ever made a showing in his state. For all his money, he has never been a contributor to party funds; so I think, making due allowances for the weakness of human nature, that a horrible example will be made of Clavering, and we shall thereby deprive you of an effective party cry in the campaign. You are really doing us a service by your course, because without your unravelling the legal tangle I doubt if anything could have been made out of the K. F. R. frauds. I have no sympathy to waste on Clavering or any of his family that I know of, except Miss Clavering. It will go hard with her."

Baskerville's tanned complexion grew a little pale, and he sat silent for some moments; so silent that Thorndyke began to suspect Mrs. Thorndyke's idea was the right one after all—Baskerville was in love with Anne Clavering. Thorndyke had laughed at it as a woman's fancy, saying to her that a woman couldn't see a man pick up a girl's handkerchief without constructing a matrimonial project on the basis of it; but Constance Thorndyke had stoutly maintained her opinion that Baskerville was in love with Anne Clavering. His attitude now certainly indicated a very strong interest in her, especially when he said, after a considerable pause:—

"If I had known Miss Clavering before this K. F. R. matter was started, perhaps I shouldn't have gone into it. There is something very painful, you must know, Thorndyke, in dealing a blow at a woman—and a woman like Miss Clavering. By heaven, for all the luxury she lives in and all the respect and admiration she commands, there is not a woman in Washington whom I pity more!"

Thorndyke had been turning over the leaves of a beautiful Apuleius, which was one of the treasures Baskerville was exhibiting to him. He opened the volume at the fifth metamorphosis and read out of it a single phrase which made Baskerville's face gain color:"'The bold, blind boy of evil ways.' There's nothing in all those old Greek literary fellows which excels this in humor, although what there is humorous in modern love I can't see. It's the most tragic thing in life, and if it is genuine, it draws blood every time."

Thorndyke had reason to say this. He had spent the eighteen best years of his life solitary and ill at ease because of a woman's love and another woman's spite, and not all the happiness of married life could ever make either him or Constance Thorndyke forget their starved hearts in those eighteen years of estrangement and separation. But as normal men deal with sentimentalities in a direct and simple manner, he added, after a minute: "Miss Clavering ought to marry. If she could be cut loose from Clavering himself and those two handsome and outrageous sisters of hers, it would be an unmixed blessing. But with all Miss Clavering's merit and charms, that family of hers will always be a handicap with a man of the sort she would be likely to marry."

"Not if he really loved her, Thorndyke." Senator Thorndyke smoked on in silence. "And," continued Baskerville, "her mother is a most worthy woman, if uneducated; and although Reginald Clavering is a great fool, I believe he is a thoroughly upright man and even a gentleman. So you see it is not wholly a family of degenerates."

Thorndyke, seeing which way the tide was setting, remarked with perfect sincerity, "Miss Clavering is worthy of any man; and I say so not only on my own judgment, but on my wife's."

"Sanest, soundest woman in Washington—except Miss Clavering herself," was Baskerville's reply to this.

When Senator Thorndyke reached home an hour afterwards, he roused his wife to tell her that he believed that Baskerville was in love with Anne Clavering after all.

"And has been ever since he knew her; but men are so dense, he didn't know it himself—much less did you know it until it became as obvious as the Washington Monument," was Mrs. Thorndyke's wifely reply.

Chapter Nine

The next day was a bright November Sunday, and after an early luncheon Baskerville started out for a walk into the country. Anne Clavering was much in his mind, and he was beginning to debate with himself in this wise: if Senator Clavering had no delicacy about inviting him to call, why should he be too delicate-minded to go? Which proves that Baskerville was in love with Anne Clavering, or he would have said that for him to go to a man's house under the circumstances in which he would enter Senator Clavering's was an outrageous breach of propriety.

When he got well out of the town, he met the scanty congregation of a small Episcopal chapel in the suburbs. Among those strolling homeward he speedily recognized General Brandon and Elizabeth Darrell—and with them Reginald Clavering. This only son of Senator Clavering's was no more like him than Anne was, and, indeed, very much resembled Anne, except that he had neither her grace nor her intelligence. He had a good and affectionate heart, and in a foolish, blundering way was both an honest man and a gentleman. His life, however, was given over to small and futile things, and even his piety, which was genuine, embodied a childish worship of ecclesiastical trifles. He was the mainstay, chief financial backer, and clerical man-of-all-work in the little chapel, while his sisters, Élise and Lydia, fought with the Brentwood-Baldwins at St. John's, and Anne, after going to an early morning service at the nearest church, devoted the rest of her Sunday to her mother.

Baskerville stopped and spoke with great cordiality to the party. He had known Elizabeth Darrell well in her girlhood, and there was a remote, seventeenth-cousin, Maryland-Virginia connection between the Baskervilles and the Brandons. His first glance at her in her mourning costume showed him that she had suffered much, and her beauty was partially eclipsed. She had gained interest, however, as the case often is, by learning the hard lessons of life, and Baskerville saw that she might regain all and more of her good looks with returning flesh and color, and a loss of the wearied and forlorn expression in her still glorious dark eyes. He asked permission to call upon her, and Elizabeth assented with outward grace and cheerfulness; but, in truth, it mattered little to her then whether she ever saw any one again, except her father, and—humiliating thought!—Pelham, once more. For, deeply incensed as she was with Pelham, the thought of ever again meeting him was profoundly agitating to her. She inquired of Baskerville about Mrs. Luttrell, and sent her a kind message; then they parted and went upon their several ways.

Half an hour afterwards, when Elizabeth Darrell was nearing her own door, Senator Clavering—who, sitting at his library window, caught sight of her graceful black figure as she stopped with her father and talked a few minutes with Reginald Clavering—started to his feet, his keen, handsome eyes fixed upon her with admiring approval. He remembered her perfectly well, that beautiful girl he had seen on the icy night ten years ago when he had watched the gay people flocking to the Charity Ball, and the little trinket he had unconsciously crushed under his foot. He had wondered a dozen times since he had been in Washington, and had often asked, what had become of General Brandon's beautiful daughter, and was told that she had married a British Army man and had disappeared in the wilderness. He had never seen General Brandon from that hour, although they lived opposite, General Brandon's hours being very different from Senator Clavering's and their habits being as dissimilar as could possibly be imagined.

Clavering was a connoisseur in feminine beauty, and all forms of it appealed to him. He thought Elizabeth twice as beautiful as he had done in that passing glimpse of her, ten years before, in the bloom of her girlhood. Strange to say, the languid, interesting, and somewhat tragic type which Elizabeth Darrell now represented was the most attractive to him—perhaps because it is the rarest. "By Jove, what a woman! I must know her," was his inward comment. He watched Elizabeth intently, her fragile figure, her peculiar grace of movement, the note of distinction in her whole person and air; and then and there he determined to resurrect his acquaintance with General Brandon, whose relationship to her was obvious, and whom Clavering had no more forgotten than General Brandon had forgotten him.

Presently Reginald Clavering entered the house, and the first sound that met his ears was something between a wail and a shout which came from the upper region. Reginald winced at the sound. His mother still held to her original Baptist faith—about the only thing pertaining to her early life which she had not meekly given up. She was at that moment enjoying the spiritual ministrations of a Baptist minister who came sometimes on Sundays to pray with her and sing camp-meeting hymns—to the intense diversion of the smart English footman and gay French maids, of whom Mrs. Clavering was in deadly fear. And to make it worse for Reginald, Anne Clavering, instead of setting her face against this unchurchmanlike proceeding, actually aided and abetted her mother in her plebeian sort of religion, and joined her clear note to the Rev. Mr. Smithers' bellowing and Mrs. Clavering's husky contralto. The whole thing offended Reginald Clavering's æsthetic sense; but it was a proof that he had much that was good in him that he bore these proceedings silently, as became a gentleman, a Christian, and an Anglican, and made no complaint to any one except Anne.

As he passed the open library door, Senator Clavering called out to him in that rich and melodious voice which the stenographers in the Senate gallery declared the most agreeable and easily followed voice of any member of the Senate: "Hello! What is the name of that infernally pretty woman whom you were escorting just now?"

"Mrs. Darrell, the widowed daughter of General Brandon. General Brandon is one of the vestrymen at St. Gabriel's Chapel," replied Reginald, stiffly.

"Yes, fine old fellow. I knew him more than thirty years ago when he was a captain of infantry out on the plains and I was a sutler, as it was called then. Handsome old chap still, and his daughter is like him. You show good taste, my boy. I thought you'd find something more entertaining than religion out at that chapel."

Reginald Clavering scorned to reply to this, but went on to his study in another part of the house. In a few minutes he heard his father's step on the stair, and dutifully opened the door for him. Clavering entered, threw himself in a great chair, and began to look around him with an amused smile. The room was a museum of ecclesiastical pictures and gimcracks.

"When I was your age," said Clavering, laughing openly, "I hadn't a room like this—I shared a board shanty with a fellow from God knows where, who had served a term in state's prison. But he was the finest smelter expert I ever saw, and had the best eye for a pretty woman. You couldn't see the boards in our walls for the pictures of ballet dancers and the like. Nothing in the least like this." And he laughed.

Reginald's pale face flushed with many emotions. His father's tone and manner expressed a frank scorn for him and all his surroundings. Clavering kept on:—

"My roommate—nobody had a room to himself in those diggings—taught me how to differentiate among pretty women." Clavering was diverted at the spectacle of a man shrinking from such a discussion. "Now, of your sisters, Anne is really the best looking—the most effective, that is. Élise and Lydia are of the tulip variety. Anne is something more and different."

"Élise and Lydia are both of them strikingly like you, sir," replied Reginald. It was the nearest approach to sarcasm he had ever made in his life. Clavering enjoyed the cut at himself immensely.

"Very neat; thank you. Now I should say that Mrs.—what's her name?—old Brandon's daughter is a remarkably attractive, even beautiful woman, although she strikes me at first glance as one of those women, not exactly young, who haven't yet found themselves. Perhaps you'll show the lady the way."

"Sir," said Reginald, after a pause, "you shock me!"

Clavering was not in the least annoyed at this. He looked at Reginald as one studies an amusing specimen, and said, as if to himself, "Good God! that you should be my son!" He then took up some of the books on the table and began to turn them over, laughing silently to himself the while. The books corresponded with the pictures and ornaments. Reginald Clavering found all of his family a cross, except his sister Anne, and his father the heaviest cross of all. He was sincerely relieved when Clavering took himself downstairs to his own library again.

It was a handsome library, and quite what the library of a senator, if not a statesman, should be. The walls were lined with encyclopædias, histories, and the English classics. Clavering, however, was a student of far more interesting documents than any ever printed in a book. He had studied unceasingly the human subject, and knew men and women as a Greek scholar knows his Sophocles. This knowledge of men had made him not only dazzlingly and superbly successful, but even happy in his way. The most saintly man on earth might have envied James Clavering his mind, ever at ease; for he knew no morals, and was unmoral rather than immoral.

Two things only in life disturbed him. One was that he would have liked to get rid of his wife, whom he had married when he was barely twenty-one. She had served his turn. Although homely, shapeless, and stupid now, she had made him comfortable—in the days when his miner's wages barely kept a humble roof over his head. She had brought her children up properly. Clavering had enough of justice in him not to hold her accountable for the fastness, the vagaries, the love of splendor, the lack of principle, that made his eldest and youngest daughters the subject of frequent paragraphs in scandalous newspapers, and had landed one in the divorce court. They were like him—so Clavering admitted to himself, without a blush. His one fear was that they would, as he expressed it, "make fools of themselves." He admired chastity in women and even respected it, so far as he could feel respect for anything; and he would, if he could, have kept all the women in his family strictly virtuous. But he never was quite at ease about either Élise or Lydia; and when he saw the simple way in which Élise had slipped off the matrimonial fetters, Clavering had begun to fear greatly—those two girls were so extremely like himself!

He knew well enough from whom Reginald inherited his temperament. Mrs. Clavering's father had been a weak, well-meaning Baptist preacher, and Reginald was a replica of him, plus a university education and a large allowance superadded. Where Anne came in Clavering frankly acknowledged himself beaten. She inherited his own strong will and her mother's gentleness of address. But she had an innate delicacy, a singular degree of social sense, a power of making herself felt and respected, that Clavering admired but the origin of which he could not trace. She was the one person in the world whom he feared and respected. It was due to her that the Claverings had any real social status whatever. It was through her, and for her alone, that certain honest, dignified, and punctilious senators and public officials came to the grand Clavering dinners and musicals, and allowed their wives to come. It was Anne who would have to be vanquished when, as Clavering had always intended, he should get a divorce from his wife and marry again. He had not attempted this, merely because, so far, the women who would have married him he did not want or could get on easier terms, and the women he might have wanted would not have him at any price. Anne was known as her mother's champion, and Clavering knew that she would fight the divorce with all the skill, courage, and pertinacity which, as Baskerville had truly said, was all she had inherited from her father. She had in her, disguised by much suavity and sweetness, a touch of aggressiveness, a noble wilfulness that would not be reasoned away. Clavering knew that the tussle of his life would come when the divorce was seriously mooted; but he was not the less ready for the tussle.

The first sight of Elizabeth Darrell had impressed him wonderfully, and the second vision of her had determined him to renew his acquaintance with General Brandon; and while he was turning the mode of this over in his mind he was summoned to luncheon. At luncheon all of the family assembled— Élise and Lydia in elaborate negligées, Anne simply but properly dressed. She sat next her mother at the table and was that poor creature's only outspoken champion.

"So you had a nice morning, with the psalm-singing and all that," said Élise to Anne.

"Very nice," replied Anne. "Mamma seemed to enjoy it very much."

"We had a nice morning, too," replied Élise. "The Brentwood-Baldwins glared at us as we went into church; they will never forgive us for getting that pew in the middle aisle, so close to the President's. Then, after church, Count Rosalka asked to walk home with me. Lydia got Laurison, the new British third secretary; so we sent the carriage on and walked out Connecticut Avenue with all the Seventh Street shopkeepers. It was very amusing, though."

"It must have been," said Clavering, gravely. "You must have recalled the time when you would have thought yourself as rich as Pierpont Morgan and Rockefeller combined if you had been as well dressed as a Seventh Street shopkeeper's daughter. It was only twelve years ago, you remember, since I struck pay dirt in mines and politics."

Élise and Lydia both smiled pleasantly. They were their father's own daughters, and along with many of his vices they inherited his superb good humor, which never gave way except to a preconcerted burst of imposing wrath.

"I remember those days quite well," said Anne. Her voice, as well as her looks, was quite different from her sisters'. Instead of their rich and sensuous tones, beautiful like their father's, Anne's voice had a dovelike quality of cooing softness; but she could always make herself heard. "I remember," she continued, touching her mother's coarse hand outspread on the table, "when mamma used to make our gowns, and we looked quite as nice as the girls who could afford to have their clothes made by a dressmaker."

"Them was happy days," said Mrs. Clavering. It was her only remark during luncheon.

They talked of their plans for the coming week, as people do to whom pleasure and leisure are new and intoxicating things. Anne was plied with questions about Mrs. Luttrell's dinner. She told freely all about it, being secretive only concerning Baskerville, merely mentioning that he was present.

"A more toploftical, stuck-up F. F. V.—or F. F. M., I suppose he is—I never saw than this same Mr. Baskerville, and as dull as ditchwater besides," said Lydia.

Here Reginald spoke. "Mr. Baskerville is very highly esteemed by the bishop of the diocese," he said.

"And by people of a good deal more brains than the bishop of the diocese," added Clavering. "Baskerville is one of the brainiest men of his age I ever knew. He is fighting me in this K. F. R. business; but all the same I have a high opinion of his gray matter, and I wish you two girls—Élise and Lydia— knew men like Baskerville instead of foreign rapscallions and fortune-hunters like Rosalka. And I wish you went to dinners such as Anne went to last night, instead of scampering over the town to all sorts of larky places with all sorts of larky people."

To this Lydia replied. So far, she had achieved neither marriage nor divorce, but she was not averse to either. "I think the dinners Anne goes to must be precious dull. Now, our men and our parties, whatever they are, they aren't dull. I never laughed so much in my life as I did at Rosalka's stories."

Clavering's face grew black. He was no better than he should be himself, and ethically he made no objection to his daughters' amusing themselves in any way but one; but old prejudices and superstitions made him delicate on the one point upon which he suspected two of his daughters were the least squeamish. He said nothing, however, nor did Anne or Reginald; it was a subject none of them cared to discuss. When luncheon was over, Mrs. Clavering and Anne made ready for their early Sunday afternoon walk—a time to which Mrs. Clavering looked forward all the week and with which Anne never allowed any of her own engagements to interfere.

Meanwhile Clavering himself, interested for the first time in the tall, shabby house across the way, walked out upon the broad stone steps of his own place and watched the windows opposite, hoping for a glimpse of Elizabeth Darrell's face. While he stood there smoking and apparently engaged in the harmless enjoyment of a lovely autumn afternoon, Richard Baskerville approached. Baskerville denied himself the pleasure of seeking Anne in her own home, but he often found himself, without his own volition, in the places where he would be likely to meet her, and so he was walking along the street in which she lived. Seeing Clavering on the steps Baskerville would have passed with a cool nod, but Clavering stopped him; and the younger man, thinking Anne Clavering might be within sight or might appear, compromised with his conscience and entered into conversation with Clavering. It was always an effort on Baskerville's part to avoid Clavering, whose extraordinary charm of manner and personality was a part of his capital. Baskerville, deep in the study of Clavering's career, felt a genuine curiosity about the man and how he did things and what he really thought of himself and his own doings. He reckoned Clavering to be a colossal and very attractive scoundrel, whom he was earnestly seeking to destroy; and his relations were further complicated with Clavering by the fact that Anne Clavering was—a very interesting woman. This Baskerville admitted to himself; he had got that far on the road to love.

The Senator, with the brilliant smile which made him handsomer than ever, said to Baskerville, "We may as well enjoy the privilege of speaking before you do me up in the matter of the K. F. R. land grants."

The younger man cleverly avoided shaking hands with Clavering, but replied, also smiling, "Your attorneys say we shan't be able to 'do you up,' Senator."

"I hope they're right. I swear, in that business the amount of lying and perjury, if placed on end, would reach to the top of the Washington Monument. Have a cigar?"

Such indeed was Baskerville's own view of the lying and perjury, but he opined that it was all on Senator Clavering's side, and he was trying to prove it. He got out of taking one of Clavering's cigars—for he was nice upon points of honor—by taking a cigarette out of his case.

"I don't know what you youngsters are coming to," said Clavering, as he smoked. "Cigarettes and vermouth, and that sort of thing, instead of a good strong cigar and four fingers of whiskey."

"I was on the foot-ball team at the university for three terms, and we had to lead lives like boarding-school misses," replied Baskerville, toying with his cigarette. "Our coach was about the stiffest man against whiskey and cigars I ever knew—and used to preach to us seven days in the week that a couple of cigars a day and four fingers of whiskey would shortly land any fellow at the undertaker's. I fell from grace, it is true, directly I was graduated; but that coach's gruesome predictions have stuck to me like the shirt of Nemesis, as your colleague, Senator Jephson, said the other day on the floor of the Senate."

"Jephson's an ass. He is the sort of man that would define a case of mixed property as a suit for a mule."

"Hardly. And he's an honest old blunderbuss."

"Still, he's an ass, as I say. His honesty doesn't prevent that."

"Well, yes, in a way it does. I'm not a professional moralist, but I don't believe there is any really good substitute for honesty." Then Baskerville suddenly turned red; the discussion of honesty with a man whose dishonesty he firmly believed in, and was earnestly trying to prove, was a blunder into which he did not often fall. Clavering, who saw everything, noted the other's flush, understood it perfectly, and smiled in appreciation of the joke. Baskerville did not propose to emphasize his mistake by running away, and was prepared to stay some minutes longer, when the entrance doors were swung open by the gorgeous footman, and Mrs. Clavering, leaning upon Anne's arm, appeared for a walk. When he saw his wife, Clavering's face grew dark; that old woman, with her bad grammar and her big hands, was always in his way. He said good morning abruptly and went indoors at once.

Anne greeted Baskerville with a charming smile, and introduced him at once to her mother. Something in his manner to Mrs. Clavering revealed the antique respect he had for every decent woman, no matter how unattractive she might be. He assisted Mrs. Clavering down the great stone steps as if she were a young and pretty girl instead of a lumbering, ignorant, elderly woman; and Mrs. Clavering found courage to address him, a thing she rarely did to strangers.

"I guess," she said diffidently, "you've got an old mother of your own that you help up and down—you do it so easy."

"No, I wish I had," answered Baskerville, with a kindness in his voice that both the old woman and the young felt. "My mother has been dead a long time; but I have a fine old aunt, Mrs. Luttrell, who makes me fetch and carry like an expressman's horse, and then she says I am not half so attentive to her as I ought to be. Perhaps Miss Clavering has told you about her—I had the pleasure of dining with Miss Clavering at my aunt's last night."

"Yes, she did, and she told me you were all real nice," answered Mrs. Clavering—and was appalled at her own daring.

Anne and Baskerville talked about the dinner, as they walked along the sunny, quiet street. Anne had enjoyed every moment spent in Mrs. Luttrell's house, and said so. Mrs. Clavering walked with difficulty, and the young man's arm at the street crossings was a real assistance to her; and without talking down to Mrs. Clavering or embarrassing her by direct remarks, he skilfully included her in the conversation.

Mrs. Clavering felt increasingly comfortable. Here was a man who did not scorn a woman because she was old and plain. For once the poor woman did not feel in the way with another person besides Anne. She ventured several remarks, such as: "People ought to be kind to poor dumb brutes, who can't tell what ails them," and "Washington is a great deal prettier for having so many trees, because trees make any place pretty,"—to all of which Baskerville listened with pleasant courtesy. He began to see in this ordinary, uneducated woman a certain hint of attractiveness in her gentleness of voice and softness of eyes that were reflected and intensified in the slim and graceful daughter by her side. Anne turned her soft, expressive eyes—her only real beauty—on Baskerville with a look of gratitude in them. Her life at home was one long fight for the happiness and dignity of her mother, for whom no one of her family had the least respect, except herself and her brother Reginald; and Reginald was but a poor creature in many ways. If Baskerville had sat up all night for a month, trying to devise a plan to ingratiate himself with Anne Clavering, he could not have done it better than by his courtesy to her mother. And he, appreciating the strong affection, the courage, the absence of false pride, the unselfishness, of Anne Clavering in this particular, admired her the more.

As they walked slowly along and talked, a kind of intimacy seemed to spring into being between them. Gratitude is a strong incentive to regard on both sides, and Baskerville's attitude toward Mrs. Clavering touched Anne to the heart. Their objective point was Dupont Circle, which at that hour was tolerably free from the colored gentry and the baby carriages which make it populous eighteen hours out of the twenty-four. But Mrs. Clavering was destined to receive further distinguished attentions during that episode of the walk. When she was seated comfortably on a bench Baskerville proposed to Anne that he show her, on the other side of the Circle, a silver ma~¹ great autumnal glory.

"Now do go, my dear," said Mrs. Clavering. "I'd like to set here awhile. Do, Mr. Baskerville, take her off—she ain't left me an hour this day, and she oughter have a little pleasure."

"Come, obey your mother," Baskerville said; and Anne, smiling, walked off with him.

Mrs. Clavering, good soul, was like other mothers, and as her darling child went off with Baskerville she thought: "How nice them two look together! And he is such a civil-spoken, sensible young man. Anne deserves a good husband, and if—"

This train of thought was interrupted by General Brandon. He, too, after his luncheon, was out for a Sunday airing, and passing the bench on which Mrs. Clavering sat, the good woman, with new-found courage, looked up at him and actually ventured upon a timid bow. She had recognized him from the first time she had seen him, when she moved into their new and splendid house; and she had a perfectly clear recollection of the old sutler days, when General Brandon was a handsome young captain, who always had a polite word for the sutler's wife. But she had never before, in the two years they had lived opposite each other, had the courage to speak to him. Her success with Baskerville emboldened her, and as General Brandon made her an elaborate, old-fashioned bow Mrs. Clavering said:—

"This used to be Cap'n Brandon—a long time ago, just before the war broke out."

"Yes, madam," replied General Brandon; "and you, I believe, are Mrs. Clavering. I remember quite well when Mr. Clavering brought you, a blooming bride, to the post."

Mrs. Clavering sighed. She was so lonely in the big house, so continually snubbed by her husband, by her daughters Élise and Lydia, by the uppish footman and the giggling maids; she was so cut off from everything she had known before, that the sight of persons connected with those early days was like water in the desert to her. She smiled a deprecating smile, and answered: "I've seen you on the streets often enough. You live opposite our house, don't you?"

"Yes," said General Brandon. Then Mrs. Clavering made a faint indication that he should sit down, and he placed himself on the bench by her side. "I recognized both you and Senator Clavering," he went on, "but as neither of you showed any recollection of me I hesitated to speak."

Mrs. Clavering sighed. "You are the first person since I came to Washington that I ever seen as far back as them days at the army post."

General Brandon, the most chivalrous of men, saw in Mrs. Clavering the timid longing to talk about old days and old ways, and he himself had a fondness for reminiscences; so the pair of old fogies entered into talk, feeling a greater degree of acquaintanceship in meeting after that long stretch of years than they had ever known before. When Anne and Baskerville returned, twenty minutes later, quite an active conversation was going on.

"Anne, my dear," said Mrs. Clavering, actually in a self-possessed manner, "this is General Brandon, who lives opposite our house. I knew him in them old times at the army post; and he's got a daughter, a widder, come home from England, to live with him. Anne, you must go and call on her."

"I shall with much pleasure," replied Anne, bestowing on General Brandon her charming smile. Then, after a little more talk, it was time to return. General Brandon gallantly offered Mrs. Clavering his arm, and the poor lady, embarrassed but pleased, was escorted with courtly grace to her door. Anne and Baskerville had meanwhile made vast strides in intimacy. It was not, however, enough for Anne to repeat her invitation to call, but Mrs. Clavering, when she arrived at the door which was by courtesy called hers, plucked up extraordinary courage and said:—

"I hope, Mr. Baskerville, you will favor us with your company on Thursday, which is our receiving day. General Brandon has promised to come, and I'll be real disappointed if you don't come, too."

It was the first invitation that Mrs. Clavering had ever given on her own initiative, and she gave it so diffidently, and in such simple good faith, that a man would have been a brute to decline it. So Baskerville accepted it with thanks, wondering meanwhile whether he were not a rascal in so doing. But he wanted very much to see Anne Clavering as often as he could, and the Montague and Capulet act came to him quite naturally and agreeably—the more so when he saw the gleam of gratification in Anne's eyes at his acceptance. She said simply:—

"I shall be glad to see you;" and then, turning to General Brandon, she added, "We shall, I hope, have the pleasure then of meeting Mrs. Darrell."

"My dear young lady, you are most kind," answered General Brandon, "but my daughter is so lately widowed—not yet a year and a half—that I feel sure it will be quite impossible to her feelings for her to appear at all in society now. Nevertheless, I shall give her your kind invitation, and she will be most gratified. I shall do myself the honor and pleasure of attending your Thursday reception."

And then they parted, Anne and Baskerville each reckoning that day to have been one of the pleasantest of their lives, and wondering when they should have the good fortune to meet in that sweet, companionable manner again.

Chapter Ten

At dinner that night General Brandon told Elizabeth about his meeting with Mrs. Clavering, and the renewal of their acquaintance. "The poor lady seemed much pleased at meeting some one associated with her former life," said the General. "She invited me to call on Thursday, which is their first reception day of the season, and especially urged that you should come. I believe their receptions are large and brilliant—the newspapers are always full of them; so I told her that owing to your very recent mourning it would be impossible for you to go to any large or gay entertainment. I have no doubt Sara Luttrell will ask you to many of her parties,—she keeps a very gay house,—and it is a source of the keenest regret to me that you cannot for the present accept invitations. But another winter I shall hope, my dear child, that you will have the spirit to enter once more into the society you are so admirably fitted to adorn."

Good General Brandon was quite unconscious that in the society to which Elizabeth had been long accustomed a year was considered the period of a widow's mourning. He never dreamed for one moment that she could have been induced to go into society at that time. As a matter of fact, it was the one thing which Elizabeth really hoped might rouse her from her torpor of mind and heart into which she had sunk in the last few months. She had a good and comprehensive mind, which had been much improved by reading under Pelham's direction. Then had come that brilliant year in London, in which she had really seen the best English society and had liked it, as every one must who knows it. During her whole married life she had taken part in the continual round of small gayeties which prevail at army posts all over the world. Her belle-ship had made this particularly gratifying and delightful to her. Society had become a habit, although very far from a passion, with her, and she had expected to return to it, as one resumes one's daily habits.

She had taken a strange interest in the Claverings from the very beginning— they constituted her first impressions of Washington; and she would have found some diversion from her sad and wearying thoughts in Mrs. Luttrell's brilliant and interesting house. But it was impossible for her to go against her father's implied ideas of propriety. He had always assumed that she was properly and dutifully heart-broken at her husband's death. She did indeed mourn good, brave, honest, stupid Jack Darrell as a woman mourns a husband for whom she feels gratitude and tenderness, without being in the least in love with him; all the sentiment which belongs to love she had secretly and hopelessly given to Pelham. She often thought that if she had not been so young, so ignorant, she never would have married Darrell.

"I think you should force yourself, however painful it may be to your feelings, to go to see Sara Luttrell some day when she is not formally receiving," said General Brandon, thinking he was proposing a tremendous sacrifice to Elizabeth; and he felt quite triumphant when she agreed to go.

When the Thursday afternoon came, there was no need to tell Elizabeth that the Clavering receptions were large and brilliant. By four o'clock carriages came pouring into the street, and by five there was almost an *impasse*. Great numbers of stylish men, both foreigners and Americans, passed in and out the splendid doors.

While Elizabeth was watching this procession with curious interest, Mrs. Luttrell's great old-fashioned coach, with the long-tailed black horses, stopped before the tall, shabby house, and Serena brought up Mrs. Luttrell's and Baskerville's cards. Mrs. Luttrell, although militant, was not the sort of woman to hit another woman when she was down, and was most gracious when Elizabeth appeared. The sight of the dingy drawing-room, of Elizabeth's pallor and evident signs of stress and trial, touched Mrs. Luttrell. She mentioned to Elizabeth that a card would be sent her for a large dinner which she was giving within a fortnight, and when Elizabeth gently declined Mrs. Luttrell was really sorry. Baskerville was sincerely cordial. He had liked Elizabeth as a girl, and her forlornness now touched him as it did Mrs. Luttrell.

When the visit was over and they were once more out of the house, Mrs. Luttrell exclaimed: "That's Dick Brandon's doings—that poor Elizabeth not going to a place and moping in that hole of a house. If she would but go about a bit, and leave her card at the British Embassy, where she would certainly be invited, she could see something of society and recover her spirits and good looks. By the way, I think she's really more enticing in her pallor and her black gown than when she was in the flush of her beauty. Of course she looks much older. Now, as I'm going into the Claverings' I suppose you will leave me."

Baskerville, with a hangdog look, replied, "I'm going into the Claverings', too." Mrs. Luttrell's handsome mouth came open, and her ermine cape fell from her shoulders without her even so much as knowing it. "Yes," said Baskerville, assuming a bullying air, now that the cat was out of the bag, "Mrs. Clavering asked me last Sunday, and I accepted."

"Where on earth, Richard Bas—"

"Did I see Mrs. Clavering? I met her out walking with Miss Clavering. Mrs. Clavering is a most excellent woman—quiet and unobtrusive—and I swear there is something of her in Miss Clavering."

"Richard Baskerville, you are in love with Anne Clavering! I know it; I feel it."

"Don't be a fool, Sara Luttrell. Because I happen to pay a visit at a house where I have been asked and could have gone a year ago, you at once discover a mare's nest. That's Sara Luttrell all over."

"And what becomes of the doubtful propriety of your going to Senator Clavering's house? And suppose you succeed in driving him out of public life, as you are trying to do?"

"I swear you are the most provoking old woman in Washington. Hold your tongue and come along with your dutiful nephew."

Grasping her firmly by the arm, Baskerville marched Mrs. Luttrell up the broad stone steps of the Clavering house. The splendid doors were opened noiselessly by gorgeous footmen who looked like the prize-winners at a chrysanthemum show. The entrance was magnificent, and through the half-drawn silken draperies of the wide doorways they could see the whole superb suite of rooms opening upon the large Moorish hall. Great masses of flowers were everywhere, and the mellow glow of wax lights and tinted lamp globes made the winter twilight softly radiant.

Half a dozen butterfly débutantes were serving tea in the huge dining room, furnished with priceless teak-wood and black oak, bright with pictures and mirrors, a magnificent Turkish carpet on the parquet floor and chandeliers from a royal palace lighting the dim splendor of the room. Here, brilliant with candelabra, was set out a great table, from which an expensive collation was served by more gorgeous footmen. This was the doing of Élise and Lydia, who overruled Anne's desire for a simple tea-table set in the library. There, however, a great gold and silver bowl was constantly replenished with champagne punch, and over this Élise and Lydia presided, much preferring the champagne bowl to the tea-table.

The library was thronged with men, old and young, native and foreign. Élise and Lydia, their handsome faces flushed and smiling, their elaborate gowns iridescent with gold and silver embroidery and spangles sweeping the floor, laughed, talked, and flirted to their hearts' content. They also drank punch with a great many men, who squeezed their hands on the sly, looked meaningly into their large, dark eyes, and always went away laughing.

Mrs. Luttrell, escorted by Baskerville, and meeting acquaintances at every turn, entered the great drawing-room, which was a symphony in green and gold. Near the door Anne Clavering, in a simple gray gown, stood by her mother, who was seated. Anne received the guests, and then introduced them to Mrs. Clavering, who made the pretence of receiving, looking the picture of misery meanwhile. The poor soul would much rather have remained upstairs; but on this point Anne was inexorable—her mother must show herself in her own drawing-room. A handsome black gown, appropriate to an elderly lady, showed Mrs. Clavering at her best, and Anne, with perfect tact, grace, and patience, silently demanded and received for her mother the respect which was due her and which there was occasionally some difficulty in exacting. As Anne caught sight of Mrs. Luttrell, she smiled with obvious pleasure; but on seeing Baskerville her face lighted up in a way which by no means escaped Mrs. Luttrell's sharp eyes.

Mrs. Clavering was nearly frightened out of her life on the rare occasions when the redoubtable Mrs. Luttrell called, but on this afternoon Mrs. Luttrell was as soft as milk and as sweet as honey itself. Mrs. Clavering was not the least afraid of Baskerville, and said to him earnestly, as he took her hand, "I'm real glad to see you."

"And I am very glad to be able to come," answered Baskerville. Then, seating himself by her side, he began to talk to her so gently on subjects the poor lady was interested in that she was more delighted with him than ever. A soft flush came into Anne's delicate cheeks; she appreciated the sweet and subtle flattery in Baskerville's attitude. It was not interest in Mrs. Clavering's conversation, nor even the pity he might have felt for her forlorn condition, which induced him to spend twenty minutes of his visit in talking to her.

Meantime the dusk was deepening. Many visitors were departing and few coming. Mrs. Luttrell was entertaining a select coterie of men around the large fireplace at the other end of the room, and Baskerville was the only person left near Anne and Mrs. Clavering.

"Will you be kind enough," he said to Anne, "to go with me to get a cup of tea? I see a table in yonder, but I am afraid of so many young girls at once. I think I can count six of them. Now if you will go with me, I shall feel as brave as a lion."

The temptation was strong, but Anne looked down at her mother. Apprehension was written on Mrs. Clavering's simple, homely face at the notion of being left alone.

"Why can't Mr. Baskerville have his tea with me?" said she. "There ain't any more folks coming. Make Peer bring a table here, Anne, and we'll have it comfortable together."

"Yes," Baskerville added, drawing up a chair. "Mrs. Clavering is far more amiable and hospitable than you. I am sure you would never have thought of so kind a solution."

Anne, with a happy smile, gave Pierre the order, and in a minute they were sitting about a little table, with an opportunity for a few minutes' talk at a moderate pitch of voice, differing from those hurried, merry meetings in a crowd of laughing, talking, moving people which usually constitute a Washington call.

While they were sitting there, all three enjoying themselves and Mrs. Clavering not the least of the three, a belated caller was announced, General Brandon. The General was in his Sunday frock coat, which had seen good service, and his silk hat, which belonged by rights on the retired list; but each was carefully brushed and clearly belonged to a gentleman. General Brandon himself, handsome, soldierly, his white mustache and hair neatly clipped, was grace, elegance, and amiability personified. His head was none of the best, but for beauty, courage, and gentleness he was unmatched. Anne received him with more than her usual cordiality, and Mrs. Clavering was so pleased at seeing him that she actually invited him to sit down at her tea-table and have tea. This he did, explaining why his daughter had sent her cards instead of coming.

"Another year, I hope, my dear madam, my daughter may be persuaded to reënter society, which, if you will pardon a father's pride, I think she adorns. But at present she is overwhelmed with grief at her loss. It is scarcely eighteen months since she became a widow and lost the best of husbands."

General Brandon prattled on, and presently said: "I had hoped to meet Senator Clavering here this afternoon, and made my visit late on purpose. His exacting senatorial duties, however, must leave him little time for social relaxation."

"I think I hear his step in the hall now," said Anne. "He will, I know, be very much pleased to meet you again."

As she spoke Clavering's firm tread was heard, and he entered, smiling, debonair, and distinguished-looking. Nobody would have dreamed from anything in his air or looks that this man was nearing a crisis in his fate, and that even then his conduct was being revealed in the newspapers and examined by his fellow-senators in a way which opened a wide, straight vista to state's prison.

Clavering was surprised, but undeniably pleased, and even amused at seeing Baskerville; and Baskerville felt like a hound, and inwardly swore at himself for letting the wish to see a woman's eyes bring him to Clavering's house. He put a bold face upon it, however, shook Clavering's outstretched hand, and called himself a fool and a rogue for so doing.

The warmth of Clavering's greeting to General Brandon delighted the simple old warrior. Clavering, who had too much sound sense to avoid allusions to his early life or to tell lies about it, recalled the time when he was a sutler and General Brandon was an officer. Then he carried the latter off to an alcove in the library, which was now deserted except by Élise and Lydia. These two young women, reclining like odalisks among the cushions of a luxurious sofa, discussed Rosalka and the rest of their swains in low voices and in terms which luckily their father did not overhear.

Into the alcove Clavering caused his choicest brands of whiskey to be brought, and at once plunged into talk; and into that talk he infused all his powers of pleasing, which soon produced upon the simple old General a species of intoxication. If any one had told him that Clavering's attention was due to the sight, more than once obtained since Sunday, of Elizabeth Darrell's graceful figure and interesting, melancholy face, General Brandon would have called that person a liar.

"You know," said Clavering, as soon as the two were comfortably established with the whiskey and the cigars, "that I am being badgered and bothered by a set of sharks, calling themselves lawyers, who want to rob me of every dollar of my fortune. You have perhaps read in the newspapers something about this K. F. R. land-grant business."

"I am aware the public prints have given considerable space to it," replied General Brandon, "but I have no knowledge of the merits of the case."

"Neither have the newspapers. The long and short of it is that the sharks, after fighting me through every court in the country, where I may say I have managed to hold my own pretty well, have contrived by political wire-pulling to get a Senate committee to investigate the matter. Now I don't want to be lacking in courtesy to my brother senators, but of all the collection of asses, dunderheads, and old women, sneaks, hypocrites, and snivelling dogs, that ever were huddled together, that select committee of my esteemed contemporaries—Good Lord! let's take a drink."

General Brandon drank solemnly. Whiskey of that brand was not to be treated lightly.

"I know well all the country embraced in and contiguous to that K. F. R. land grant," said the General, putting down his glass reverently. "I scouted and fought and hunted over all that region more than forty years ago, when I was a young lieutenant just turned loose from West Point."

"Why, then," cried Clavering, his handsome eyes lighting up with a glow like fire, "you might be of real service to me." He did not specify what manner of service he meant, and General Brandon innocently thought Clavering meant about the K. F. R. land grants. But no man who ever lived could tell Clavering anything he did not know about any piece of property he had ever owned; least of all could simple, guileless General Brandon tell him anything.

"I should be most happy," replied the General. "I have a considerable quantity of memoranda, maps and surveys of the region, which are quite at your service."

"Capital," said Clavering, his deep eyes shining with a keen delight. "Now as the investigation is going on, which you have seen in the newspapers, I shall have to make immediate use of any information you might be able to give me. Suppose you were to let me come over to your house to-night and take our first view of what you have? And of course you'll stay and dine with me."

"I thank you very much, Senator, but I cannot leave my daughter to dine alone—she is too much alone, poor child. And immediately after dinner I am engaged to spend an hour with an old friend, General Mayse, a former classmate of mine who is now inflicted with paralysis and to whom I pay a weekly visit. Besides, I should have to rummage among my papers to find those that we require. To-morrow night I shall be at your service."

But it was not Clavering's nature to delay the accomplishment of any wish. He wanted to see and know Elizabeth Darrell, so he said cordially: "At all events I should like to talk the matter over with you. Would you allow me to come in this evening then, after you have returned from your visit?"

"Certainly, Senator. I shall be at home by half after nine."

Then Clavering, seeing that General Brandon was his, began to talk about other things, even to hint at chances of making money. To this General Brandon only sighed and said: "Those enterprises are for men with capital. I have only the equity in my house and my salary, and I cannot, for my daughter's sake, jeopardize what little I have. She was left with but a small provision from her husband's estate, which was strictly entailed." Clavering could not refrain from smiling at General Brandon's simplicity in refusing such an offer, if even but a hint, for such a reason; but he said no more on the subject.

As the General passed into the drawing-room to say good-by to Mrs. Clavering, he was surprised to find Baskerville still sitting at the tea-table. Baskerville had not been asked to stay to dinner, but when Mrs. Luttrell was ready to leave a very mild invitation from Mrs. Clavering, who had no notion of the duration of fashionable visits, had made him ask permission to remain—a permission which Mrs. Luttrell gave with a wink. Anne was not displeased with him for staying—her eyes and smile conveyed as much; and man-like, Baskerville had succumbed to the temptation. But when General Brandon came in and found him the very last visitor in the drawing-room he felt himself distinctly caught, and made his farewells with more haste than grace. Mrs. Clavering urged him to come again, and Anne's tones conveyed *auf wiedersehen* to him as eloquently as a tone can without specific words; nevertheless, when Baskerville found himself out in the cool, crisp night, he began to doubt, as he had ever doubted, the propriety of his going to Senator Clavering's house at all. But General Brandon was saying to him most earnestly, as they stood under the lamp-post before going their different ways:—

"Senator Clavering is a very cruelly maligned man; of that I am certain. And I think, Mr. Baskerville, that most of the testimony you and the Civil Service League and the K. F. R. attorneys have collected will break down when it is introduced before the committee. Why, Senator Clavering tells me that he has been accused, on evidence that wouldn't hang a dog, of wholesale bribery, of having bought his seat in the Senate, of having bought up courts and legislatures. But he will be triumphantly vindicated—I make no doubt at all of that."

"I wish he might be," replied Baskerville, with a degree of sincerity that would scarcely have been credited; "but I don't think he can be."

When General Brandon let himself into his own house, dinner was ready to be served. He was full of enthusiasm about the Claverings. At the table he assured Elizabeth of his entire belief in Clavering and of his respect for him. Mrs. Clavering he pronounced to be a most excellent and unpretending woman, Anne altogether admirable, Reginald Clavering a worthy fellow and a sound churchman, and Élise Denman and Lydia Clavering two much-abused young women, in whom mere high spirits and unconventionality had been mistaken for a degree of imprudence of which he felt sure they could never be guilty. Then he mentioned Clavering's proposed visit, and asked Elizabeth if she would, the next day, find the trunk in which he kept certain papers, open it, and get out of it everything dated between '56 and '61.

When dinner was over and General Brandon had gone out to pay his weekly visit to his paralyzed comrade, Elizabeth went upstairs to a small back room, called by courtesy the study. Here were General Brandon's few books; he was not, and never had been, a man of books, but he liked to be considered bookish. There was in the room an open grate fire, a student's lamp, and some old-fashioned tables and easy-chairs. To this room Elizabeth had succeeded in imparting an air of comfort. She sat down before the fire to spend the evening alone, as she had spent so many evenings alone in the last eighteen months, and would, she feared, continue to spend her evenings for the rest of her life. She had expected to find her life in Washington dull, but the weeks she had been at home had been duller than she had thought possible. Her father's old friends had called upon her, but they were all staid and elderly persons, and the circle had grown pitifully small in her ten years of absence. Those ten years had practically obliterated her own acquaintances in the ever changing population of Washington, and the few persons left in the gay world whom she knew, like Mrs. Luttrell, it was plain that her father did not expect her to cultivate.

One resource—reading—occurred to her on this particular evening. She had a mind well fitted for books, but she had never been thrown with bookish people, except Pelham, and reading had formed no essential part of her life. Pelham was a man of great intelligence, and a reader; but both his intelligence and his reading were confined to his profession. No matter where Elizabeth's thinking began, Pelham was sure to come into it somewhere. She started up from her chair as the recollection of him, which always hovered near her, took shape in thought and almost in speech, and going to the book-case took out the first volume her hand fell upon. It was an old translation of Herodotus, and Elizabeth, determined upon a mental opiate, opened it at random and read on resolutely. She fell upon that wonderful story of Cyrus, the reputed son of Mithradates the herdsman; and in following the grandly simple old narrative, told with so much of art, of grace, of convincing perspicacity, that not even a translation can wholly destroy its majestic beauty, Elizabeth lost herself in the shadowy, ancient past. She was roused by Serena's voice and Serena's hand, as black as the Ethiopians in Herodotus's time, who worshipped no other gods save Jupiter and Bacchus. Serena produced a card. It was simple and correct, and read: "Mr. James Clavering," with the address.

"It is Senator Clavering," said Elizabeth, in a moment. "Tell him that General Brandon is not at home."

"De gent'mun seh he got er 'p'intment wid de Gin'l, an' he gwine ter wait for him. I t'ink, Miss 'Liz'beth, you better lemme ax him up heah. De parlor is jes' freezin' col'," answered Serena, who never forgot that people should be made comfortable.

"Ask him up, then," replied Elizabeth. She was somewhat flurried at the thought of receiving Clavering alone, but there was no help for it. She was not, however, disappointed; on the contrary she felt a deep and curious interest in seeing this man and tracing if possible that singular recollection of him, so sharp yet so impalpable and still actually inexplicable to herself.

In a few minutes Serena ushered Clavering into the room. At close range he was even more attractive than at a distance. It was difficult to associate any idea of advancing age with him. Maturity was all that was indicated by his handsome, smooth-shaven face, his compact and elegant figure, his iron-gray hair. Manual labor had left but one mark upon him—his hands were rough and marred by the miner's tools he had used. He was perfectly well dressed and entirely at his ease. He introduced himself with the natural and unaffected grace which had been his along with his sutler's license and miner's tools.

"This, I presume, is Mrs. Darrell. I thank you very much for allowing me to wait for General Brandon's return." He said no word about his appointment with General Brandon being at half-past nine while then it was only a little past eight.

Elizabeth invited him to sit down, and herself took a seat opposite him. The color which came into her pale face very much enhanced her looks, and Clavering thought he had never seen so interesting a woman. Her slender black figure unconsciously assumed a pose of singular grace and ease, the delicate color mounted slowly into her pale cheeks, and she was indeed worthy of any man's notice. And as her personality had struck Clavering with great force at the very first glimpse he had had of her ten years before, so, seeing her close at hand and her attention fixed on himself, she overpowered him quickly, as the warm, sweet scent of the jessamine flower is overpowering. It was what he would have called, had he been thirty years younger, love at first sight.

Clavering's coming into the room was, like some new, strong force, making itself felt over everything. The small room seemed full of him and nothing else. He was by nature a dominant personality, and he dominated Elizabeth Darrell as strangely and suddenly as she had cast a spell over him.

"My father will regret very much not being here when you came. Perhaps he misunderstood the hour of your appointment," she said.

Clavering's white teeth shone in a smile. "Don't trouble about that. Besides, it has given me the pleasure of seeing you."

Elizabeth was not unmindful of the fact that Clavering was a married man, with a wife across the street; and his words, which would have been merely those of courtesy in most men, could not be so interpreted, for Clavering was not a man of pretty speeches.

He picked up the volume of Herodotus which lay on the table. "So you've been reading old Herodotus! That's pretty heavy reading for a young woman, isn't it?"

"I took it up at random just now, and became interested in it," answered Elizabeth.

"You are a great reader, I suppose?"

"N-no. Hardly, that is. But I am very much alone, and I have read a good deal since I have returned to America."

"Why should a woman like you be alone? Why shouldn't you go about and see people and live like other women of your age?"

Elizabeth made no reply to this; she could scarcely admit that her seclusion was more of her father's doing than her own. She was struck by the beauty of Clavering's voice and by the correctness of his speech, which was better than that of many college-bred men.

"How long have you been a widow?" he asked.

"A year and a half."

"And have you any children?"

"No, I lost my only child when he was a baby."

"That's hard on a woman. You women never forget those dead babies. But all your life is before you yet."

"It seems to me it is all behind me."

"Why? Did you love your husband very much?"

Elizabeth had suffered Clavering's questions partly through surprise and partly because Clavering could say and do what he chose without giving offence—a quality which had been one of the great factors in raising him from the shaft of a mine to a seat in the United States Senate. But the question put to Elizabeth was so unexpected,—it had never been asked of her before,—it was so searching, that it completely disconcerted her. She remained silent, while her eyes, turned upon Clavering, wore a look of trouble and uncertainty.

"A great many women don't love their husbands," said Clavering, "and if they are left widows, their feelings are very complex. They think they ought to grieve for their husbands, but they don't."

The color fled suddenly out of Elizabeth's cheeks. Clavering's words fitted her case so exactly and so suddenly that she was startled and frightened. It was as if he had looked into her soul and read at a glance her inmost secrets. She half expected him to say next that she had loved another man than her husband. And as for applying the common rules of behavior to a man like Clavering, it was absurd on the face of it. He was leaning toward Elizabeth, his elbow on the arm of his chair, his eyes fixed upon her with a kind of admiring scrutiny. He found her quite as interesting as he had expected, and he ardently desired to know more about her and, what is as great a mark of interest, to tell her more about himself.

Elizabeth remained silent for a while, and then forced herself to say: "My husband was one of the best of men. He was as good as my father."

"That settles it," replied Clavering, with grim humor. "I never knew a woman in my life who spoke of her husband's goodness first who was really in love with him. When a woman is in love with a man, it isn't his goodness she thinks of first; it is his love. Now don't fly off at that; I'm not a conventional man, and you must know it if you ever heard of me before. And I don't mean to be disrespectful. On the contrary, I want your good opinion—I have wanted it ever since the first time I ever saw you. I was very much struck with you then. I have wanted to know you and I have planned to know you. Have I committed any crime?"

"But—but—you are a married man," said Elizabeth, faltering, and conscious that she was talking like an ingénue.

Clavering laughed as he replied: "That's downright school-girlish. Any boarding-school miss would say the same. Well, I can't help it now that I married a woman totally unsuited to me before I was twenty-one years old. Come, Mrs. Darrell, we are not children. I wanted to know you, I say, and I always try to do what I want to do. Don't you? Doesn't everybody? Well, let us then know each other. I swear to you I know less of women than I do of any subject I have ever tried to master. True, I never had time until lately; and, besides, I was a middle-aged man before I ever met any educated and intelligent women. In the class of life from which I spring women are household drudges and bearers of children, and I never knew them in any other aspect until I was over forty years of age. Then you can't imagine what a stunning revelation to me a woman was who had never done anything but amuse herself and improve herself. Suppose you had never met any educated men till now—wouldn't you find them captivating?"

When a man talks to a woman as she has never been talked to before he is certain of finding an interested listener, and, it follows, a tolerant listener. So Elizabeth could not disguise her interest in Clavering, nor was it worth while to pretend to be offended with him. The superficial knowledge she had of the vicissitudes of his life was calculated to arouse and fix her attention; and there was so little to do in her present life that she would have been more or less than mortal if she had turned from the first object of interest she had yet met with in her new and changed and dreary life.

She paused awhile before answering Clavering's last question. "I dare say I should feel so," she answered. "I remember how it was when I was first married and went to India. Everything interested me. I could not look at a native without wanting to ask all manner of questions of him and about him, which of course I could not be allowed to do; and the life there is so strange—their race problem is so different from ours, and all my modes of thought had to be changed. I was in India over eight years, and it was as strange to me when I left it as when I arrived."

Elizabeth had got the talk away from the personal note upon which Clavering had pitched it, and he, seeing he had said enough for a beginning, followed Elizabeth's conversational lead. He asked her many questions about her life in India, all singularly intelligent and well put, because drinking at the fountain of other people's talk had been his chief source of education during his whole life. And Clavering, without being widely read, was far from being an ignorant man. Although he knew not a word of any language except his own, nor the history of any country except his own, he was well acquainted with the history of his own times, and he knew who every living man of importance in his own country and Europe was, and what he was doing. Seeing that Elizabeth was susceptible to the charms of conversation and had a distinct intellectual side, Clavering appealed to her on that side. He told her with an inimitable raciness and humor some of the incidents of his early life in the West, his later adventures, even of his career in the Senate.

"I think I never worked so hard in my life as I have during the five years I've been in the Senate," he said. "No man can come to the Senate of the United States with the education of a sutler, miner, promoter, speculator, and what not—such as I have had—and not work hard; that is, if he expects to be anything else than a dummy. But it isn't in James Clavering to be a dummy anywhere. So I have thought and read and worked and slaved, and bought other men's brains in the last five years as earnestly as any man ever did. The result is that when I open my mouth now the senators listen. At first the lawyers in the Senate used to hide a grin when I began to speak, and I admit I did make some bad breaks in the beginning. But I saw my way out of that clearly enough. I found a man who was really a great constitutional lawyer, although he had never been able to make more than a bare living out of his profession in Chicago. I have always invested liberally in brains. When you can actually buy brains or news, you are buying the two most valuable commodities on earth. Well, when I took up a question I had my man go over the legal aspects of it and put them down in black and white. Then I knew well enough how to use them, and I may say without boasting that I have done as well, or better, than any man of my opportunities now in the Senate. However, I don't compare myself with such men as Andrew Johnson. You know his wife taught him to write, and that man rose to be President of the United States. Of course he wasn't what you would call a scholarly man, like many of the senators, but good Lord! think of the vast propelling force that took an illiterate man from the tailor's bench and gave him such a career as Andrew Johnson's, and made him Vice-President of the United States. Those men—and men like me, too—can't be called all-round men, like Senator Thorndyke, for example. All of us have got great big gaps and holes in our knowledge and judgment and conduct that the normal well-educated man hasn't. But where we are strong, we are stronger than they. Do you know anything about Thorndyke?"

"I have heard my father speak of Mrs. Thorndyke, whose family he knew many years ago, and he visits occasionally at Senator Thorndyke's. Mrs. Thorndyke sent me a request that I would call to see her, but—but—I don't pay any visits now."

"It's a shame you don't—a woman like you. Mrs. Thorndyke is charming, but not so charming as you. And I lay claim to great nobility of soul when I praise Mrs. Thorndyke, or Thorndyke either, for that matter. Mrs. Thorndyke has no use for me or for anybody of my name, except my second daughter. And Thorndyke, although he isn't leading the pack of hounds who are baying after me to get me out of the Senate, is quietly giving them the scent. Yet I swear I admire Thorndyke—or, rather, I admire his education and training, which have made him what he is. If I had had that training—a gentleman for my father, a lady for my mother, association with the sons of gentlemen and ladies, a university education, and then had married a lady—"

Clavering got up and took a turn about the narrow room. Finally he came and sat down in a chair closer to Elizabeth, and continued: "Thorndyke is one of the lawyers in the Senate who used to bother me. It seemed to me at first that every time I opened my mouth in the Senate chamber I butted into the Constitution of the United States. Either I was butting into the shalls or the shall nots, and Thorndyke always let me know it. I could get along from the first well enough in the rough-and-tumble of debate with men like Senator Crane, for example,—a handsome fellow, from the West, too, very showy in every way, but not the man that Thorndyke is. It was the scholarly men that I was a little afraid of, I'm not ashamed to say. I am a long way off from a fool; consequently I know my own limitations, and a want of scholarship is one of those limitations."

Elizabeth listened, more and more beguiled. She could not but see a sort of self-respect in this man; he respected his own intellect because it was worth respecting, and he had very little respect for his own character and honor because he knew they were not worth respecting. As Elizabeth studied him by the mellow lamplight, while his rich voice echoed through the small room, she could not but recognize that here was a considerable man, a considerable force; and she had never known a man of this type before. She noted that he was as well groomed as the most high-bred man she had ever known—as well as Pelham, for example. He had come into the room with ease and grace. No small tricks of manner disfigured him; he was naturally polished, and he had the gift, very rare and very dangerous, of saying what he would without giving offence,—or, rather, of disarming the person who might be offended. And in spite of his frank talking of himself Elizabeth saw in him an absence of small vanity, of restless self-love. Unconsciously she assumed an air of profound interest in what Clavering was saying,—a form of flattery most insidious and effective because of its unconsciousness.

Elizabeth herself, in the eighteen months of loneliness, poverty, and desperate anxiety which she had lately known, had almost lost the sweet fluency which had once distinguished her; but presently Clavering chose to make her talk, and succeeded admirably. She found herself speaking frankly about her past life and telling things she had never thought of telling a stranger; but Clavering seemed anything but a stranger. In truth, he had probed her so well that he knew much more about her than she had dreamed of revealing.

When at last General Brandon's step was heard, Elizabeth started like a guilty child; she had forgotten that her father was to return. General Brandon was delighted to see Clavering, and took a quarter of an hour to explain why he had been ten minutes late.

"I didn't expect to see any papers to-night," replied Clavering, "but I should like to talk over some things with you. Please don't go, Mrs. Darrell; what I have to say you are at perfect liberty to hear."

Elizabeth hesitated, and so did General Brandon; but Clavering settled the matter by saying: "If I am to drive you out of your sitting room, I shall feel obliged to remain away, and thereby be deprived of General Brandon's valuable services." Elizabeth remained.

Clavering then began to give the history from his point of view of the K. F. R. land grants. It was a powerfully interesting story, told with much dramatic force. It embraced the history of much of Clavering's life, which was in itself a long succession of uncommon episodes. It lost nothing in the telling. Then he came to the vindictive and long-continued fight made on him politically, which culminated in the bringing of these matters before a Senate committee by a powerful association of Eastern railway magnates and corporation lawyers, aided by the senators in opposition and others in his own party who, because he was not strictly amenable to party discipline, would be glad to see him driven out of the Senate. But Clavering was a fighting man, and although driven to the wall, he had his back to it; he was very far from surrender, and so he said.

Elizabeth listened with breathless interest. Nothing like this had ever come into her experience before. It struck her as being so much larger and stronger than any of the struggles which she had heretofore known that it dwarfed them all. Everybody's affairs seemed small beside Clavering's. Yet she was fully conscious all the time that this was special pleading on Clavering's part. She admired the ingenuity, the finesse, the daring, that Clavering had shown and was showing; but it all seemed to her as if there must be something as large and as strong on the other side.

No such idea, however, came into General Brandon's kind, simple wooden head. When Clavering had finished speaking, the General rose and, grasping him by the hand, said solemnly: "My dear sir, I sympathize with you profoundly. I am convinced that you have been the victim of misplaced confidence, and that this unprincipled hounding of you on the part of men who wish to rob you, not only of your property and your seat in the Senate, but your high character and your priceless good name, is bound to come to naught. I offer you my sincere sympathy, and I assure you that I place entire credence in every word that you have told me."

This was more than Elizabeth did; and when Clavering thought of it afterward, sitting over his library fire, he laughed to himself. On the strength of it, however, he had secured opportunities of seeing General Brandon's daughter very often, and he did not mean to let the grass grow under his feet.

Chapter Eleven

The season opened with a bang on the first of December. The smart set could barely get six hours in bed from going to parties at all hours. This did not apply to Mrs. Luttrell, who, although she was out every night, did not disturb herself to appear in public until four o'clock in the afternoon. That particular form of barbaric entertainment known as a ladies' luncheon had no charms for Mrs. Luttrell, because there were no men to be found at them; for this woman, who cherished with an idolatrous recollection the memory of the only man she had ever loved, and who had refused more offers of marriage than any other woman of her day, frankly admitted that she couldn't enjoy anything without a masculine element in it. And men she contrived to have in plenty, with a success but little inferior to that of Ninon de l'Enclos.

For that reason Richard Baskerville was not only the person Mrs. Luttrell loved best in the world, but was really her most intimate friend. There was nothing Mrs. Luttrell enjoyed so much as a midnight tête-à-tête over her bedroom fire with Baskerville, he just from his books and she just from her nightly gayety. Mrs. Luttrell scorned a boudoir,—or the modern version of it, a den. She had a huge, old-fashioned bedroom, with an ancient four-poster mahogany bed, with green silk curtains, and a lace valance; and everything in the room was big and square and handsome and comfortable, like the bed. There was a large fireplace, with shining brass fire-dogs and a monumental brass fender; and Mrs. Luttrell frequently admitted that when she got her feet on that fender and her dressing-gown on, she grew so communicative that she would tell the inmost secrets of her soul to the veriest stranger, if he had his feet on the fender at the same time.

It was on a night early in January that Mrs. Luttrell nabbed Baskerville at her door, as she was being let in by the sleepy black butler. Baskerville followed her upstairs into her room, considerately turning his back while the old lady got out of her black-velvet gown, and whisked off her flannel petticoat, into her comfortable dressing-gown—an operation she performed without the least regard for his presence. Then, when her delicate, high-bred feet were on the fender before the glowing wood fire, she said:—

"Now you can turn around—and I'm a great deal more clothed than the women you take down to dinner or dance with at balls."

"I don't dance at a great many balls. Let me see—I haven't danced for—"

"Oh, I know. Well, I'm just from a dinner at Secretary Slater's, where that ridiculous little Mrs. Hill-Smith, his daughter, was in great feather, and also the Baldwin girl and Anne Clavering."

"You ought to beg Miss Clavering's pardon for bracketing her with Mrs. Hill-Smith and Eleanor Baldwin."

"My dear boy, it would make you die laughing to see the patronizing air Mrs. Hill-Smith and Eleanor Baldwin put on with Anne Clavering. As the Slater family is at least forty years old and the Brentwood-Baldwins quite twenty years old, they regard the Claverings, who have come up within the last six years, very much as the old French nobility regarded the *bourgeoisie*. But I think Anne Clavering is a match for them. Indeed, she proved herself a match for a much more considerable antagonist—that is, myself—this very night."

"Have you been impertinent to Miss Clavering?"

"Well, Richard, my dear boy, I am afraid I have been. But it was all the fault of those two foolish creatures, Mrs. Hill-Smith and Eleanor Baldwin. It was in this way. The gentlemen,"—Mrs. Luttrell still used this antique word,—"the gentlemen had come into the drawing-room after dinner—very prim and proper they were after their cigarettes and two glasses of hock. In my time, when the gentlemen came in after dinner they were always as merry as lords and delightfully free: I have been slapped on the back by Daniel Webster at a dinner, when I was sixteen years old. But nothing so agreeable happens now—and there aren't any Daniel Websters, either. Well, when I was talking to that ridiculous Mrs. Hill-Smith something unluckily started me off upon the new people in Washington. Mrs. Hill-Smith, you know, assumes that she has sixteen quarterings, so she has to grin and bear it when I begin telling about people; and I always say to her, 'You and I, Mrs. Hill-Smith, who knew some people before 1860.' Somebody was speaking about Mrs. James Van Cortlandt Skinner's private chaplain—that woman has added much to the gayety of nations. There's a story going around that she had a darling of a fight over it, not only with the bishop, but with the bishop's wife; and I was giving a very amusing account of it, when Anne Clavering quietly remarked that she happened to know that Mrs. Skinner had not spoken of it yet to the bishop. Of course this spoiled my story, and I was a little cross about it. Judge Woodford was present, and he told a pleasant little tale about my grandfather having been very cross on one occasion, and having pulled somebody's nose, and I said my crossness was a case of atavism on my part. And so it was turned into a joke. When we were leaving I was sorry I had been short with Anne Clavering, so I went up and asked her to come and see me on my next day at home, and to pour tea for me—that I still held to the good old fashion of keeping a day at home and seeing my friends. And what do you think the minx said? She was very sorry, but she had an attack of atavism, too,—her grandfather wasn't used to afternoon tea and she had never acquired any real taste for it!"

Baskerville laughed delightedly.

"Oh, it wasn't so clever, after all," said Mrs. Luttrell, smiling with that unshakable good humor which was the most exasperating thing on earth to all her enemies and her friends alike. "It is just because you're in love with Anne Clavering; and I think she likes you pretty well, too."

Baskerville sat up then, sobered in an instant. What Mrs. Luttrell knew or suspected all Washington would shortly know. "Why do you say that?" he asked quietly.

"Because I think it, that's why. It's one of the strangest things in the world that people in love think all the rest of the world blind and deaf. And a woman lets her secret out just as readily as a man. I say Anne Clavering likes you. I don't say she is pining and can't eat and sleep for you; but I do say she likes you, though. And I feel sorry for the girl—such a family! You ought to see how that divorcée, Mrs. Denman, goes on with Count von Kappf, who, I believe, has been sent over here by a syndicate to marry an American heiress. Nobody knows what Anne Clavering has to suffer for the conduct of that sister of hers."

"And you, who call yourself a Christian, had to add to Miss Clavering's mortification."

"Oh, it was only a trifle, and she came out ahead."

"Anyhow, you shall apologize to her. Do you understand me, Sara Luttrell? You shall apologize, and before me, too."

"Very well," replied Mrs. Luttrell, unabashed. "The first time I catch you and Anne Clavering together I'll apologize."

Baskerville sat silent for a while as Mrs. Luttrell luxuriously toasted her toes. Presently he said, "So people are kind enough to say that I am in love with Miss Clavering?"

"Yes, indeed. People are always kind enough to say things—and a great many people are saying that you are in love with her. You haven't escaped notice as much as you thought."

"I don't desire to escape notice. And I only hope enough people will say it so it will get to Miss Clavering's ears. Then she may not be so surprised as to throw me over when—the opportunity comes. I may be a good many sorts of a blamed fool, Sara, but I am not such a fool as to be anything but flattered when my name is associated with Miss Clavering's."

"Very decently said. But how are you going to manage about this senatorial investigation—trying to ruin the father as a preliminary to marrying the daughter?"

Baskerville grew grave at once. The investigation was on in earnest. The committee which had been appointed before the adjournment of Congress had begun its sittings directly upon the meeting of Congress, and Baskerville had at once come into prominence as one of the representatives of the Civil Service League. The question of Clavering's culpability with regard to the land grants was complicated with the open barter and sale of Federal offices, and the Civil Service League had taken it up actively. The League was in no way bound by senatorial courtesy, and it had a formidable array of evidence to produce, which pointed straight to criminal as well as civil indictments. Baskerville found himself in a difficult position. He had gone too far in one direction toward exposing Senator Clavering, and his heart had carried him too far in another direction, for he was at last beginning to realize that he had fallen in love with Anne Clavering—a path upon which a strong man never halts. It is your weakling who falls halfway in love and then stops.

Mrs. Luttrell studied Baskerville keenly. Herself a sentimentalist in disguise, she loved Baskerville the better for doing what she had long dreaded—for she had a woman's jealousy of another woman's usurping the first place with this nephew-in-law, who was son, companion, and comrade in one. But at least he did not contemplate foisting a pink-and-white nonentity upon her; Mrs. Luttrell always declared herself afraid of silly women. She not only liked Anne Clavering, but she saw in her a large and generous spirit, who would not, by small artifices, try to come between Baskerville and Mrs. Luttrell. And the ineradicable interest which is every woman's inalienable right in a love-affair was strong in Mrs. Luttrell's breast. She began to wish that Baskerville and Anne would marry; and after sitting quite silent for ten minutes watching Baskerville's moody face, she suddenly got up, went over to him, and smoothing the hair back from his forehead, kissed it tenderly. Two tears dropped upon his brow. Baskerville looked up and took her hands in his. He spoke no word, but he knew that the memory of the man so long dead was poignant still; and Mrs. Luttrell, after a pause, said in a low voice:—

"I hope Anne Clavering will love you as I loved my Richard. And if you can make her as happy as he made me—Good night. I can't bear to speak much of it, even to you."

"If any woman ever loves me as you loved my uncle, I should think myself eternally blessed with such love. Good night, Sara dear."

He kissed her warmly, went out of the room and downstairs and across the garden to his own house, and into his library. The first thing he saw upon the big library table was a mass of documents relating to the K. F. R. land grants. Baskerville pushed them away, and taking up a well-thumbed volume of Theocritus tried to forget himself in the pictures of the fair shining of the Sicilian sun, in the sound of the pipe of Daphnis, in the complainings of the two poor old fishermen lying by night in their wattled cabin on the sand dunes.

All was in vain. His thoughts were no sooner diverted from Anne Clavering than they turned to Clavering and his affairs. How amazing was this man who had rough-hewn his way to a high place, to enormous wealth, to great power, from which he was likely to be thrown headlong into an abyss of shame! Baskerville had very little doubt that, no matter how successful might be the suits against Clavering, he would manage to retain great tangible sums of money. Men of the Clavering type hold on to their money more intelligently than to their supposititious honor. And finding it impossible to get away from his own thoughts, even in books which had heretofore been an unfailing sedative, Baskerville went to bed, and tossed in true lover's fashion half the remaining night, before he fell into a troubled sleep to dream of Anne Clavering.

Chapter Twelve

It is said that all truly benevolent women are matchmakers, and although Mrs. Thorndyke would have indignantly denied the charge of being a matchmaker, it was an indisputable fact that within a fortnight of dining at Mrs. Luttrell's she contrived an impromptu dinner at which Anne Clavering and Baskerville were the first guests to be asked; and if they had declined, it is doubtful if the dinner would have come off at all. However, they both accepted; and Mrs. Thorndyke, whether by inadvertence, as she stoutly alleged, or by design, as Thorndyke charged, had Baskerville take Anne in to dinner.

Some faint reflection of the rumor which was flying about Washington concerning Baskerville's devotion had reached Anne Clavering's ears. It gave a delightful shyness to her eyes, a warm color to her usually pale cheeks. Something in Baskerville's manner—the ingenuity with which he managed to perform every little service for her himself, conveyed subtly but plainly to Anne his interest in her. She had been deeply flattered and even made happy by Baskerville's calling at last at her house. There was every reason why he should remain away—so much Anne had admitted to herself often, and always with a burning blush, remembering what she knew and had read about the investigation through which her father was passing. But Baskerville had come, and there must have been a powerful force, much stronger than her mother's timid invitation, to bring him. Perhaps he came because he could not stay away.

At this thought Anne, who was sitting at her dressing-table after the dinner at the Thorndykes', caught sight of her own face in the mirror. A happy smile hovered about the corners of her mouth, her eyes became eloquent. Women, being close students of their own emotions, can always detect the dawning and the development of this silent but intense interest in a certain man, an interest which is born, grows, and often dies for want of nourishment, but sometimes lives and thrives on neglect—and sometimes,—O glorious consummation!—comes into its kingdom of love. Anne Clavering, who had passed her twenty-seventh birthday, and who, shamed and indignant at the conduct of her sisters, had maintained a haughty reserve toward men and had hitherto found it easy, knew that it was not without meaning she felt herself watching for Baskerville's entrance into a room; that she was secretly uneasy until he had placed himself beside her; that when he talked, an instant, sweet, and positive mental sympathy came into being between them which seemed to bring them together without any volition on their part.

January was flying by. Anne Clavering went out quite as much as Mrs. Luttrell, but with a different motive. To Mrs. Luttrell society was a necessity, as a thing becomes after a lifetime of habitude. Anne Clavering would have liked society well enough if it had been merely a means of pleasure. But she had to maintain before the world a position which her father and her two sisters jeopardized every hour. The place of the Claverings in society was by no means a fixed one. All the idle and careless people, all the worshippers of money, all those who love to eat and drink at somebody else's expense, all those who pursue pleasure without conscience or delicacy, thronged the Clavering house.

Clavering himself was seldom invited out, and did not regret it. The small talk of society bored him, and he was conscious that he did not shine unless he had the centre of the stage. Occasionally he met a man who interested him, and semi-occasionally a woman who did the same. But no woman had ever interested him as much as Elizabeth Darrell. He was amazed, himself, at the power she had of drawing him to her; for, under the specious pretence of getting information from General Brandon concerning the K. F. R. land grants, Clavering soon managed to spend two or three evenings a week in Elizabeth's company. He speedily found out General Brandon's ways—his hour or two at the club in the evening, his visits to his old friends, all of which were clock-like in their regularity. On these evenings, when General Brandon returned to meet an appointment, Clavering would invariably be found established in the study. Any other man in the world but General Brandon would have had his suspicions aroused, but the General was born to be hoodwinked. His chivalric honor, his limpidness of character, his entire innocence, were strong forces, as all these things are. He radiated good influences upon honest men, and gave active encouragement to every rogue of every sort who had dealings with him.

Elizabeth Darrell, however, was not so simple as her father. After that first evening she saw that Clavering was determined to secure her society. She wondered at herself for submitting to it, but in truth it would have been more remarkable if she had not done so. The extreme dulness of her life made almost any companionship a resource, and Clavering had certain fascinating qualities which were very obvious. Without making himself the hero of his own recitals, he gave the most vivid and interesting pictures of life on the wide Wyoming ranges, on the Staked Plains, in California mining camps, amid the boulders of the Yellowstone. Elizabeth listened under a kind of bewitchment, while Clavering, in his rich voice, told the story of those years—a story pulsing with movement, brilliant with adventure, with life and death at issue every moment. She began to understand this man's power over men, and to recognize a kind of compulsion he exercised over her. She might have remained out of the study, where, with a map spread out, to amuse General Brandon, Clavering talked to him and at Elizabeth. She was present not only because she wished to be, but she recognized distinctly that she also came because Clavering wished her to come. Especially was this true with regard to those odd half-hours which she spent with Clavering alone.

Once she went out of the room when Serena brought Clavering's card up. In a minute or two Serena came with a message: "De gent'mun seh he mus' see you, Miss 'Liz'beth, 'bout some dem papers outen de Gin'l's trunk." And Elizabeth, obeying this strange compulsion, went back into the room, and saw Clavering's eyes light up with lambent fire at sight of her.

That he was deeply and even desperately in love with her from the start there could be no question to any woman, and least of all to a woman as clever as Elizabeth Darrell. She received a profound shock when this was quickly revealed to her, not by any explicit word of Clavering's, but by all his words, his looks, his course of conduct. He knew too much to venture to make open love to Elizabeth, and in other ways she made him keep his distance in a manner which Clavering had never experienced in his life before. He would no more have dared the smallest personal liberty with Elizabeth Darrell than he would have ventured to put a stick of dynamite into the fire. He had never really been afraid of a woman before, and this of itself added a powerful interest to Elizabeth. He realized fully the difficulties which beset him when he thought of his chances of making Elizabeth his wife. He could manage a divorce from his present wife in a way not known by the poor soul herself, or by Anne, or by any one else in the world except Clavering. That once accomplished, though, Elizabeth remained still to be won. She probably inherited the Southern prejudice against divorce, and it might not be easy to overcome it. And there was General Brandon to be considered. Clavering, studying that honest, simple, handsome face across the table from him, bent earnestly over the ridiculous maps and useless memoranda, remembered that the General still cherished an ancient pair of duelling pistols, which he had inherited from his grandfather. He had taken these antique shooting-irons out of the old escritoire in the corner and had shown them, not without pride and reverence, to Clavering, saying solemnly:—

"These weapons, my dear sir, have never been used since my grandfather purchased them in 1804, when he unfortunately became involved in a dispute concerning politics with a gentleman of the highest character in Virginia. They had a hostile meeting and shots were exchanged, but no blood was spilled. I am exceedingly glad that the old practice of duelling over trifles is gone, never to return. But there is one class of cases left in which a gentleman has but one resource—the duello. That is, when the honor of the ladies of his family is impugned. In most instances the transgressor should be shot down like a dog. But there are other cases when, owing to imprudence on the lady's part, the code must be invoked. Thank God, the honor of Southern women is safe in their own keeping. But behind her, every woman, sir, of every country, should have the protection of a man with arms in his hands, if need be. I am aware that my ideas are antiquated; but I have always held them and I always shall."

Clavering listened to this without a word or smile. Nothing would be more likely, if he should betray his design toward Elizabeth, than that he should find himself looking down the barrel of one of those queer old pistols in the hands of this soft-voiced, gullible, guileless old Don Quixote. These, however, were but obstacles; and obstacles, in Clavering's lexicon, were things to be overcome.

In the narrowness and dulness of her life, Elizabeth naturally thought much of Clavering. If she had been asked at any moment whether she would marry him, should he get a divorce, she would instantly and with horror have answered "no." But she had seen enough of the great, self-indulgent world to know that divorce and remarriage are by no means the impossible and unheard-of things which simple people in staid communities think they are. She began to speculate idly, in her lonely afternoon walks and in the evenings when Clavering did not come, as to what would happen if she should marry Clavering. Whenever she caught herself at this she would recoil from the idea in horror. But it returned. Pelham's conduct had shattered all her ideals of man's love. If he could act as he had done, where was the difference between the love of the best and the worst of men?

This bitterness toward Pelham was much increased by the receipt of a letter from Mr. McBean, the solicitor, more hard, more peremptory, more insulting, than any he had yet written her. There had been no trouble in finding Elizabeth's whereabouts, for although she had not thought fit to notify McBean of her leaving England, it was known that she had returned to America, and McBean's letter reached her promptly. In it threats of legal proceedings were repeated, with an earnestness terrible to Elizabeth. This letter made her ill in bed. She called it a neuralgic headache, to soothe her father, but in truth it was a collapse from alarm and grief. It was an emergency which could only be helped by money; and a large sum of money, it seemed to Elizabeth—twenty-five hundred dollars to begin with, and then cost and expense which she could not understand added to it. This referred solely to the necklace. What else had to be accounted for nearly staggered her,—but where was she to get two or three thousand dollars? Her father could not have produced it had he converted his blood into money; and the poor old house, plastered with mortgages from roof to cellar, would scarcely sell for more than what had been borrowed on it.

It was now the height of the season, and the whirl of gayety and of politics made Washington seethe like a caldron. Carriages were dashing about from the early afternoon to all hours of the morning. Houses were lighted up, music resounded, men and women rushed hither and thither in the race after pleasure.

At the great white building on Capitol Hill history was being steadily and rapidly made. One subject, not wholly political, aroused deep interest on the House side as well as in the Senate. The investigating committee on the K. F. R. land grants had already held several meetings, and it was known that for some reason of political expedience the party in power wished the question settled at the earliest possible date. There was, among certain senators who did not really understand the matter, a disposition to throw Clavering overboard like Jonah. Those senators who really understood the question reckoned Clavering to be perfectly deserving of a long term in state's prison. There was no hope of acquittal for him from the moment the whole evidence against him was known to be available; and for this nobody deserved so much credit as Richard Baskerville. He had been more than two years unravelling the tangled web of litigation, and only a very astute lawyer, with money and time to spend on it, could have done it at all. It was quite clear now, compact and available. A lesser man than Clavering would at this stage of the proceedings have resigned from the Senate and decamped.

Clavering, however, was incapable of understanding defeat, and had no more thought of surrender than the Old Guard at Waterloo. His entertainments, always lavish and frequent, grew more lavish and more frequent. Washington was not big enough to supply half the luxuries he required; New York was called upon, and Paris and Vienna, for rarities of all sorts to make the dinners and balls at the Claverings' more brilliant, more startling. Élise and Lydia revelled in this; Anne's good taste and good sense revolted against it. She read every word in the newspapers concerning her father, and she began to see that ruin and disgrace were threatening him with fearful quickness. Even Reginald Clavering, dull and self-centred, became frightened and ashamed. Not so Clavering; he was not the man to "roll darkling down the torrent of his fate." He would go if he had to go, with all the splendor which unlimited money and assurance could contrive. It gave him little spells of laughter and amusement when he thought how much Washington would miss his princely entertaining, in case he should be struck down by his enemies. If that should occur, however, he reflected that Washington was not the only city, nor America even the only country, in the world. He was not really much grieved at the possibility of leaving public life, although he fought with a gladiator's courage against being thrown out. He had accomplished much of what he had gone into public life for,—the making of a vaster fortune than the vast one he had before. And then, that new dream which had come into his life— Elizabeth Darrell. If he should win her, as he fully intended and expected, she might not find Washington a very comfortable place of residence. He would give her a splendid hotel in Paris, or a grand establishment in London.

He would spend half the year in America, in the West, which he liked far better than the East; and the other half he could spend having what he would have called "a great big bat" in Europe. He might go into European financiering and teach those old fogies a thing or two—Clavering indulged in many Alnaschar dreams about this time.

One afternoon in the latter part of January Elizabeth went out for her usual solitary walk. It had been very cold, with snow, and the thermometer that day suddenly jumped into the sixties, bringing a damp white fog which enveloped everything. Elizabeth walked straight down the street on which she lived, without regard to where she was going; she meant to be out of doors only for so many hours, and to find in the loneliness of a walk a change from the loneliness of the house. It was within a week of the time she had received McBean's letter, and it lay heavy on her heart.

She had walked but a few squares, when she heard a step behind her which she recognized as Clavering's. She stopped involuntarily, the red blood surging into her pale face. In a moment Clavering was by her side.

"I saw you go out, and followed you," he said.

Elizabeth made no reply. He had never joined her on the street before, although sometimes she had passed him getting in and out of his automobile or driving behind a notable pair of sorrels. But this time he had not only joined her—he had followed her. Elizabeth's sudden flushing was by no means lost on Clavering.

They walked on due east through the mist which enveloped all things, the snow still piled in drifts along the edges of the streets. They spoke little, but Elizabeth felt instinctively that Clavering had something of consequence to say to her when they got into the unfamiliar part of the town, where he could be certain of being unobserved. The street, which had been fashionable as far as Sixteenth Street, grew semifashionable, and then became a region of lodging-houses, places with dressmakers' signs, and an occasional small shop. Then, growing more and more remote, it became a street of comfortable, quiet houses, tenanted by people to whom the West End of Washington mattered as little as the west end of Bagdad. By that time they had gone a mile. They came to one of those small triangular parks which abound in Washington, where there are seats under the trees and asphalt walks winding in and out of shrubbery.

Elizabeth, under the spell of compulsion which Clavering had cast upon her, made no objection to entering the park with him. Usually it was completely open to observation, but now the soft and clinging fog drew a misty curtain between the little park and the world. Clavering led the way to a bench among a clump of evergreens, and Elizabeth, without a word of protest, sat down upon the bench, the Senator at her side.

"There are places within half a mile of everywhere in this town," he said, "where one can be as secure from observation as if one were in a back street of the city of Damascus. And if I had designed this afternoon for meeting you and talking confidentially with you, nothing could have been better. The people who live in these houses seem always to be asleep or dead, and if they knew our names, they couldn't recognize us ten feet off. Now," he continued, "tell me what is troubling you—for I have seen ever since that first glimpse of you that something is preying upon you."

Elizabeth remained silent.

"What is it?" asked Clavering again, with authority in his voice. And Elizabeth, still with that strange feeling of being obliged to do what Clavering required, told him the whole story of the necklace.

Clavering listened attentively. Elizabeth had tried to keep out of it the personal note, the shame and disappointment and resentment she felt at Pelham's conduct; but she was dealing with a very astute man, who read her with extraordinary keenness, and who saw the good policy, from his own point of view, of still further embittering her feelings toward Pelham.

"I should say that fellow Pelham ought to have shown you a little more consideration, especially as you say he inherited everything."

"Yes."

"A woman, standing alone, is almost bound to fall in with just such brutes as Pelham and that Scotch solicitor. Mind, I say that you were obliged to meet with some men who were traitors, all in fact except those who happen to be in love with you. Look—" he opened his watch, and on the inner case Elizabeth saw a Greek sentence engraved, [Greek: memnêstein apistein]. "You didn't think I knew Greek. Of course I don't. No man born and raised in my circumstances ever knew Greek, and I never expect to know it. I have heard about some one of those old classics learning to play the fiddle when he was eighty, and always thought him a great fool for so doing. No, I only had this put in Greek to puzzle fools; it means, 'Remember to distrust.' It was a pity that you had not remembered to distrust that Pelham scoundrel."

Elizabeth remained silent and almost stunned at this characterization of Pelham, and Clavering, seeing he had gone far enough in that direction, said:—

"If the diamond broker—pawn-broker, I should call him—gave you five hundred pounds on the necklace, it was probably worth fifteen hundred. However, fifteen hundred pounds is a small matter."

"It is a great deal to me and always was, except for that short time in London when we thought ourselves the richest people in the world," replied Elizabeth.

"You may, if you choose, be one of the richest women in America."

ill236

"THE LITTLE PARK WAS WHOLLY DESERTED EXCEPT FOR THEMSELVES."

Elizabeth's face had grown deathly pale. She was sensible of the dishonor of any proposal Clavering might make to her. All of the stories she had heard from the beginning about Clavering's intention to divorce his wife rushed upon her mind—all of her own vague and haunting speculations for the past few weeks. She remained silent, but every moment she grew more agitated.

Clavering was silent for a few moments, allowing the leaven to work. Then he continued: "Of course there is but one way to do this. I can get a divorce and then you must marry me. No doubt you have a lot of unpractical ideas about divorce, but let me tell you that when a man and a woman are indispensable to each other—as you are to me—what does anything on earth matter?"

No one listening to Clavering's cool and measured tones would have surmised what he was proposing to Elizabeth; nor did he attempt the smallest endearment, free as they were from observation, for the fog grew denser every moment and the little park was wholly deserted except for themselves.

At his last remarks Elizabeth attempted some faint protest, which went unheeded by Clavering, who spoke again: "People call me a successful man. So I am, with money, politics, cards, and horses. But I have no luck with women. First, I married before I was twenty-one—cursed folly that it was! You have seen my wife—I'll say no more. Then, my eldest and youngest daughters—well, they are like me in some ways, that's enough. Élise has been through the divorce court. It cost me something like fifty thousand dollars to keep the truth about her from coming out. Lydia will go the same way. My best plan with them will be to marry them to men who will get the upper hand of them—keep a tight rein over them. So far, I haven't succeeded; and I am seriously considering giving them each a handsome fortune, marrying them to foreigners, and getting them out of the country."

Elizabeth's pale face had grown red while Clavering was speaking. He was close enough to see it, even by the uncertain light that penetrated the mist.

"You think I'm a brute, eh? No, on the contrary I have a strong hankering after decency in my womenkind."

"Your daughter Anne—" Elizabeth spoke falteringly.

"Ah, yes, bad luck again. Anne has twice the sense of her sisters, is really more attractive and is perfectly certain to behave herself. But she is on her mother's side, and if—or when—I do get a divorce, I shall have to fight her, and she is the only one of my children whose opposition would amount to anything. You know what a Miss Nancy Reginald is."

"But—but—how can you get a divorce if Mrs. Clavering—"

"Doesn't want it? Well, I never was properly married to her in the first place. She didn't know it at the time, and I was a youngster and didn't know it, either; but our marriage wasn't regular at all. I should have got the license in Kentucky instead of in Ohio, where we crossed the river to get married. So we are not really married and never have been, according to law. When I mention the subject to Mrs. Clavering, I shall offer to get the divorce; if she is contumacious, I shall simply prove that we have never been married at all. That will be hard on the children, and on that account I think there is no doubt she would agree to the divorce, if it were not for Anne. Anne, however, doesn't know anything about the defect in the marriage, and I rather think she will back down when she finds out just where we stand."

Elizabeth listened to this with horror. But it was horror of the deed, not of the man. Clavering's calm and lucid presentation of the case, the absence of hypocrisy, his quiet determination, seemed to lift him out of the class of vulgar criminals and make him almost respectable. And then he went on to give his side of the case, and his voice had in it a strange note of longing.

"I have before me twenty years yet, and although I am reckoned a man who can live on bonds and stocks and lawsuits and fighting other men, still I've had my dreams—I have them still. If I could find a woman who would be a wife to me, and yet could be an intellectual companion for me—that would be something that all my money hasn't brought me. Do you blame a man for longing after it? Don't you think I am more nearly human for wanting it than if I were satisfied to go on all my life as I have done for the last thirty-five years?"

"Yes." Elizabeth spoke unwillingly, but the assent was forced out of her. And whether it was his words, his voice,—always singularly captivating,—his compelling glance, or his powerful personality, Elizabeth began to feel a toleration, along with a reprehension, of him. For Clavering, like all men, was made up of things to admire and things to abhor; only he possessed both in a stronger degree than common. He was much older than Elizabeth, but he had not lost the fire and vigor of youth.

Elizabeth's agitation had subsided somewhat, but she was still unable or unwilling to speak. The gray mist was becoming denser, and they could see the gas-lamps studding the fast-falling darkness like jewels; the sound of wheels and hoofs upon the asphalt was deadened by the fog and grew fainter, the street was quieter, more deserted even than Washington streets usually are. In the little park, with the masses of evergreen shrubbery around them, they were as alone, as little subject to intrusion, as if they had been on a desert island. After a considerable pause Clavering spoke again.

"I saw you first, just ten years ago, one night as you were waiting on the street with your father, for some lady to take you to a ball. You dropped a little trinket from around your neck."

Elizabeth started with surprise. "That was the night I first met my husband—and Hugh Pelham. And I lost my little pearl heart and never found it."

"I was the guilty man," said Clavering, with a smile. "I crushed your heart under my foot." It was an accidental joining of words, but Clavering wished he had expressed himself otherwise. The words had an ominous sound, and Elizabeth, after looking at him intently for a few minutes, turned her head away.

Clavering, hastening to recall his lost ground, added: "The day will come when I will give you the most superb diamond locket that the South African mines can produce. I will make duchesses envy you your jewels and princesses cry with envy of them. I remembered you ever after that night, and a month ago I met you. Don't think people are fools who talk of love at first sight for anybody at any age, or under any circumstances. The moment my eyes fell upon you I was anxious to know you. When I knew you, I wanted to know you better. When I knew you better, I became willing to do anything for you, to jeopardize anything in order to marry you. And I will give you a great fortune, millions of money, of which I shall get very little benefit, because you will outlive me many years and probably marry some other man and endow him, by gad, with my money. I will go anywhere you may desire to live, for I don't believe you would consent to live in Washington. You may have a splendid house in London or Paris, a great country house, a château, any and everywhere you like, and you may command me as no other woman has ever commanded me. Now will you marry me after I am divorced?"

Elizabeth felt dazed. She had known from the first what was coming, but when Clavering put his wish into words it was as strange and staggering as if the idea had never before occurred to her. The thought of committing so great a wrong upon another woman, as Clavering suggested, appalled her— a wrong so vast and far-reaching that she turned away from the contemplation of it. But she did not fly from the temptation, and the temptation which is not fled from is the conqueror.

Clavering interpreted her silence with ease. He took her hand, pulled off her glove, and held her soft palm between his two strong ones. Five minutes passed; they seemed an hour to Elizabeth, frightened yet fascinated, her mind overwhelmed with what Clavering had told her, had promised her, had urged upon her. Through it all came the cry of her heart for Pelham. Had he been true to her, this temptation would never have come in her way. And as he had forgotten her and had even persecuted her, what did it matter what became of her, so she had ease instead of this frightful poverty, companionship instead of this dreadful loneliness, security instead of this perpetual terror over the small and sordid matter of a few hundred pounds? Clavering was too clever a man to urge her overmuch when he saw that he had a tempter always with her in her own self. At last, after five minutes of agitated silence, she managed to withdraw her hand and rise. Clavering, without a word, walked with her out of the little park, hailed a passing hansom in the dusk and put her in, only saying at the last:—

"I will see you again as soon as possible. Meanwhile, remember you have but to say one word and all is yours."

The hansom rolled off, and Clavering, putting his hands in his pockets, walked away at a quick gait. The expression on his face was like that of a successful gladiator. It was not pleasant to see.

Chapter Thirteen

The next night but one, Clavering had an appointment with General Brandon at the usual hour of half-past nine. And at nine o'clock promptly he was sitting with Elizabeth in the little study, waiting for General Brandon's return.

The first thing he said to her was: "Of course that affair about the necklace must be straightened out at once. I can cable to my London agent, and he can find out all about it and recover it, for it can be easily traced and recovered. And leave me to deal with the solicitor on the quiet."

"I hardly think you know what you are offering," replied Elizabeth, with involuntary haughtiness. "I could not accept money or services from you. It is not to be thought of for a moment."

"Then what are you going to do about it?" asked Clavering, coolly, in the words of a celebrated character.

Ah, what was she going to do about it? thought poor Elizabeth. Tell her father and see him turned out of the only shelter he had for his aged head? If only she had been more experienced, had known more! She had been so very, very ignorant in those London days. If Pelham had not behaved so basely to her!

Clavering talked on, quietly assuming that he would take charge of the matter for her; but Elizabeth, after listening to him in silence and even in weakness, suddenly and impulsively rose and said, "I desire you never to speak to me on that subject again."

Then General Brandon's step was heard upon the stair, and nothing more was said between them. Elizabeth remained in the room while Clavering was there, and he honestly thought he was progressing quite as fast as he had any right to expect.

It was now the middle of January, and the investigating committee continued to sit and the newspapers to print the proceedings. This did not tend to make it any pleasanter for Clavering's family. Anne, with a touch of her father's courage, continued to go out and to entertain, but it was with an aching heart. To add to her other anxieties, Mrs. Clavering was very ailing and unhappy. By some strange accident—for the poor lady never read the newspapers— she got an inkling that Clavering was under fire, and she often asked questions which Anne had difficulty in answering. Whatever love Mrs. Clavering had ever felt for Clavering had long since been cast out by fear; but she had the true feminine instinct which makes a dove fierce in the presence of the despoiler of her nest. Reginald Clavering redoubled his attention to his mother, and was of more help to Anne than she had thought possible.

It had been determined, chiefly at Clavering's suggestion, that a grand musical, followed by a ball, should be given at the Clavering house on Shrove Tuesday, as a wind-up to the splendid entertainments for which the house had long been noted; and the undisguised intention was to eclipse everything that had hitherto been done in Washington in the way of entertaining. Anne opposed it, but Élise and Lydia carried the day, backed up by their father.

Only Clavering suspected that it was likely to be the last entertainment given there. He felt confident of knowing the decision of the committee before Shrove Tuesday, and he fully realized the possibility that it might mean expulsion from the Senate on his record alone; as, unluckily for him, there was a very complete and authentic legal record of his doings, which Baskerville had unearthed. So far Clavering had kept out of jail; but there had been more than one true bill found against him, and even verdicts in criminal cases, which had never been enforced. He was still fighting, and meant to go down fighting; but he devoted far more thought to planning what he would do if he were compelled to leave public life than if he were permitted to stay in it. He reckoned that by expediting matters he could get the divorce granted and the decree entered by the first of June, when he would marry Elizabeth Darrell, go abroad for the summer, and then arrange his life for the future. And while he was taking it for granted that he could marry Elizabeth, and was seeing her in private two or three times a week by General Brandon's innocent connivance, Clavering had touched her hand but once and had never pressed his lips to her cheek, nor had she ever allowed him one word of acknowledged love-making. And this was a woman he was ready to dower with millions, which, as he grimly thought, a young husband, his successor, would get! Clavering concluded that some women were ungrateful. At the same time, he did not seriously doubt that he could marry Elizabeth in June.

He began to congratulate himself on his good luck in his constant presence at General Brandon's house escaping notice. No one but himself, the General, and Elizabeth seemed to have any knowledge of his visits, although General Brandon, at his club, did some innocent bragging about the assistance he was giving to Senator Clavering "in the unholy warfare against a man incapable of the smallest dishonesty." "Why, sir," he would say to any one who would listen to him, "Senator Clavering has assured me, on his word of honor, that there is not one scintilla of truth in the shameful allegations brought against him in the public prints. Wait, however, until the senatorial committee has made its report. Then you will see Senator Clavering triumphantly vindicated; mark my words, sir, triumphantly vindicated."

Nobody but General Brandon, however, really believed this. Certainly Anne Clavering did not, and every day that she read the newspaper accounts of what had occurred and what had not occurred at the meeting of the investigating committee, her heart sank lower. To keep her mother from suspecting anything, Anne pursued her usual course of life; but it required all her resolution to do it. Every time she entered a drawing-room she called up all her courage to meet an affront, if one should be offered her. Not one was passed upon her, but she lived in dread of it.

During this time Baskerville had gone everywhere he thought it likely that he should meet Anne Clavering, but so far he had not been fortunate. He did not repeat his visit to Clavering's house. He had doubted the propriety of his going in the first instance, and he doubted it still more as time passed on. But it did not keep him from falling deeper and deeper in love with the image of Anne Clavering in his mind. On the Thursday which was Constance Thorndyke's day at home, he felt tolerably confident that Anne Clavering would be paying her dinner call; and so on the stroke of four he presented himself, armed and equipped as the law directs, at Mrs. Luttrell's door, to accompany that redoubtable person upon a round of Thursday visits.

After several perfunctory calls where Baskerville was bored to death but behaved himself beautifully, he arrived with Mrs. Luttrell at Constance Thorndyke's door precisely at five o'clock. Constance Thorndyke received them with the same charming grace and cordiality which always distinguished her and which was powerful enough to draw within her circle, as her guest on her reception day, her husband. Thorndyke never felt so proud of his wife as when he saw her in his own drawing-room, and she collected about her, from the wide field of Washington, persons who made her drawing-room shine. He frankly admitted to Constance that hers were the only receptions in Washington which he really enjoyed. He was delighted to see Baskerville and Mrs. Luttrell, the latter being to him, as to most men, an ever blooming tree of delight. He came up and established Mrs. Luttrell in a chair by the fireside, with a good cup of tea and with a man on each side of her; and Mrs. Luttrell found herself as happy as it is given to mortals to be on this distressful planet. Thorndyke's conversation interested her on the one side, and Admiral Prendergast, a superb specimen of the old-time chivalrous naval officer, with whom Mrs. Luttrell had had an intermittent flirtation for not less than forty years, on her other side.

"What a blessed comfort it is," sighed Mrs. Luttrell to a listening group, "to be able to come into a drawing-room like this and have a good cup of tea, with some cups and saucers and tea-spoons that did not come out of a curio shop, and some honest bread and butter. I declare I am tired to death of these brazen retired tradespeople who have come to this town and undertaken to receive in their Louis Quinze drawing-rooms, and in their English dining rooms, with a great big table full of pink and green kickshaws, and candelabra three feet high all over it, and a big placque of roses just like an old-fashioned feather bed."

"Will you listen to Sara?" asked her dutiful nephew. "She has hauled me about this day from one retired tradesman's house to another, scattering compliments as she went, and embracing every man, woman, and child she met of the smart set—the smarter the better. She couldn't be kept from going with those people unless she were chained up."

"Well," faintly replied Mrs. Luttrell, "one has to be a hypocrite in this world; but I do say, Constance, that next my own yours is the best drawing-room in Washington."

"That is indeed high praise," replied Constance Thorndyke, smiling, "and I am vain enough to believe it is sincere, especially when I can get my own husband to come home early Thursday afternoon."

Mrs. Thorndyke had never been strictly beautiful nor even remarkably pretty before her marriage, but since then she had developed a late-flowering loveliness which was much more than beauty. She was happy, she loved and was beloved; she had it in her power to assist the man she loved without making him hate her; she had, in fact, all that she had ever asked of high heaven, except one thing—she was childless. But that one supreme disappointment gave to her face and to her soul a touch of softness, of resignation, that disarmed fate. With a tender feminine superstition, she believed that, this last gift having been denied her, she would be suffered to retain the happiness already hers. Thorndyke himself had to be both husband and children to her, and on him she concentrated all the love and solicitude of her nature. That he was happy there could be no doubt. In Constance he had all that he had ever wished for.

The Thorndyke house was one of the few in Washington which Baskerville could enter with a clear conscience in the matter of duty calls. He always paid them promptly to Constance Thorndyke, and often went when there was no obligation for him to go. He had some one besides Constance Thorndyke in view, however, in paying that particular visit; it was Anne Clavering whom he had really come to see. Mrs. Thorndyke found means to let him know that Anne had not been there yet; and while Baskerville was taking what comfort he could out of this Anne walked into the drawing-room. She looked pale and worn and much older than she really was. Baskerville's keen eye took this in at a glance; but like a sincere lover he admired her none the less for not being in a flush of spirits, and felt an increased tenderness for her. A delicate rosy color flooded her face when she saw who was present, and rosier still when Baskerville established her in a corner, that he might have a monopoly of her sweet company.

Bearing in mind his promise to discipline his aunt, almost the first words Baskerville said to Anne were: "I hear my aunt was quite impertinent to you the other night; but before I slept I made her promise to apologize to you."

This was quite loud enough for Mrs. Luttrell to hear, and she promptly turned her smiling, sharp old face toward Anne. "My dear, he did, as I am a sinner! Well, it's a great thing at my time of life to discover a new sensation, and I've found one in the act of apology. Now listen, all of you—Constance, make these people stop chattering—Jack Prendergast, be quiet, and Senator Thorndyke, stop laughing. Miss Clavering, I was rather impertinent to you at Secretary Slater's the other night, but I declare it was those two foolish women, Mrs. Hill-Smith and Eleanor Baldwin, who were really to blame. However, I think you got the better of me—ha, ha! I always liked you, and like you better for your spirit. I offer you my sincere apologies—on condition that you never again make the least objection to anything I say or do—for, look you, Sara Luttrell has been used to speaking her mind too long to change. But I apologize."

At which Admiral Prendergast remarked piously, "Lord, now lettest Thou thy servant depart in peace."

Anne rose and took Mrs. Luttrell's hand in hers. "I'll forgive you," she said, smiling; "but don't think I am afraid of you—I like you too much for that."

"I know you're not afraid of me—you and my nephew, Richard Baskerville, are the only two creatures yet who openly defy me—and when you join forces, as you have done to-day, you are too strong for me."

This coupling of their names did not lose anything by Mrs. Luttrell's emphatic manner of saying it, and it deepened the color in Anne's face and brought the light to Baskerville's eyes. And as if directly inspired by Satan, the old lady kept on:—

"You ought to have seen how angry my nephew was with me when he heard of my behavior—we were having a quiet chat in my bedroom while I was undressing, and he gave me such a rating as you never heard in your life. Oh! he took it to heart much more than you did. His language to me was something shocking. He threatened to tell my age all over town, and to throw my ermine cape into the fire if I ever misbehaved to you again. I never saw him in such a way before."

How much inadvertence and how much malice aforethought there were in this speech only Sara Luttrell knew, but it was distinctly disconcerting to Anne Clavering, and visibly shortened her visit. Mrs. Luttrell went out at the same time, and, after being helped into her big coach by Baskerville, turned to speak to him as the carriage rolled off.

"Didn't I do it handsomely? Why, he isn't here!" And at that moment she caught sight of Baskerville sitting by Anne Clavering's side in her brougham, then whirling around the corner. Mrs. Luttrell smiled and then sighed. "The scamp," she said to herself. "I remember how once—" She took from her pocket the miniature which never left her, and her memory went back to the days when to recline in that man's arms and to feel his kisses upon her lips were Paradise, a paradise to which the gate had been forever closed to any other man.

Baskerville had got into his present agreeable situation by simply not waiting for an invitation, and furthermore by saying authoritatively to the footman, "Miss Clavering wishes to drive out Connecticut Avenue until she directs you to turn."

It was all done so suddenly that Anne did not realize it until it was over; but what woman who loves is averse to having the man of her choice sitting by her side in the intimate seclusion of a brougham at dusk of a winter's evening? Baskerville, however, was there for a purpose—a purpose quickly formed but to be resolutely carried out. He said to Anne: "I saw that my aunt's heedless words embarrassed you, and I felt sorry for you. But it was quite true—I made her promise to apologize to you; and as long as I live, as far as I have the power, I shall force everybody who injures you to make you amends."

Baskerville's eyes, fastened upon Anne, gave a deeper meaning to his words. The flush faded from Anne's cheeks, and she looked at Baskerville with troubled eyes, knowing a crisis was at hand. "I am very bold in forcing myself on you," he said, "but the time has come for me to speak. I have not the same chance as other men, because I can't go to your father's house. I went once upon your mother's kind invitation, but I doubt whether I should have done so; I can only plead my desire to see you, and I feel I can't go again. You know, perhaps, that I am one of the lawyers engaged in prosecuting this investigation before the Senate. If I had known you before I began it, I would have never gone into it. But being in it I can't honorably withdraw. Perhaps you can't forgive me for what I have done, but it has not kept me from loving you with all my soul."

Anne shrank back in the carriage. At any other time she would have heard these words with palpitating joy; and even now they opened to her a momentary glimpse of Paradise. But the memory of all that was said and done about her father, the conviction of his impending disgrace, overwhelmed her. She sat silent and ashamed, longing to accept the sweetness of the love offered her, conscious of her own integrity, but with a primitive honest pride, reluctant to give any man the dower of disgrace which she felt went with her father's daughter.

Silence on the part of the beloved usually augurs well to the lover, but when Anne's silence was accentuated by two large tears that dropped upon her cheeks Baskerville realized that they were not happy tears. He would have soothed her with a lover's tenderness, but Anne repulsed him with a strange pride. "You are not to blame for what you have done in my father's case, but I know, as well as you do, that before this month is out my father may be a disgraced man. And although you may not believe it—you with your generations of ladies and gentlemen behind you"—she spoke with a certain bitterness—"may not believe that the daughter of people like my father and my mother can have any pride, yet I have—whether I am entitled to it or not. I would not take a disgraced name to any man."

Baskerville's answer to this was to take her two hands in his. It became difficult for her to be haughty to a man who plainly indicated that he meant to kiss her within five minutes. And he did.

Anne's protests were not those of a woman meaning to yield; Baskerville saw that she felt a real shame, the genuine reluctance of a high and honorable spirit. But it was swept away in the torrent of a sincere and manly love. When they parted at Anne's door Baskerville had wrung from her the confession of her love, and they were, to each other, acknowledged lovers.

That night Anne and her father dined alone. Élise and Lydia were dining out with some of their "larky" friends, and Reginald was out of town. Clavering noted that Anne was rather silent. Anne for her part looked at her father with a kind of resentment she had often felt before. What right had he to dower his children with his own evil deeds? Why, instead of acquiring a vast fortune, which he spent on them, as on himself, with lavishness, should he not have given them a decent inheritance. Was it not wholly through him that she had not been able to give herself freely and joyfully to the man who loved her and whom she loved? With these thoughts in her mind she sat through the dinner, silent and distrait; but she could not wholly subdue the happiness that Baskerville had given her, even though happiness with her could never be without alloy.

When dinner was over she went up to her mother's room, and spent the rest of the evening cheering and comforting the poor soul. After Mrs. Clavering was in bed Anne came downstairs to remain until Élise and Lydia returned from their party. She sat in the library with a book in her hand, but her thoughts were on Baskerville. And, thinking of him, she fell into a soft, sweet sleep to dream of him. When she awakened it was almost midnight, and Élise and Lydia had not returned.

To keep herself from falling asleep again she took up at random one of a pile of periodicals on the table. It was a scurrilous newspaper which she loathed; but the first paragraph in it which, before she could lay it down, fell under her eye enchained her attention. An hour afterward Élise and Lydia came in and tiptoed softly up to their rooms; but Anne remained in the same position in the great library chair in which she had been for the last hour, still holding the newspaper in her hand.

Clavering had gone out directly after dinner, and after a visit to the club, which he found rather chilling, went to General Brandon's house, as usual in advance of his appointment. It seemed to Clavering on that evening as if Elizabeth relaxed a little of her reserve, which was at the same time both timid and haughty. Later he went down town and managed to put up a tolerably stiff game of poker, and it was two o'clock in the morning before he found himself at his own door. He let himself in, and went into the vast, luxurious library, where the fire still glowed. He turned up the electric light in a superb bronze electrolier on his library table, stirred the fire, and then perceived Anne sitting in a chair drawn up to the fender.

"Why, what are you doing here?" asked Clavering, good-naturedly.

"I wanted to speak to you to-night," Anne replied quietly.

"Go on," said Clavering, seating himself and lighting a cigar. "Make it short, because when a woman wants to 'speak' to a man it always means a row."

"I hope this does not," replied Anne.

Her father looked at her closely. She had a wearied and anxious look, which belied her youth, and she had good cause to be both wearied and anxious a good part of the time. She handed him the newspaper which battened upon scandal, and the first paragraph in it announced the forthcoming divorce of Senator Clavering and his subsequent marriage to a Chicago widow, nearly his age, with a fortune almost as large as his own. Clavering's strong-beating heart gave a jump when he began reading the paragraph, but when he found how far off the scent was the report his countenance cleared. It was as good an opportunity as he could have desired to have it out with Anne, and he was not sorry she had broached the subject.

"Well," he said, laying the paper down, "are you surprised?"

"No," replied Anne, looking at him steadily.

"Then we may proceed to discuss it," said Clavering. "I intend to provide handsomely for your mother, and I dare say she will be a hundred times happier out in Iowa among her relations and friends than she can be here."

"I hardly think my mother would look at it from that point of view," said Anne. She controlled her agitation and her indignation admirably, and Clavering saw in her his own cool courage and resource. "Of course my mother has felt and known for years that you had no further use for her, now that her drudgery is not necessary to you. But she is, as you know, a very religious woman. She thinks divorces are wrong, and, timid as she is, I believe she would resist a divorce. She would, I am sure, be willing to go away from you and not trouble you any more—and I would go with her. But a divorce—no. And I have the same views that she has, and would urge her to resist to the last; and she will."

She had not raised her tones at all, but Clavering understood her words perfectly. She meant to fight for her mother. He smoked quietly for several minutes, and Anne knew too much to weaken her position by repeating her protest. Then Clavering leaned over to her and said: "I think, when you know the circumstances, you will be more than willing to let your mother get the divorce. We were never legally married."

The blood poured into Anne's face. She rose from her chair, and stood trembling with anger, but also with fear. "I don't believe—I can't believe—" She stopped, unable to go on.

"Oh, there's no reflection on your mother or on me, either. We ran away to be married—a couple of young fools under twenty-one. I got the license in Kentucky, but we crossed the Ohio River into Ohio. There we found a minister, an ignorant old fellow and a rogue besides, who didn't know enough to see that the license had no effect in Ohio. And then I found out afterwards that he had been prohibited from performing marriage services because of some of his illegal doings in that line. I knew all about it within a week of the marriage, but being ignorant then myself, I thought the best way was to say nothing. Afterward, when I came to man's estate, I still thought it best to keep it quiet for the sake of you children. And I am willing to keep it quiet now—unless you force me to disclose it. But, understand me, I mean to be divorced in order to marry a lady to whom I am much attached—not this old whited sepulchre from Chicago"—for so Clavering alluded to the widow with millions—"but a lady without a penny. Have you any suspicion to whom I refer?"

"I have not the least suspicion of any one," Anne replied, as haughtily as if she had all the blood of all the Howards, instead of being the nameless child she was.

Clavering was secretly surprised and relieved to know this. Then the tongue of gossip had not got hold of his attentions to Elizabeth Darrell. This was indeed rare good fortune. He spoke again. "So now you know exactly where you stand. If you will let me have my way, the thing can be managed quietly. If you oppose me, you will be sorry for it."

"And you mean, if my mother doesn't consent, that you will brand us all—us, your children—as—as—I can't speak the word." Anne fixed a pair of blazing eyes on her father, and Clavering never felt more uncomfortable in his life. He had no shame and no remorse, but he really wished that Anne Clavering would not gaze at him with those eyes sparkling with anger and disgust.

"I think you don't exactly understand the masculine nature," he said. "I simply mean that I shall have a divorce, and if you don't choose to accept my terms—for, of course, I am dealing with you, not your mother—it will be you and not I who proclaim to the world what I have kept quiet for thirty-five years."

The interview lasted barely ten minutes, but to Anne Clavering it seemed as if æons of time separated her from the Anne Clavering of half an hour ago. Clavering was unshaken. He had been contemplating this event in his life ever since it happened, thirty-five years before, and had reckoned himself a magnanimous man in determining not to reveal the truth about his marriage unless he was compelled to—that is to say, unless he could not get the divorce by other means. But Anne had forced his hand, as it were; so let her take the consequences. The repudiation of his wife cost Clavering not a pang. He took no thought of her patience, her years of uncomplaining work for him, her silence under his neglect and abandonment. The thought, however, that he had admitted to any one the illegitimacy of his children, gave him a certain degree of discomfort; he felt an inward shock when he spoke the words. But it was not enough to turn him from his will.

Anne sat still for so long that Clavering did not know what to make of it. She had grown very pale, and Clavering suspected that she really had not the strength to rise, which was the truth. The room was so profoundly still that when a smouldering log in the fireplace broke in two and fell apart with a shower of sparks, the slight noise made both Clavering and Anne start.

Anne rose then, somewhat unsteadily. Clavering would have liked to offer his arm and to have assisted her to her bedroom, but he was afraid. She walked out of the room without looking at him or speaking to him again. Halfway up the broad and splendid staircase he heard her stop, and, looking out of the half-open door, he saw her shadowy figure sitting on the stairs. After a few moments more she went on up, and he could hear only the faint sound of her silken skirts as she moved. Opposite her mother's door she stopped. There was no sound within, and she passed on.

It was one of Elizabeth Darrell's sleepless and harassed nights. About three o'clock she rose from her bed and went to the window. In the great house opposite, Clavering's library windows were lighted up, and so were the windows of Anne's boudoir. A sudden suspicion of the truth flashed into Elizabeth's mind.

"His daughter suspects something—has discovered something," she thought to herself, panting and terrified. "They have had a scene."

Neither Elizabeth nor Clavering nor Anne had any sleep that night.

Chapter Fourteen

The next day was Mrs. Luttrell's day at home, and in spite of her declared preference for small receptions, a choice little circle of friends, tea and good plain bread and butter, she contrived to have crowds of visitors, resplendent drawing-rooms, and in the dining room a brilliant table, glowing with floral feather beds and sparkling with lights, whereon were served most of the kickshaws which Mrs. Luttrell had so severely animadverted on the day before.

It was a field-day with Mrs. Luttrell. All the Cave-dwellers and all of the smart set seemed to be in evidence at one time or another during the afternoon. The street was blocked with carriages, lackeys stood ten deep around the handsome doors, and the air fluttered with the tissue paper from the many cards that were left. The splendid and unique drawing-rooms were at their best, and Mrs. Luttrell, arrayed in the immortal black-velvet gown, was standing in the centre of the middle drawing-room, dispensing flatteries to the men and civilities to the women with great gusto. Baskerville was present, doing his part as host, helping out the shy people like Eleanor Baldwin's mother, the handsome, silent Mrs. Brentwood-Baldwin, who was known to be cruelly dragooned by her up-to-date daughter. But there are not many shy people to be found in Washington. Mrs. James Van Cortlandt Skinner was not at all shy when she came sailing in, toward six o'clock, with a very handsome young man, dressed in the height of ecclesiastical elegance. The private chaplain was, at last, an attained luxury.

"My dear Mrs. Luttrell," she said cooingly, "may I introduce to you the Reverend Father Milward of the Order of St. Hereward?"

Mrs. Luttrell's handsome mouth widened in a smile which was subject to many interpretations, and she shook hands cordially with Mrs. James Van Cortlandt Skinner's protégé. Father Milward himself gave Mrs. Luttrell a far-away, ascetic bow, and then, turning to Baskerville, began discussing with him the status of the English education bill. Father Milward gave it as his solemn opinion that the bill did not go far enough in opposing secular education, and thought that the Dissenters had been dealt with too favorably by it and under it.

Mrs. Van Cortlandt Skinner had felt a little nervous at the way her newest acquisition might be received by Mrs. Luttrell, but had determined to put a bold face upon it. And why should anybody be ashamed of achieving one's heart's desire, so long as it is respectable? And what is more respectable and likewise more recherché, than a domestic chaplain? And the Reverend Father Milward had been domestic chaplain to an English duke. Nor had his severance with the ducal household been anything but creditable to Father

Milward, for the duke, a very unspiritual person, who kept a domestic chaplain on the same principle as he subscribed to the county hunt, had said that he "wouldn't stand any more of Milward's religious fallals, by gad." The chaplain had therefore discharged the duke, for the young clergyman's fallals were honest fallals, and he was prepared to go to the stake for them. Instead of the crown of martyrdom, however, he had fallen into Mrs. James Van Cortlandt Skinner's arms, so to speak; and he found it an ecclesiastical paradise of luxury and asceticism, God and mammon, full of the saintliness of the world.

Before Mrs. Van Cortlandt Skinner had a chance to tell what position the Reverend Father Milward held in her family, Mrs. Luttrell said to her, aside: "So you've got him! I thought you'd get the upper hand of the bishop. The fact is you're cleverer than any of the Newport people I've heard of yet. They've got their tiaras and their sea-going yachts and they have the Emperor to dinner, but not one of them has a private acolyte, much less a full-grown chaplain. You've done something really original this time, my dear."

Mrs. Van Cortlandt Skinner did not know exactly how Mrs. Luttrell meant to be taken, but smiled faintly and said: "You can't imagine, my dear Mrs. Luttrell, the blessed privilege of having Father Milward under my roof. He has been with me a week, and every day we have had matins, compline, and evensong. I have had the billiard room turned into a chapel temporarily, and it is really sweet; but of course I shall have an early English chapel built at each of my houses. I have plenty of ground for a chapel at my Washington house. My servants have been most attentive at the services, and when Lionel or Harold is absent my butler, a very high churchman, acts as clerk. It is really edifying to see and hear him. You know persons in very humble walks of life sometimes possess great graces and virtues."

"So I have heard," replied Mrs. Luttrell, earnestly.

"I am determined to take Father Milward everywhere with me. I want his holy influence to be shed in the best society. It is beautiful to see him with Lionel and Harold. I hope that one or both of them will develop a vocation for the priesthood. I could do so much for them—build them beautiful parish houses and everything. If one of them should wish to organize a brotherhood, in America, as you once suggested, I would build a beautiful brotherhood house at my place on the Hudson. To give to the Church is such a privilege, and to give to these beautiful and poetic orders which our beloved Mother Church in England is organizing has a peculiar charm for me."

"I see it has," answered Mrs. Luttrell; "and if you have everything else you want, why not get a domestic chaplain, or a couple if you like, just as the

Empress Elizabeth of Russia used to get her a new lover whenever she wanted one?"

Mrs. Skinner gave a little start at this. She was a guileless woman and never knew when people were joking unless they told her so. She had never heard of the Empress Elizabeth, and moreover she was sincerely afraid of Mrs. Luttrell.

"And," continued Mrs. Luttrell, "now that you have walloped the bishop of the diocese, for I understand that he made a terrible row about the domestic chaplain, I would, if I were in your place, get an archbishop to preside over the Church in the United States. The archbishop is clearly the next move in the game, after the domestic chaplain. One wants a little elegance now in religion, you know, and an archbishop is just twice as stylish as a mere bishop; and in time"—Mrs. Luttrell laid her hand approvingly on Mrs. Van Cortlandt Skinner's imperial sable boa—"Lionel or Harold may live to be Archbishop Skinner. There isn't any reason in the world why you people who have loads of money shouldn't have everything you want. Don't forget that, my dear Mrs. Skinner."

Mrs. Skinner felt that she was being trifled with; so she laughed a little and moved away, saying: "I see Bishop Slater, the secretary's brother, across the room, and I must speak to him. I think the secretary is a dear, and so is the bishop, so nice and high in his Church views."

Mrs. Luttrell turned to face an accusing mentor in Richard Baskerville, who had heard a part of the "trying out" of Mrs. James Van Cortlandt Skinner; but before he could speak he caught sight of Anne Clavering entering the wide doors. He had not thought to see her that day, feeling that what had passed between them in the brougham would keep her away from Mrs. Luttrell's as a place where she would be certain to meet him; for Anne Clavering had all the delicate reserve which a man would wish in the woman he loves. Therefore, not expecting to see her, Baskerville had early in the day despatched to her a basket of violets and a brief note, in which he asked permission to speak at once to her father. He had received no reply, but expected one before he slept. Anne's appearance, however, in Mrs. Luttrell's drawing-room surprised him; she evidently sought him, and this she would not be likely to do unless she were in some emergency.

To Baskerville's keen eye her face, glowing with an unusual color, her eyes, which were restlessly bright, betrayed some inward agitation. She was very beautifully dressed in velvet and furs, with more of magnificence than she usually permitted herself; and her white-gloved hand played nervously with a superb emerald pendant that hung around her neck by a jewelled chain. Baskerville was the first person who greeted her, and Mrs. Luttrell was the next.

"This is kind of you," said the latter, all sweetness and affability. "It shows what a nice disposition you have, to come to me to-day, after the way my nephew made me kowtow to you yesterday. Richard, give Miss Clavering a cup of tea."

Baskerville escorted Anne through the splendid suite of rooms, each speaking right and left and being stopped often to exchange a word with a friend or acquaintance. People smiled after the pair of them, as they do after a pair of suspected lovers. When they came to the high-arched lobby that led into the dining room, Baskerville opened a side door, partly concealed by a screen and a great group of palms, and showed Anne into a little breakfast room, which opened with glass doors on the garden. A hard-coal fire burned redly in the grate, and the dying sunset poured its last splendors through a huge square window. Baskerville shut the door, and Anne and he were as much alone as if they had the whole house to themselves.

"I have practised a gross fraud upon you about the tea," said he, smiling; "but here is a chance for a few minutes alone with you—a chance I shall take whenever I can get it." He would have taken her hand, but something in her face stopped him. She had protested and denied him the day before, when he told her of his love; but it had not stood materially in his way. Now, however, he saw in an instant there was something of great import that made a barrier between them.

"I wished very much to see you alone and soon; I came here to-day for that purpose," she said. She spoke calmly, but Baskerville saw that it was with difficulty she restrained her agitation. "Yesterday," she went on, "I told you what I feared about my father—"

"And I told you," Baskerville interrupted, "that I would marry you if I could, no matter who or what your father is."

"You were most generous. But you don't know what I know about my father—I only found it out myself last night. I had an interview with him. There was something in a newspaper about his divorcing my mother."

"If he does and you will marry me, I shall engage to treat your mother with the same respect and attention I should my own. Mrs. Clavering is one of the best of women, and I have the greatest regard for her."

Anne raised to him a glorified, grateful face. The poor, despised mother for whom she had fought and was still fighting, the helpless, unfortunate woman who seemed to be in everybody's way except in hers—the offer of kindness and consideration went to Anne Clavering's heart. She wished to say something in the way of thanks to Baskerville, but instead she burst into a sudden passion of tears. Baskerville, with a lover's ardor, would have comforted her upon his breast, but she kept him at a distance.

"No, no!" she pleaded, weeping, "hear me out—let me tell you all." Baskerville, although at her side, did not perforce so much as touch her hand. Anne continued, strangely recovering her calmness as she proceeded: "I can't repeat all my father said—I have neither the strength nor the time now; but he told me there was an—an invalidity about his marriage to my mother. She, poor soul, knew nothing of it, for—for our sakes, his children. But it was no marriage. And last night he told me plainly that if I persuaded my mother to resist the divorce, he can prove that she never was—that we are—" She stopped. Her tears had ceased to flow, her face was deathly pale; a heart-breaking composure had taken the place of her emotion.

Baskerville, however, had become slightly agitated. He comprehended instantly what she meant. She was not even the legitimate child of James Clavering. Small as the credit of his name might be, it was not hers. Baskerville, as a man of honorable lineage, had a natural shrinking from ignoble birth, but it did not blind him to the inherent honor in Anne Clavering nor turn his heart away from her. He recovered his coolness in a moment or two and was about to speak, when she forestalled him hurriedly.

"So, you see, you must forget all that happened yesterday. I thank you a thousand times for—for—what you once felt for me. If things were different—if I were—but, as you see, it is quite impossible now."

"And do you suppose," said Baskerville, after a pause, "that I would give you up—that I could give you up? I am afraid you don't yet know what love is."

Their conversation had gone on in tones so low that they might have been discussing the affairs of total strangers. Baskerville made no attempt to take her hand, to beguile her with endearments. It was a moment solemn for both of them, and Baskerville spoke with the calm appeal of a noble and steadfast love. It was not the sweet seduction of passion, but the earnest claim and covenant of love upon which he relied.

Anne remained with her eyes fixed on the floor. Baskerville said no more. He scorned to plead his right, and his silence wrought for him far more than any spoken words. His manner was one of questioning reproach, a reproach most dear to a loving and high-minded woman. The meaning of it came softly but inevitably upon Anne Clavering. It was no light sacrifice for a man of sensitive honor, of flawless repute, to link himself in any way with a woman dowered as Anne Clavering was dowered by her father's evil-doing, but Baskerville reckoned it as nothing when weighed in the balance against his honorable love. At last the whole beauty of his conduct dawned full upon her; Baskerville knew the very instant when she grasped all that he meant. The color began to mount to her pale cheeks; she sighed deeply and raised her eyes, now softly radiant, to his face.

"You are very, very generous," she said. "It is good to have known a man so generous, and it is sweeter than I can tell you to have been loved by such a man. But I can be generous, also. It is too great a sacrifice for you. I cannot accept it."

To this Baskerville only replied: "Tell me but this—one word will settle it forever. Do you love me?"

ill280

"THE NEXT MINUTE SHE WAS FAST IN BASKERVILLE'S ARMS."

Anne remained silent, but the silences of a woman who loves are more eloquent than words. The next minute she was fast in Baskerville's arms, who would not let her go; and they had a foretaste of Paradise, such as only those know whose love is mingled with sacrifice, which is the ultimate height of the soul's tenderness. But their time was of necessity short, and what Anne had told Baskerville required instant consideration. When Anne would have persisted in her refusal Baskerville would not listen, but turned to the matter of her interview with Clavering.

"This is a question which must be met at once, because I believe your father quite capable of carrying out his threat. And your mother must be the first one to be considered. What do you think she would wish?"

It was the first time in her life that Anne Clavering had ever heard any one say that her mother was to be considered at all. A great wave of gratitude surged up in her heart—the poor, helpless, ignorant, loving mother, who had no friend but her—and Baskerville. She looked at him with eyes shining and brimming and laid a timid, tender hand upon his shoulder.

"I ought not to accept your love—but—"

"You can't prevent it," replied Baskerville.

"Then, if gratitude—"

But when lovers talk of gratitude it means more kisses. The pale dusk of winter now filled the room, and there was no light except the red glow of the fire. Baskerville would have asked nothing better in life than an hour in that quiet, twilighted room, nor would Anne either; but, woman-like, Anne remembered that there were some other persons in the world besides themselves, and made as if to go, nor would she heed Baskerville's pleadings to remain longer.

As they reached the door Baskerville said: "Think over what you wish me to do, and write me when you determine. Of course I must see your father immediately. And we must take my aunt into our confidence, for it is through her that we must meet."

Poor Anne had not had much time for that sweet trifling which is the joy of lovers, but at the idea of Mrs. Luttrell being taken into any one's confidence a faint smile came to her quivering lips. "The whole town will know all about it."

"No, I can frighten my aunt, and she shan't tell until we are ready."

Anne's cheeks were flaming, and she said, as all women do who have to face inspection directly after a love scene, "If I could but get away without being seen."

"It is easy enough; this glass door opens."

Baskerville led her through the glass door into the garden and around to the front of the house, where in the throng of arriving and departing visitors not even the lynx-eyed Jeems Yellowplush who opened the brougham door suspected that Miss Clavering had not walked straight from Mrs. Luttrell's drawing-room.

Anne lay back in the carriage, lost in a dream of love and gratitude. All her life long she had fought alone and single-handed for the poor, oppressed mother. She knew perfectly well all her mother's ignorance, her awkward manners, but Anne knew also the patience, the goodness, the forgiving and unselfish nature which lay under that unpromising exterior. Not one point of Baskerville's conduct was lost on Anne Clavering, and if love and gratitude could repay him, she meant that he should be repaid. And in the coming catastrophes she would have Baskerville's strong arm and masculine good sense to depend upon.

She had read the newspapers attentively, and she believed that her father and his associates would be found guilty of all that was alleged against them; and she knew that the divorce was a fixed thing, not to be altered by anybody. That of itself might be expected, in the ordinary course, to exile the family from Washington, but Anne doubted it. Élise and Lydia would not have delicacy enough to go away if they wished to remain, and their fondness for the smaller fry of the diplomatic corps was quite strong enough to keep them in Washington when it would be better for them to live elsewhere. Reginald, in spite of his weakness and narrowness, had a sense of dignity that would make him keep out of the public eye.

For herself, Anne had determined, before her interview with Baskerville, that a quiet home in the little Iowa town where her mother was born and bred would be the place for her mother and herself; and she had thought with calm resignation of the change in her life from the gayety and brilliance of Washington to the quiet seclusion of a country town. It would not be all loss, however, for her path in Washington had not been entirely roses. Washington is a place of great and varied interests, where one may live any sort of life desired; and it is not easy to adapt those who have lived there to any other spot in America. But now these words of Richard Baskerville's, his manly, compelling love, had changed all that for her. She felt it to be her destiny—her happy destiny—to live with him in Washington. His name and high repute would protect her. She would not ask of him to have her mother always with her, although a more submissive and unobtrusive creature never lived than Mrs. Clavering. It would be enough if she could pass a part of the year with Anne, while Reginald took care of her the other part, and both of them would vie with each other in doing their duty. Her heart swelled whenever she thought of the consideration Baskerville had shown toward Mrs. Clavering; it would make the poor woman happy to know it, for this woman, used to the bread of humiliation, keenly felt the smallest attention paid her. And then Anne fell into a sweet dream of delight, and was happy in spite of herself. She came down from heaven only when the carriage stopped in front of the great stone house of Senator Clavering.

At the same hour Mrs. Luttrell sat before the fire in the great empty drawing-room, from which the guests had just departed. Mrs. Luttrell was burning with curiosity to know what had become of Baskerville and Anne Clavering when they disappeared so mysteriously—for Baskerville had not returned, either. The fact is, while Anne was lost in a soft ecstasy, Baskerville, smoking furiously at a big black cigar, was walking aimlessly about the streets, his heart beating high. He looked at his watch. It was seven o'clock, and it occurred to him that it was time to go back to Mrs. Luttrell and make provision for future meetings with Anne Clavering and, possibly, their marriage from Mrs. Luttrell's house, if circumstances should follow as he expected.

When he walked in, Mrs. Luttrell's greeting was, "Where's Anne Clavering?"

"Safe at home, I trust," replied Baskerville, throwing the end of his cigar into the fire.

"And what became of you, pray, when you two went prancing off, and never came back?"

"I took Miss Clavering into the morning-room."

"You did, eh?"

"I did."

"And what happened in the morning-room?"

"I decline to state, except that Miss Clavering and I are to be married—perhaps in this house. Senator Clavering, you know, and I are at feud, and the coming revelations about him make it very likely that he won't have a house here very long"—Baskerville had in mind Clavering's divorce—"and our meetings, Miss Clavering's and mine, are to take place under your roof, with yourself to play gooseberry. Even if you are due at the biggest dinner going at the house of the smartest of the smart and the newest of the new, you shall stay here, if we have to chain you up."

"Upon my word!"

"And you are not to open your mouth to a living being about what I am telling you, until I give you permission. I know your idea of a secret, Sara Luttrell—it means something that is worth telling. But if you let one ray of light leak out, I shall never speak to you again, and shall tell your age all over Washington."

Mrs. Luttrell looked at Baskerville with admiring eyes. "That's the way your uncle used to talk to me. No one else in the world ever did it, except you and him."

"Now, will you obey me?"

"You are an impudent rogue. Yes, I will obey you."

"Then go to your desk this minute and write Miss Clavering a note offering the hospitality of your roof and your services as chaperon whenever she requires it; and mind you make it a very affectionate note."

Baskerville led Mrs. Luttrell to her desk, where she wrote her note. "Will this do?" she asked, and read to him:—

"DEAR ANNE CLAVERING: My nephew, Richard Baskerville, tells me you and he are to be married, and as he is at feud with your father he can't go to your house. Therefore you must come to mine. I need not say that my services as chaperon are at your disposal. I think you know that I am a sincere person, and when I tell you that I think Richard Baskerville would do well to marry you even if you hadn't a rag to your back, you may be sure I think so. And you will do well to marry him. He is like another Richard who died long ago—the husband of my youth.

"Affectionately yours,

"SARA LUTTRELL."

"That will do," replied Baskerville, and taking Mrs. Luttrell's small, white hand in his he kissed it, kissed it so with the air and look and manner of the man dead fifty years and more that Mrs. Luttrell's bright old eyes filled with sudden tears—she, the woman who was supposed to have been born and to have lived without a heart.

Chapter Fifteen

Anne Clavering was engaged to dine out, as usual during the season, the evening of the afternoon when happiness had come to her in Mrs. Luttrell's morning-room. She was so agitated, so overcome with the tempests of emotion through which she had passed in the last twenty-four hours, that she longed to excuse herself from the dinner and to have a few hours of calming solitude in her own room. But she was too innately polite and considerate to slight and inconvenience her hostess, and so resolutely prepared to fulfil her engagement. She could not resist spending in her mother's room the half hour which intervened from the time she returned home until she should go to her room for a short rest and the making of her evening toilet.

Mrs. Clavering was not usually keen of apprehension, but Anne scarcely thought she could conceal from her mother's affectionate and solicitous eyes all the feelings with which she palpitated. Mrs. Clavering loved the excuse of a trifling indisposition that she might keep her room and be free from the necessity of seeing visitors and of being seen by the army of insubordinate foreign servants in the Clavering household. She was full of questions about Anne's afternoon at Mrs. Luttrell's, and the first question she asked was whether that nice young man, Mr. Baskerville, was there. At that Anne blushed so suddenly and vividly that it could not escape Mrs. Clavering.

"Why, Anne," she said, "I believe Mr. Baskerville must have been paying you some compliments! Anyhow, he's the nicest and politest man I've seen in Washington, and I hope when you marry, you'll marry a man just like him. And I do hope, my dear, you won't be an old maid. Old maids don't run in my family."

This was Mrs. Clavering's guileless method of suggestive matchmaking. Anne, with a burning face, kissed her and went to her room for a little while alone in the dark with her rapture—and afterward purgatory, in being dressed to go out. She had already begun to debate whether it would be well to tell her secret to her mother at once. The poor lady was really not well, and any thought of impending change for her best beloved might well distress her. But her simple words convinced Anne that Mrs. Clavering would not be made unhappy by the news that Richard Baskerville and Anne loved each other. Rather would it rejoice her, and as there had been no time to talk seriously about the date of the marriage she need not be disturbed at the thought of an immediate separation from Anne.

All this Anne thought out while her hair was being dressed and her dainty slippers put on her feet and her Paris gown adjusted by her maid. In that little interval of solitude before, when she lay in her bed in the soft darkness, she had thought of nothing but Richard Baskerville and the touch of his lips upon hers. But with her maid's knock at the door the outer world had entered, with all its urgent claims and insistence. But through all her perplexities still sounded the sweet refrain, "He loves me." She thought as she fastened the string of pearls around her white neck, "The last time I wore these pearls I was not happy, and now—"

And so, on her way to the dinner and through-out it and back home again, the thought of Richard Baskerville never left her; the sound of his voice in her ears, the touch of his lips upon hers, and above all the nobility of his loving her purely for herself—rare fortune for the daughter of a man so rich, even if not so wicked, as James Clavering. Anne tasted of joy for the first time, and drank deep of it. She was glad to be alone with her love and her happiness, to become acquainted with it, to fondle it, to hold it close to her heart. She was very quiet and subdued at the dinner, and by a sort of mistaken telepathy among the others present it was understood that Miss Clavering felt deeply the situation in which Senator Clavering was placed. But Anne Clavering was the happiest woman in Washington that night. Even the impending disgrace of her father, of which she was well assured, was softened and illumined by the lofty and self-sacrificing love bestowed upon her by Richard Baskerville.

When she came home, after eleven o'clock, she stopped as she always did at her mother's door. Mrs. Clavering calling her softly, Anne went into the room. With her mother's hand in hers she told the story of her love and happiness. If she had ever doubted whether it would be well to tell Mrs. Clavering, that doubt was dispelled. The poor lady wept, it is true, being tender-hearted and given to tears like the normal woman, but her tears were those of happiness.

"I've been a-wishin' and a-hopin' for it ever since I saw him that Sunday," said the poor soul. "I want you to have a good husband, Anne, the sort of husband my father was to my mother; never a cross word between 'em before us children, Ma always havin' the dinner on time and the old leather arm-chair ready for Pa—we didn't have but one easy-chair in the house in them days. And Pa always sayin' Ma was better lookin' than any one of her daughters, and kissin' her before us all on their weddin' anniversary, and givin' her a little present, if it wasn't no more than a neck ribbon; for they was always poor; but they loved each other and lived as married folks ought to live together."

"If Richard and I can live like that I shouldn't mind being poor myself, dear mother, because I remember well enough when we were poor, and when you used to sew for us, and do all the rough work, and indulged us far too much;

and I was happier then than I have been since—until now," Anne replied softly.

Mrs. Clavering sighed. "All the others, except you, seem to have forgot all about it." This was the nearest Mrs. Clavering ever came to a complaint or a reproach.

And then Anne, with loving pride, told her of Baskerville's kind words about her, of his voluntary offers of respect and attention. Mrs. Clavering, sitting up in bed, put her large, toil-worn hands to her face and wept a little.

"Did he say that, my dear, about your poor, ignorant mother? I tell you, Anne, there are some gentlemen in this world, men who feel sorry for a woman like me and treat 'em kind and right, like Mr. Baskerville does. Now, you tell him for me—because I'd never have the courage to tell him myself— that I thank him a thousand times, and he'll never be made to regret his kindness to me; and tell him anythin' else that would be proper to say, and especially that I ain't goin' to bother him. But I tell you, Anne, I'm very happy this night. I wouldn't have gone without knowin' this for anythin'—not for anythin'."

Then the mother and daughter, woman-like, wept in each other's arms, and were happy and comforted.

The next morning brought Anne a letter from Baskerville. Clouded as Anne Clavering's love-affair was, with many outside perplexities, restraints, shames, and griefs, she did not miss all of what the French call the little flowers of love—among others the being wakened from sleep in the morning by a letter from her lover. Her first waking thought in her luxurious bedroom was that a letter from Baskerville would soon be in her hands. And when the maid entered and laid it on her pillow and departed Anne held it to her heart before breaking the seal. Then, lighting her bedside candle in the dark of the winter morning, she read her precious letter. In it Baskerville told her that he was urgently called to New York that day, but would return the next; and his first appointment after his return would be to see Senator Clavering, for they must arrange, for obvious reasons, to be married at the earliest possible moment. There were not many endearing terms in the letter—for Baskerville, like most men of fine sense and deep dealing, did not find it easy to put his love on paper; but those few words were enough—so Anne Clavering thought. And Baskerville told her that she would receive a letter from him daily, in lieu of the visit which he could not pay her at her father's house.

Baskerville returned to Washington on the following night, for a reason rare in the annals of lovers. The last meeting of the investigating committee was to be held the next day, and Baskerville, having succeeded in exposing

Clavering, must be on hand to complete the work. But before doing this he had to tell to Clavering his intention to marry his daughter.

The committee met daily at eleven o'clock, but it was not yet ten o'clock on a dull, cold winter morning when Baskerville took his way to the Capitol, certain of finding Clavering at work by that hour; for the Senator had most of the best habits of the best men—among them, industry, order, and punctuality in a high degree.

Baskerville went straight to the committee-room set apart for Clavering, for, not being a chairman of a committee, he had no right to a room. His colleagues, however, on the same principle that a condemned man is given everything he wishes to eat, supplied Clavering generously with quarters in which to prepare his alleged defence. Two of the handsomest rooms in the Senate wing were therefore set apart for him, and to these Baskerville made his way. The messenger at the door took in his card, and he heard Clavering, who was walking up and down the floor dictating to a stenographer, say in his agreeable voice, "Show the gentleman into the room at once."

Baskerville entered, and Clavering greeted him politely and even cordially. He did not, however, offer to shake hands with Baskerville, who had purposely encumbered himself with his hat and coat; so the avoidance on the part of each was cleverly disguised.

"Pray excuse me for calling so early, Senator," said Baskerville, composedly, "but may I have a word in private with you?"

Clavering was infinitely surprised, but he at once answered coolly: "Certainly, if you will go with me into the next room. It is my colleague's committee-room, but there is no meeting of the committee to-day, and he allows me the privilege of seeing people there when it is vacant. You see, I am snowed under here," which was true. The masses of books and papers and type-writers' and stenographers' desks filled the room in an uncomfortable degree.

Clavering led the way into the next room. It was large and luxuriously furnished with all the elegances with which legislators love to surround themselves. He offered Baskerville one of the large leather chairs in front of the blazing fire, took another one himself, and fixed his bright, dark eyes on Baskerville, who took the advice of old Horace and plunged at once into his subject.

"I presume that what I have to tell you will surprise you, Senator, and no doubt displease you. I have asked your daughter, Miss Anne Clavering, to marry me, and she has been good enough to consent. And I feel it due to you, of course, to inform you at the earliest moment."

Clavering was secretly astounded. No such complication had dawned upon him. He knew, of course, that Anne and Baskerville were acquainted and met often in society; he had by no means forgotten that solitary visit of Baskerville's, but attached no particular meaning to it. His own pressing affairs had engrossed him so that he had given very little thought to anything else. But it was far from James Clavering to show himself astonished in any man's presence, least of all in an enemy's presence. His mind, which worked as rapidly as it worked powerfully, grasped in an instant that this was really a good stroke of fortune for Anne. He knew too much of human nature to suppose that it counted for anything with him. Men like Baskerville do not change their characters or their principles by falling in love. Baskerville might possibly have altered his methods in the investigation, but this happened to be the very last day of it, and things had gone too far to be transformed at this stage of the game. However, it gave Clavering a species of intense inward amusement to find himself in a position to assume a paternal air to Baskerville. After a moment, therefore, he said with a manner of the utmost geniality:—

"Displease me, did you say? Nothing would please me better. Anne is by long odds the best of my children. She deserves a good husband, and I need not say that your high reputation and admirable character are thoroughly well known to me, as to all the world."

All interviews with prospective fathers-in-law are embarrassing, but perhaps no man was ever more embarrassingly placed than Baskerville at that moment. He could not but admire Clavering's astuteness, which made it necessary for Baskerville to explain that while seeking to marry Clavering's daughter he would by no means be understood as countenancing Clavering. Baskerville colored deeply, and paused. Clavering was entirely at ease, and was enjoying the humor of the situation to the full. It is a rare treat to be enabled to act the benevolent father-in-law, anxious only for the welfare of his child, to a man who has been trying for two years to railroad the prospective father-in-law into state's prison.

"I think, Senator," said Baskerville, after a moment, "that we needn't beat about the bush. My course in this investigation has shown from the beginning my views on the case. They are not favorable to you. I have no right to expect your approval, but Miss Clavering is of age and can make her own choice. She has made it, and I have no intention of giving her time to back out of it. It is, however, due to you as her father that I should speak to you of certain matters—my means, for example. I can't give your daughter the luxuries, I may say magnificence, with which you have surrounded her, but I can give her all that a gentlewoman requires. She does not ask for more."

Clavering stroked his chin meditatively, and with a gleam of acute satisfaction in his eye looked at Baskerville, uncomfortable but resolute, before him. "My dear boy," said he, "I've given my consent already; and I rather think, with such a pair as you and my daughter Anne, it wouldn't do much good to withhold it."

Baskerville could have brained him with pleasure for that "My dear boy," but he only said: "Quite right, Senator. I also ask the privilege of speaking to Mrs. Clavering."

"Mrs. Clavering is very ailing—hasn't been out of her room for a week. But she's the last person in the world likely to oppose Anne."

"I shall try to persuade Miss Clavering to have our marriage take place very shortly," said Baskerville, presently.

"Certainly, as soon as you like." Clavering sat back in his chair, smiling. Never was there so obliging a father-in-law.

Baskerville rose. The interview had lasted barely five minutes, and both men were conscious of the fact that Clavering had had the best of it from beginning to end. He had gotten a great deal of amusement out of what Baskerville would not have gone through with again for a great pile of money.

"Thank you very much for your acquiescence. Good morning," said the prospective bridegroom, bowing himself out. Not one word had been said about any fortune that Anne might have, nor had Baskerville touched Clavering's hand.

The Senator went back to his stenographers. He was thoughtful and did not get into full swing of his work for at least fifteen minutes. He felt a kind of envy of Richard Baskerville, who had no investigations to face and never would have. He had no divorce problem in hand and never would have. His love was not of the sort which had to be forced upon a woman, and the woman coerced and overborne and almost menaced into accepting it. On the whole, Clavering concluded, looking back upon a long career of successful villany, that if he had his life to live over again, he would live more respectably.

That day the last meeting of the committee was held, and within an hour the two men, Baskerville and Clavering, faced each other in the committee-room, each a fighting man and fighting with all his strength. Baskerville took no part in the oral arguments, but, sitting at one end of the long table in the luxurious mahogany-furnished and crimson-curtained committee-room, he supplied data, facts, and memoranda which proved Clavering to have been a habitual thief and a perjurer.

The committee-room was only moderately full. The hearings had been open, but the crush had been so great that it was decided to exclude all except those who were directly interested in the hearing and those lucky enough to get cards of admission. It was an eager and even a sympathetic crowd. The same personal charm which had been a great factor in Clavering's success was still his. As he sat back, his leonine face and head outlined against the crimson wall behind him, his eyes full of the light of combat, cool, resolute, and smiling, it was impossible not to admire him. He had no great virtues, but he had certain great qualities.

As the hearing proceeded, Clavering's case grew blacker. Against some of the most damning facts he had some strong perjured evidence, but the perjurers were exposed with the evidence. Against all, he had his own strenuous denial of everything and the call for proof. But proof was forthcoming at every point. And it was all Richard Baskerville's handiwork. Clavering knew this so well that although perfectly alert as to the statements made by the keen-eyed, sharp-witted lawyers from New York, he kept his eyes fixed on Baskerville, who was handing out paper after paper and making whispered explanations—who was, in short, the arsenal for the weapons so mercilessly used against Clavering.

The two men engaged in this deadly and tremendous strife, which involved not only millions of money and a seat in the United States Senate, but also the characters and souls of men, eyed each other with a certain respect. It was no man of ordinary mould whom Baskerville had sought to destroy, and that Clavering would be destroyed there was no reasonable doubt. The last day's work meant expulsion from the Senate, a disgrace so huge, so far-reaching, that it was worse than sentencing a man to death. Apart from the degree of honesty in Clavering's own party, it was perfectly well understood that no party would dare to go before the country assuming the burden of the gigantic frauds of which he was being convicted. And it was due to Baskerville that the evidence to convict had been found. All that the other lawyers had done was insignificant beside the two years of patient research, the disentangling of a thousand complicated legal threads, which was Baskerville's work. Some of the evidence he presented had been collected in the wildest parts of the West and South at the imminent risk of his life; all of it had required vast labor and learning.

Being a natural lover of fighting, Baskerville in the beginning had taken a purely human interest in tracking this man down and had thought himself engaged in a righteous work in driving him out of public life. He still knew he was right in doing this, but it had long since become a painful and irksome task to him. He had come to love this man's daughter, of all the women in the world,—to love her so well and to confide in her so truly that not even her parentage could keep him from marrying her. But he knew that he was stabbing her to the heart. She had forgiven him in advance; like him, love and sacrifice had asserted their rights and reigned in their kingdom, but that she must suffer a cruel abasement for her father's iniquities Baskerville knew. And, with this knowledge, nothing but his sense of duty and honor kept him at his post.

The committee sat from eleven in the morning until two in the afternoon. Then, after a short adjournment, it met again. It sat again, with another short recess, until nearly nine o'clock, and a final adjournment was reached at midnight. Not a person of those entitled to be present had left the room, during that long and trying stretch of hours. All were acting a part in a great tragedy, a tragedy of which the last act was to take place in the United States Senate chamber, and was to be one of the most fearful ever enacted in that historic spot. Clavering had gone down fighting. The committee recognized as much, and when, in the midst of a deep silence, the chairman declared the meeting adjourned and Clavering rose to go, every man present, acting involuntarily and quite unconscious of what he was doing, rose as if to do honor to the man whose infamy had been proved before them. A line was made for Clavering, and he passed out of the room. It was as if his crimes were so great, his audacity so huge, his courage so vast and unquenchable, that they saluted him, as a firing squad salutes a guilty officer condemned to be shot.

When James Clavering walked out into the sharp January night, the Capitol behind him showing whitely in the gleaming of the multitude of stars, he knew himself a beaten and ruined man, beaten and ruined by two men— James Clavering and Richard Baskerville.

Baskerville determined to walk the long stretch between the Capitol and his own house; he wanted the fresh air and the solitude, in order to recover himself—for he, too, had been under a terrific strain. As he walked rapidly down the hill Clavering's carriage passed him—the same brougham in which Baskerville had told Anne Clavering of his love. An electric lamp shone for a moment into the carriage and revealed Clavering sitting upright, his head raised, his fists clenched; he was a fighting man to the last.

Chapter Sixteen

It was the gayest season Washington had ever known. There was a continuous round of entertaining at the White House, unofficial as well as official. The different embassies vied with one another in the number and splendor of their festivities; and the smart set entered into a merry war among themselves as to which should throw open their doors oftenest, collect the largest number of guests, and make the most lavish and overpowering display of luxury.

The Claverings did their part, chiefly engineered by Clavering himself, and abetted by Élise and Lydia. Clavering had good reason to suspect that the report of the investigating committee would be ready within the month. It was now the middle of January. Shrove Tuesday came on the fourteenth of February, St. Valentine's Day, and this was the evening selected for the grand ball and musical which were to complete the season. Other musicals had been given in Washington, but none like this; other balls, but this was meant to surpass them all. It had heretofore been enough to get artists from the Metropolitan Opera in New York; it remained for Clavering to import a couple of singers from Paris for the one occasion. A Hungarian band, touring America, was held over a steamer in order to come to Washington and play at the ball. The shops of Vienna were ransacked for favors for the cotillon; and the champagne to be served came from a king's cellars.

All this Anne Clavering regarded with disgust and aversion. She felt sure that her father was soon to be hurled from public life, and deservedly so. Her mother's health was giving her grave alarm. She was at all times opposed to the excess of luxury and fashion which delighted the pagan souls of Élise and Lydia, and now it was an additional mortification to her on Baskerville's account. He, she felt convinced, was conscious of the brazen effrontery, the shocking bad taste, of it all, and considerate as he was in not speaking of it, her soul was filled with shame to suppose what he thought. She began to hate the lavish luxury in which she dwelt, and looked forward eagerly to the time when she could live modestly and quietly in a house not so grand as to excite the transports of all the society correspondents who got a sight of its stupendous splendors.

Mrs. Clavering's illness, though slight, continued, and gave Anne a very good excuse for withdrawing somewhat from general society. And it also gave her time for those charming meetings at Mrs. Luttrell's house, where she and Richard Baskerville tasted the true joy of living. Mrs. Luttrell nobly redeemed her promise, and would have sent every day for Anne to come to tea. As Mrs. Luttrell did not often dine at home without guests, the best tête-à-tête she could offer the lovers was tea in the little morning-room by the firelight. But Anne, with natural modesty, did not always accept Mrs. Luttrell's urgent invitations. When she did, however, she and Baskerville always had an enchanted hour to themselves in the dusk, while Mrs. Luttrell considerately disappeared, to take the half hour's beauty sleep which she declared essential, during some part of every day, for the preservation of her charms.

The lovers also met more than once at the Thorndykes', at little dinners à quatre. Mrs. Thorndyke would write a note to Anne, asking her on various pleas to come and dine with Thorndyke and herself; and as soon as Anne had accepted there would be a frantic call over the telephone for Thorndyke, in which Mrs. Thorndyke would direct him at the peril of his life to go immediately in search of Baskerville and to bring him home to dinner. And Thorndyke, like the obedient American husband, would do as he was bidden, and produce Baskerville with great punctuality. How far Constance Thorndyke's own acute perceptions were accountable for this, and how far Mrs. Luttrell's incurable propensity for taking the world into her confidence, nobody could tell. At all events, it made four people happy; and if anything could have made Baskerville and Anne more in love with the ideal of marriage it was to see the serene happiness, the charming home life, of Senator and Mrs. Thorndyke.

Baskerville had not ceased to press for an early date for his marriage, but Mrs. Clavering's indisposition and the position of Clavering's affairs deferred the actual making of the arrangements. It was to be a very simple wedding, Anne stipulated; and Baskerville, with more than the average man's dread of a ceremony full of display, agreed promptly. Some morning, when Mrs. Clavering was well, Anne and he would be quietly married, go from the church to the train, and after a few days return to Baskerville's house. And Anne promised herself, and got Baskerville to promise her, the indulgence of a quiet domestic life—a thing she had not known since the golden shower descended upon James Clavering.

Clavering had said nothing to Anne in regard to Baskerville's interview with him, nor had the father and daughter exchanged one word with each other, beyond the ordinary civilities of life, since that midnight conversation in which Mr. Clavering had announced his intention of getting a divorce. Neither had he said anything to Mrs. Clavering, and his plans were entirely unknown to his family. By extraordinary good fortune not the smallest suspicion fell on the pale, handsome, silent Mrs. Darrell across the way, with her widow's veil thrown back from her graceful head.

In those weeks, when Anne Clavering saw as little of the world as she could, she occasionally took quiet and solitary walks in which Baskerville would gladly have joined her. But Anne, with the over-delicacy of one who might be open to the suspicion of not being delicate enough, would not agree to see him except under the chaperonage of Mrs. Luttrell. And twice in those solitary walks she met Elizabeth Darrell, also alone. Both women regarded each other curiously, meanwhile averting their eyes.

Anne knew quite well who Elizabeth was, and at their second meeting, which was quite close to Elizabeth's door, Anne was moved by the true spirit of courtesy and neighborly kindness to speak to her. She said, with a pleasant bow and smile: "This, I believe, is Mrs. Darrell, our neighbor, and I am Miss Clavering. I have the pleasure of knowing your father, General Brandon."

Elizabeth received this advance with such apparent haughtiness that Anne, her face flushing, made some casual remark and went into her own house. In truth Elizabeth was frightened and surprised beyond measure, and felt herself so guilty that she knew not where to look or what to say, and literally fled from the sight of James Clavering's innocent daughter as if she had been an accusing conscience.

Meanwhile the preparations for the grand St. Valentine's musical and ball went gayly on. Clavering himself showed unwonted interest in it. He was as insensible of public approval or disapproval as any man well could be; nevertheless, he hoped that the report of the investigating committee would not be made public until after the great function on Shrove Tuesday. It pleased his fancy for the spectacular to think that the last entertainment he gave in Washington—for he well knew it would be the last—should be full of gorgeous splendor, so superbly unique that it would be remembered for a decade.

He told this to Elizabeth Darrell, for although the investigation was closed Clavering trumped up some specious requests for more of General Brandon's information and assistance on certain alleged general points, and by this means still contrived to see Elizabeth once or twice a week. He tried to persuade Elizabeth to come to the grand festivity, and was deeply in earnest in his effort. He counted on its effect upon her when he should tell her that she could have similar entertainments whenever she liked, in a much larger and more splendid city than Washington—London or Paris, for example.

Elizabeth, however, recoiled with something like horror from the idea of going to Clavering's house and being hospitably received by his wife and daughters; for she had reached the point when Clavering's bribes—for so his love-making might be considered—were always in her mind. At one time she would feel so oppressed with her loneliness, her poverty, her disappointments, that she would be almost eager for the splendid destiny which Clavering offered her; at another time she would shrink from it with horror of it and horror of herself. All her social and religious prejudices were against divorce and were strong enough to have kept her from marrying Clavering if he had ever really been married to Mrs. Clavering, but as he had never been married to her no moral obligation existed. Elizabeth would also have been incapable of the meanness, the iniquity, of taking Clavering away from another woman who had a much better right to him than she; only she knew that Mrs. Clavering would suffer nothing in parting with Clavering. The feeling that his children might be wounded made no strong appeal to Elizabeth.

However, Clavering's best argument—his stupendous wealth—was always in some form before her eyes. Every time she went out of doors, or even looked out of her window, she saw the evidences of Clavering's fortune— his magnificent house, his army of servants, his superb equipages, his automobiles of every description. She could not get away from it, and it made her own shabby home seem the shabbier and the narrower every day she lived in it. Moreover, she was at that dangerous age when a woman is brought face to face with her destiny; when she is forced to say good-by to her girlhood and to reckon upon life without first youth or first love.

And after Hugh Pelham's behavior, why should she reckon on love at all? Was there such a thing as love? He had apparently loved her with the noblest love; it had lasted many years, and finally, in a day, in an hour, for the merest paltry consideration of money, he had not only forgotten her, he had persecuted her. If it were not her fate to know the very ultimate sweetness of love, at least she might have known its consolation. Now that Pelham was lost to her she began to think reproachfully, as women will, of what he might have done for her. If he had been true to her, or even decent to her, she would never have been in those desperate straits in London; she would never have been in her present cruel position, for the instant her father knew of her embarrassments she knew he would sell the roof over his head to pay back the debt; and she would never have dreamed of marrying Clavering. All these troubles came from her having believed in love—and perhaps there was no such thing, after all. But in thinking of marrying Clavering and exchanging her present miserable existence for that promised dazzling London life, a shadow would fall across it—Hugh Pelham's shadow. How would she face him? How could she conceal from him that she had sold herself to this man? And how could she visit him with the scorn lie deserved if she had so easily bartered herself away?

Clavering saw the conflict in Elizabeth's mind, and it gave him a species of sardonic amusement at his own expense. Here he was, ready to sacrifice so much for this woman who had nothing, who could scarcely be brought to look upon what he offered her, and who had kept him at such a distance that he had but once touched her hand in private. He felt himself in many ways at a disadvantage with Elizabeth Darrell. He was, like all men, brought up in humble surroundings, unused to clever and highly organized women, and he did not exactly know how to appeal to such women or how to classify them. One moment Elizabeth would appear to him cleverer than the cleverest man, the next he saw in her some feminine foible that made her seem like a precocious child.

Yet all the time Clavering maintained, in his quietly overbearing way, that the whole affair of the marriage was fixed; but he was not so certain as he professed. He would talk of their plans: they would be married and go to London, and Elizabeth might have any sort of an establishment she liked. She was already well known and well connected there, and he candidly admitted to himself that it would probably be a season or two before London society would find out exactly what sort of a person he was. He warned Elizabeth not to expect any attention from the American ambassador, and was, in short, perfectly frank with her.

He saw that the idea of a life of splendor in London had its attraction for Elizabeth. If she should marry, she would not dare to remain in Washington, and she had no ties elsewhere in her own country. Clavering's manners, in spite of his origin and career, were admirable, and she would have no occasion to blush for him in society—a point on which well-bred women are sensitive. She knew, in externals, he would compare favorably with any of the self-made Americans who buy their way into English society. For herself, her birth and breeding lifted her far above the average titled American woman, whose papa or mamma has bought her a title as they bought her a French doll in her childhood. And London was so large, and so little was really understood there of American life and manners, that Elizabeth felt they would be comparatively safe in London—if—if—

She had taken to reading the newspapers attentively, and had followed the investigation closely. She made herself some sort of a vague promise that should Clavering be exonerated she would marry him, but if he should be proved a scoundrel she would not. But she was already inwardly convinced that he was guilty. He told her, the first time he had a chance, of Baskerville's interview with him—told it with such humor, such raciness, such enjoyment of Baskerville's uncomfortable predicament, that Elizabeth, though little given to merriment, was obliged to laugh.

"Of course," he said, "they will be married shortly. Baskerville has a fine position here—not showy, you know, but the right sort. He has a comfortable fortune, too. Gad! at his age I would have thought myself as rich as Rockefeller if I had had as much. Now it wouldn't keep me in automobiles. I shall provide for Anne handsomely, and besides she will get everything I give her mother, which will be in itself a handsome fortune. Oh, I'm not mean about giving money to my family. Just as soon as Élise and Lydia get the cash I intend to give them, when I get the divorce, they will both be sure to marry some foreign sprig. They have a whole forest of them here and at those foreign watering-places. I shall give Reginald quite as much as he will know how to use, and that will still leave me enough to make you one of the richest women in the world."

Then he redoubled his urging that Elizabeth should come to the grand musical; but she refused his proposition with such violence that he thought it prudent to say no more about it. General Brandon, however, had accepted with pleasure, and quite looked forward to the event. But the very day before, he came home from his office with a bad attack of rheumatism, and was forced to take to his bed.

In the afternoon of the next day, while Elizabeth was sitting by her father's bedside reading to him, and occasionally giving furtive glances at the great masses of palms and magnificent flowering plants being carried into Clavering's house, a card was brought up to her. It was inscribed, "Mr. Angus McBean." So the solicitor had carried out his threat at last. Elizabeth's heart gave a great jump, and then seemed as if dead within her. But she maintained some outward composure, and said she would see the gentleman in a few moments; and telling General Brandon that it was an acquaintance of other days, she left the room. She went to her own room to recover herself a little before descending to meet the man through whom Hugh Pelham had persecuted her ever since her husband's death.

When she entered the drawing-room, the Scotchman rose and greeted her politely. Elizabeth answered his greeting coldly, and McBean, who had seen several Scotch duchesses at a distance, thought he had never beheld anything quite so haughty as this American woman. She remained standing, and Mr. McBean, perceiving she was not likely to ask him to sit, coolly took a chair; and Elizabeth, perforce, sat too.

"I have come in the interests of my client, Major Pelham, to endeavor to reach a basis of settlement with you, madam, concerning the matter we have been corresponding about," blandly remarked Mr. McBean.

"So I supposed," said Elizabeth, icily.

Mr. McBean continued, still blandly: "I may recall to you that you have persistently refused to answer my letters or to refer me to a lawyer, and as the affair involves jewels of considerable value, as well as large sums of money, I thought myself justified in coming to America to seek a settlement of the matter. May I inquire if you will now give me the name of your lawyer? For it would be far more to your interests—I may say it is necessary to your interests—that this matter be settled promptly."

These words were of vague but dreadful import to Elizabeth. She remained silent. She knew nothing of law or lawyers, and the mere thought of consulting a lawyer seemed to her to be giving away her case. There was one,—yes, Richard Baskerville,—the only lawyer she knew in Washington, if she might still be said to know him. She recalled the few times she had seen him since her return to Washington. But she had known him well in the old days. He seemed to have retained his former kindness to her; she might consult him. All this passed rapidly through her mind. What she said was in a calm voice: "I think I need not consult any lawyer on the point of retaining my husband's gift. The pendant to the necklace was my husband's wedding present to me."

Mr. McBean sighed patiently. He had had many dealings with lady clients, and all of them were like this, quite haughty and impossible, until they were frightened; then they would do anything that was asked of them. The only thing left, then, was to frighten Mrs. Darrell, and to give her to understand that the rights of property were the most sacred rights on earth—from the Scotch point of view.

"I think, madam, if you will kindly consent to see your solicitor, or—I believe you use the generic term in the States—your lawyer, and will afterward, have him kindly accord me an interview, you will change your mind upon this matter. The necklace, without counting the additions made to it by your husband, or the pendant, which I understand is of no great value, all of which will be restored to you, is worth at least fifteen hundred pounds. Such a piece of property is not to be disposed of lightly."

So, then, being driven into a corner, helpless and alone, Elizabeth flatteringly consented to consult a lawyer. Mr. McBean left as his address a second-class hotel, and bowed himself out, promising to repeat his call as soon as he was permitted.

Had the Scotch solicitor known it, he had done more toward driving Elizabeth into marrying Clavering than any of Clavering's offers, vows, urgings, and inducements. As she stood, pale and frightened, with a wildly beating heart, her eyes fell involuntarily on the superb house opposite her.

At that moment Clavering dashed up in a magnificent automobile, and got out. Elizabeth noticed that he did not walk with his usual graceful and springy step, and that he leaned against one of the stone pillars of the doorway, before the ever ready, gorgeously caparisoned flunky opened the entrance door. In truth, James Clavering had in his breast pocket a type-written document, which acted like a drag upon his footsteps and a weight upon his shoulders. It was a stolen copy of the report of the committee of investigation, for he always had those in his pay who served him on like occasions.

The next moment, Élise and Lydia drove up in a gem of a victoria. They were enveloped in the costliest furs, and so were the immaculate coachman and footman. The pair of perfectly matched bay cobs was worth a fortune. The harness was gold-mounted, with the Clavering initials upon it. As the two girls got out of the victoria Elizabeth caught the gleam of a long chain dotted with diamonds around Élise's neck. Both of them seemed to radiate wealth; and there stood she, forlorn and despairing for the lack of a few hundred pounds!

Nor was this all. Even if the value of the necklace could be raised by her father's sacrificing everything he had,—his interest in his mortgaged house,—what might not be done to her because she could not produce the necklace itself? Clavering had told her that with money enough it could easily be traced and recovered; but that would mean more money still, and she might as well ask for a star as for any more than the small sum her father could raise. And when she thought that by saying one word she could step from this unstable, bitter, and humiliating position into the very acme of luxury and all the ease of mind which money could give, it seemed to her almost a paradise. It was well for her that Clavering was not on the spot at that moment.

She went back to her father's bedside and to reading the book she had laid down. She uttered the words, but her mind was far off. As she dwelt upon Mr. McBean's phrases and thinly disguised threats, she grew more and more panic-stricken. At last Serena brought up General Brandon's dinner, and Elizabeth went down to her own solitary meal in the dingy dining room. Action was forced upon her; she must see a lawyer, and Richard Baskerville was her only choice. She must try to see him that very night. As she knew he would not be at the Claverings', she thought her chance of finding him at home was excellent.

When dinner was over Elizabeth gave Serena a note to take to Richard Baskerville, asking him to call that evening to see her upon a matter of pressing importance. She put her request upon the ground of old acquaintance, coupled with present necessity. Serena returned within a half-hour, with a note from Baskerville saying he would be pleased to call to see Mrs. Darrell that evening at half-past nine o'clock.

General Brandon having been made comfortable for the night, Elizabeth descended to the drawing-room. The gas was lighted, but turned low. Elizabeth went to the window, whence she could see the Clavering house blazing with light and an army of liveried servants moving to and fro. A fraction of the cost of that one entertainment would have made her a free woman.

Shortly after half-past nine o'clock Baskerville arrived. Like Elizabeth, he gazed with interest at the Clavering house. It was undoubtedly the last great entertainment there at which Anne would preside, and Baskerville had a conviction that it was the last entertainment the Claverings would ever give in Washington. He had private information that the committee of investigation had agreed upon its report, and he believed it would deal severely with Clavering.

He had been surprised to receive Elizabeth's note, but he recognized at once that she was in great trouble, and he had come willingly, as a gentleman should. When he saw Elizabeth, he realized how great was her trouble. Then, sitting in the dimly lighted drawing-room, Elizabeth, with many pauses and palpitations and hesitations, began her story. Baskerville gently assisted her, and the telling of the first part was not so hard. When it came to the further history of it Elizabeth faltered, and asked anxiously, "But wasn't the necklace mine entirely, after my husband gave it to me?"

Baskerville shook his head. "I'm afraid not, Mrs. Darrell, and I am afraid that Major Darrell made a mistake—a perfectly natural and excusable mistake—in thinking it was his to give you in perpetuity. Of course I am not so well informed on these points as an English lawyer would be, but from what you tell me of the other jewels, and the course of the solicitor concerning them, I cannot but think that he knows what he is doing, and that you will have to give up the necklace, retaining of course your pendant, and perhaps the stones your husband bought."

Elizabeth looked at him with wild, scared eyes; and then, bursting into tears, told him the whole story of pawning the necklace, of finding it gone, and her unwillingness to own what she had done. Baskerville was startled, but allowed her to weep on, without trying to check her. He saw that she was in a state of trembling excitement, excessive even under the circumstances, and she must have her tears out. She had, so far, avoided mentioning Pelham's name.

"But what of the heirs of Major Darrell? Surely, when they know how you were straitened in London after your husband's death and the good faith in which you pledged the necklace, they would not wish to distress you unnecessarily about it."

Then Elizabeth was forced to speak of Pelham. "Major Darrell's heir is his cousin, Major Pelham, the man—next my husband and my father—whom I thought my truest friend. He is in West Africa now, or was when my husband died, and I have not heard of his return to England since. But he has countenanced all this, and seems to delight in persecuting me through this man McBean. And it is quite useless, too, as I have no means of paying the money. I have only a small income, about a hundred pounds a year. But if my father learns of my trouble, as he eventually must if this persecution is kept up, he will certainly sell this house—his only piece of property, and mortgaged at that. Oh, I didn't think a man could be so cruel as Hugh Pelham has been!"

"Does McBean claim to be acting under Major Pelham's instructions?"

"Yes. In everything he writes me or says to me he uses Hugh Pelham's name."

"There is hut one thing to do, Mrs. Darrell. I shall see McBean to-morrow and endeavor to see what I can do with him. If I fail with him, I shall appeal to Major Pelham."

"Oh, no, not that—not that!"

She spoke with so much of feeling, of anger, of mortification in her voice, that Baskerville could not but suspect that there was something more concerning Pelham which Elizabeth had not chosen to tell him; but his duty to her as a friend and a lawyer remained the same. "Pardon me," he said kindly, "but I think it almost necessary to inform Major Pelham of the state of the case. I shall not, however, do it unless you consent. But I think you will consent."

Elizabeth grew more composed, and they talked some time longer—talked until the rolling of carriages began under the porte-cochère of the Clavering house, and women wrapped in gorgeous ball cloaks and trailing behind them rich brocades and velvets and sparkling chiffons began to pour through the great entrance doors into the regions of light and splendor beyond. The rhythmic swell of music began to be heard; the great festivity had begun.

Both Elizabeth and Baskerville, sitting in the quiet room only a stone's throw away, were thinking about what was going on in the great mansion across the street. Elizabeth was asking herself if, after all, there were any alternative left her but to agree to marry Clavering. One word, and all her troubles and perplexities about money, which had spoiled her life from the time of her girlhood, would disappear. And if she did not marry Clavering—here her dread and apprehension became so strong that she was sickened at the contemplation.

In spite of her preoccupation with her own troubles she could not but regard Baskerville with interest, knowing of his relations with Anne Clavering. Here was another man, like Pelham, who seemed the very mirror of manly love and courage; but perhaps he would be no better than Pelham in the long run.

He might marry Anne under an impulse of generous feeling and live to repent it. Elizabeth was becoming a sceptic on the subject of man's love.

Baskerville had no suspicion that Elizabeth Darrell knew anything of his relations with Anne Clavering, nor did he connect Clavering in any way with Elizabeth. He was thinking of Anne while talking to Elizabeth, remembering how she had disliked and dreaded this great function. She was to do the honors of the occasion, Mrs. Clavering being still ailing. The town had been ringing with the magnificence of the coming festivity, but Anne had been so averse to it that Baskerville had said little about it to her. It was out of the question that he should go, and so no card had been sent him; and he agreed fully with Anne that the affair was most unfortunately conspicuous at the present time.

A silence had fallen between Baskerville and Elizabeth, while listening to the commotion outside. A sudden wild impulse came to Elizabeth to tell Baskerville, of all men, her struggles about consenting to marry Clavering, without mentioning any name. Baskerville had been kind and helpful to her; he had come to her immediately at her request; and before she knew it she was saying to him, in a nervous voice: "I could be free from all these anxieties about money, my father could end his days in ease—all, all if I would but marry a divorced man—a man to be divorced, that is. And after all, he never was actually married, it was a mistake."

Baskerville had been looking abstractedly out of the window at the carriages flashing past, but at this he turned quickly to Elizabeth. "You mean Senator Clavering?" Baskerville was a remarkably self-contained man, but in his burst of surprise the name fell from his lips before he knew it.

Elizabeth sat dumb. She had yielded to a mad impulse, and would have given a year of her life to have unsaid those words. Baskerville hesitated for a minute or two, and then rose. Elizabeth's silence, the painful flushing of her face, her whole attitude of conscious guilt, proclaimed the truth of Baskerville's surmise. He looked at her in pity and commiseration. She had just told him enough to make him understand how great the temptation was to her; and yet so far she had not yielded. But that she would yield he had not the least doubt. And what untold miseries would not she, or any woman like her, bring upon herself by marrying Clavering!

It was a question which neither one of them could discuss, and Baskerville's only words were: "I have no right to offer you my advice, except on the point upon which you have consulted me, but I beg of you to consider well what you are thinking of. You are hovering over dreadful possibilities for yourself. Good night."

He was going, but Elizabeth ran and grasped his arm. "You won't speak of this to Miss Clavering! You must not do it! You have no right!"

Baskerville smiled rather bitterly. Whether Elizabeth were afraid or ashamed he did not know—probably both.

"Certainly I shall not," he said, and to Elizabeth's ears his tone expressed the most entire contempt.

"And I haven't promised him—I haven't agreed yet," she added, tears coming into her eyes; and then Baskerville was gone.

Elizabeth sat, stunned by her own folly, and burning with shame at the scorn she fancied Baskerville had felt for her. He had been kind to her and had agreed to do all that was possible with McBean, but by her own act she had lost his good will and respect. Well, it was part of the web of destiny. She was being driven to marry Clavering by every circumstance of her life—even this last. Pelham's unkindness was the beginning of it; McBean's persecution helped it on; General Brandon's goodness and generosity, Baskerville's contempt for her—all urged her on; she supposed Baskerville would probably have nothing more to do with her affairs and would leave her to face McBean alone, and that would be the end of her resistance to Clavering.

She went up to her own room and, with a cloak huddled about her, sat by the window in the dark, looking out upon the splendid scene of a great ball in a capital city. Elizabeth in the cold and darkness watched it all—watched until the ambassadors' carriages were called, followed rapidly by the other equipages which were parked in the surrounding streets for blocks. At last, after three o'clock in the morning, the trampling of horses' hoofs, the closing of carriage doors, and the commotion of footmen and coachmen ceased— the great affair was over. Quickly as in the transformation scene at a theatre, the splendid house grew dark—all except the windows of Clavering's library. They remained brilliantly lighted long after all else in the street was dark and quiet.

Elizabeth, for some reason inexplicable to herself, remained still at her window, looking at the blaze of light from Clavering's library windows. What was keeping him up so late? Was it good news or bad? Had the report of the committee been made?

Within the library sat Clavering in his accustomed chair. In his hand he held a type-written document of many pages, which had cost him many thousands of dollars to have purloined and copied from another one which was locked up in the safe of the secretary of the Senate. Every page of this document proclaimed in some form or other his guilt, and at the bottom was written in the handwriting of a man he knew well, and who had stolen and copied the report for him:—

"Resolution of expulsion will be introduced immediately after reading of report, and will pass by three-fourths majority."

And the hired thief had not played fair with him. He had discovered that at least three newspapers had bought the stolen report, and at that very moment he knew the great presses in the newspaper offices were clanging with the story of his disgrace to be printed on the morrow.

Then there was a bunch of telegrams from his state capital. If the Senate did not vote to expel, the legislature would request him to resign; so there was no vindication there. To this, then, had his public career come! Clavering was not honest himself, nor did he believe in honesty in others; but he believed it possible that he might have been more secret in his evil-doing. He had thought that with money, brains, and courage he could brazen anything out. But behold! he could not. He was fairly caught and exposed. Those stray words of Baskerville's, uttered some months before, recurred to him, "There is no real substitute for honesty."

He had heard the news on his way home that afternoon, from an out-of-town expedition. It had unnerved him for a little while; it was that which made him get out of the automobile so heavily when Elizabeth, unseen, was watching him. He had gone through the evening, however, bravely and even cynically. Many senators had been asked to the great function, but scarcely half a dozen had appeared; and all of them were inconsiderable men, dragged there by their womenkind. In the course of some hours of reflection—for Clavering could think in a crowd—a part of his indomitable courage and resource had returned. He had no fear of the criminal prosecution which would certainly follow. William M. Tweed had been caught, but Tweed was a mere vulgar villain and did not know when he was beaten. Clavering rapidly made up his mind that he could afford to restore eight or even ten millions of dollars to the rightful owners, and that would satisfy them; they wouldn't be likely to spend any part of it in trying to punish him.

As for any part the state and federal government might take he was not particularly concerned. The party had done enough to clear its skirts by expelling him from the Senate, and if he satisfied all the claims against him, nobody would have any object in entering upon a long, expensive, and doubtful trial. But after paying out even ten millions of dollars he would have twice as much left, which nobody and no government could get, though it was as dishonestly made as the rest. With that much money and Elizabeth Darrell—for Elizabeth entered into all his calculations—life would still be worth living.

When the mob of gayly dressed people were gone, when the laughter and the dancing and the music and the champagne and the feasting were over, and Clavering sat in his library alone under the brilliant chandelier, he grew positively cheerful. He was not really fond of public life, and although he would have liked to get out of it more gracefully, he was not really sorry to go. He had found himself bound in a thousand conventions since he had been in Washington. He had been hampered by his family: by his wife because she was old and stupid and ignorant, by Élise and Lydia because they were so bad, by Anne and Reginald because they were so honest. It would be rather good to be free once more—free in the great, wide, untamed West, free in the vast, populous, surging cities of Europe. He would have Elizabeth with him; he did not much care for any one else's society. She had never heard him admit his guilt, and he could easily persuade her that he was the victim of untoward circumstances.

While he was thinking these things, he heard a commotion overhead. Presently the whole house was roused, and servants were running back and forth. Elizabeth Darrell, still watching at her window, saw the sudden and alarming awakening of the silent house. Mrs. Clavering had been taken violently ill. Before sunrise the poor lady was no longer in any one's way. A few hours of stupor, a little awakening at the last, a clinging to Anne and Reginald and telling them to be good, and Mrs. Clavering's gentle spirit was free and in peace.

When the undertaker was hanging the streamers of black upon the door-bell, the morning newspaper was laid on the steps. On the first page, with great head-lines, was the announcement that Senator Clavering had been found guilty of the charges against him and that expulsion from the Senate was certain to follow. The newspaper omitted to state how the information was obtained.

Chapter Seventeen

The morning of Ash Wednesday dawned cold and damp and cheerless. Baskerville had heard a rumor at the club the night before that there had been a leak between the committee-room, the office of the secretary of the Senate, and the room of the investigating committee; that the big iron safe had been entered and a stolen copy of the report of the committee had been made and would be published in the morning. So he had the morning newspaper brought to him. On the first page, with a huge display head, together with the recommendation of expulsion against Senator Clavering, the report was printed in full.

Baskerville immediately wrote a note to Anne Clavering, asking that their engagement might be announced and also suggesting an immediate marriage. Within an hour came back an answer from Anne. In a few agitated lines she told him of her mother's death. She did not ask Baskerville to come to her; but he, seeing that it was no time for small conventions, replied at once, saying that he would be at her house at twelve o'clock, and begged that she would see him.

Elizabeth Darrell was the first person outside of Clavering's family who knew that he was a free man. There had been no time to get a doctor for Mrs. Clavering, although several had been called. When they arrived, all was over. Elizabeth had seen the sudden shutting of the windows; she knew, almost to a moment, when Mrs. Clavering died.

At seven o'clock in the morning Serena, with the morbid anxiety to communicate tragic news which is the characteristic of the African, came up to Elizabeth's room full of what she had gleaned from the neighboring servants. Elizabeth listened and felt a sense of guilt enveloping her. Then, when General Brandon was dressed, he came up to her door to discuss the startling news, and his was the first card left for the Clavering family. On it the good soul had written:—

"With heartfelt sympathy in the overwhelming sorrow which has befallen Senator Clavering and his family."

Elizabeth remained indoors all that day. She drew her window curtains together, so that she could not see the house which might have been hers, where had lived the dead woman of whom she had considered the spoliation.

At twelve o'clock Baskerville came, and was promptly admitted into the Clavering house. There had been no time to remove the festal decorations. The Moorish hall was odorous with flowers; the mantels and even the hand-rail of the staircase were banked with them. Masses of tall palms made a mysterious green light through the whole of the great suite of rooms. The ceilings were draped with greenery, and orchids and roses hung from them. The huge ball-room was just as the dancers had left it, and everywhere were flowers, palms, and burnt-out candles on girandoles and candelabra. The servants, in gorgeous liveries, sat about, more asleep than awake; and over all was that solemn silence which accompanies the presence of that first and greatest of democrats, Death.

Baskerville was shown into a little morning-room on the second floor, which had belonged to the poor dead woman. It was very simply furnished and in many ways suggested Mrs. Clavering. Baskerville, remembering her untoward fate in being thrust into a position for which she was unfitted, and her genuine goodness and gentleness, felt a real regret at her death. Being a generous man, he had taken pleasure in the intention of being kind to Mrs. Clavering; he knew that it would add extremely to Anne's happiness. But, like much other designed good, it was too late. He remembered with satisfaction the little courtesies he had been able to show Mrs. Clavering and Anne's gratitude for them; and then, before he knew it, Anne, in her black gown, pale and heavy-eyed, was sobbing in his arms.

She soon became composed, and told him calmly of the last days. She dwelt with a kind of solemn joy upon her last conversation with her mother about Baskerville, and the message she had sent him. "My mother had not been any too well treated in this life," added Anne, the smouldering resentment in her heart showing in her eyes, "and you are almost the only man of your class who ever seemed to recognize her beautiful qualities—for my mother had beautiful qualities."

"I know it," replied Baskerville, with perfect sincerity, "and I tried to show my appreciation of them."

It was plain to Baskerville, after spending some time with Anne, that she knew nothing of the news concerning her father with which all Washington was ringing. Baskerville felt that it would never do for her to hear it by idle gossip or by chance. So, after a while, he told her—told her with all the gentleness, all the tenderness, at his command, softening it so far as he could.

Anne listened, tearless and dry-eyed. She followed him fairly well, and asked at last, "Do you mean that—that my father will be expelled from the Senate, and then—there will be no more trouble?"

"Dearest, I wish I could say so. But there will be a great deal more of trouble, I am afraid—enough to make it necessary that you and I should be married as soon as possible."

"And you would marry the daughter of a man so disgraced, who may end his days in a prison?"

"Yes—since it is you."

He then inquired her plans for the present. Mrs. Clavering's body was to be taken for burial to her old home in Iowa. Baskerville asked, or rather demanded, that within a month Anne should be prepared to become his wife. "And haven't you some relations out in Iowa from whose house we can be married?" he said.

"Yes," replied Anne, "I have aunts and cousins there. I warn you they are very plain people, but they are very respectable. I don't think there is a person in my mother's family of whom I have any reason to be ashamed, although they are, as I tell you, plain people."

"That is of no consequence whatever. I shall wait until after your mother's funeral before writing your father and having our engagement announced, and within a month I shall come to Iowa to marry you."

And Anne, seeing this sweet refuge open to her, took heart of grace and comfort.

Clavering himself, sitting in his darkened library, was in no way awed by death having invaded his house. He had been brought face to face with it too often to be afraid of it; he was a genuine, throughgoing disbeliever in everything except money and power, and he regarded the end of life as being an interesting but unimportant event.

His wife's death was most opportune for him; it made it certain that Elizabeth Darrell would marry him. He had fully realized that stubborn prejudice on Elizabeth's part against divorce, and although he had not seriously doubted his ability to overcome it, yet it had been stubborn. Now all was smoothed away. He would act with perfect propriety, under the circumstances; he surmised enough about the women of Elizabeth's class to understand that a breach of decorum would shock her far more than a breach of morals. There would be no outward breach of decorum. He would wait until after the funeral before writing her; but it would be useless, hypocritical, and even dangerous to postpone writing longer.

With these thoughts in his mind he sat through the day, receiving and answering telegrams, scanning the newspapers, and digesting his own disgrace as exposed in print. Even that had come at a fortunate time for him—if there is a fortunate time to be branded a thief, a liar, and a perjurer, a suborner of perjury, a corrupter of courts, a purchaser of legislatures. Elizabeth would feel sorry for him; she wouldn't understand the thing at all. He would insist on being married in the autumn, and Elizabeth would no doubt be glad to be married as far away from Washington as possible. Perhaps she might agree to meet him in London and be married there. He would go over in the summer, take the finest house to be had for money, and transport all the superb equipment of his Washington establishment to London. He also remembered with satisfaction that he had now nothing to fear on the score of divorce from that soft-spoken, wooden-headed, fire-eating old impracticable, General Brandon, with his fatal tendency to settle with the pistol questions concerning "the ladies of his family."

In these reflections and considerations James Clavering passed the first day of his widowerhood. On the third day after Mrs. Clavering's death the great house was shut up and silent. The Claverings left it, never to return to it. It stood vacant, a monument of man's vicissitudes.

The day after Mrs. Clavering's burial took place, in the little Iowa town where her family lived, a line appeared in the society column of a leading Washington newspaper, announcing the engagement of Anne Clavering and Richard Baskerville. Coming as it did on the heels of the tragic events in the Clavering family and Baskerville's share in a part of these events, the announcement was startling though far from unexpected. Mrs. Luttrell took upon herself the office of personally acquainting her friends with the engagement and declaring her entire satisfaction with it. Being by nature an offensive partisan, much given to pernicious activity in causes which engaged her heart, Mrs. Luttrell soon developed into a champion of the whole Clavering family. She discovered many admirable qualities in Clavering himself, and changed her tune completely concerning Élise and Lydia, whom she now spoke of as "a couple of giddy chits, quite harmless, and only a little wild." These two young women had speedily made up their minds to fly to Europe, and arranged to do so as soon as Anne was married, which was to be within the month.

The catastrophes of the Clavering family made a profound impression on Washington. Their meteoric career was a sort of epitome of all the possibilities of the sudden acquisition of wealth and power. Whatever might be said of them, they were at least not cowards—not even Reginald Clavering was a coward. They were boldly bad, or boldly good. Anne Clavering had won for herself a place in the esteem of society which was of great value. Not one disrespectful or unkind word was spoken of her when the day of reckoning for the Claverings came.

The Senate allowed James Clavering two weeks to recover from his grief at his wife's death before annihilating him as a senator. Clavering improved the time not only by arranging for his second marriage, but by forestalling, when he had no fighting ground, the criminal indictments which might be expected to be found against him. He paid out secretly in satisfaction money, and reconveyed in bonds, nearly three millions of dollars. There were several millions more to be fought over, but that was a matter of time; and he would still have a great fortune remaining, if every suit went against him.

It would very much have simplified his property arrangements had Elizabeth Darrell consented to marry him within a few weeks of his widowerhood. But this Clavering knew was not to be thought of. A week after his wife's death he wrote to Elizabeth. He quietly assumed that all arrangements had been made for their marriage, as soon as he should have got his divorce. In his letter he reminded Elizabeth there could now be no question or scruple in regard to her marrying him. He told her he would be in Washington at the end of the week, when the proceedings in the Senate would take place, and that he should expect to see her. He asked her to write and let him know where they should meet.

Elizabeth realized that she had gone too far to refuse Clavering a meeting, nor, in fact, did she desire to avoid him. Her feelings toward him had become more and more chaotic; they did not remain the same for an hour together. She felt that a powerful blow had been dealt her objection to marrying him in the removal of the divorce question; she doubted in her heart whether she ever could have been brought to the point of marrying him had his wife not died.

And then there had been another interview with McBean. He had told Elizabeth he was about to leave Washington to be absent a month, as he was combining pleasure with business on his visit to America, but that on his return, if the necklace were not forthcoming, he should begin legal proceedings immediately. Mr. McBean was fully persuaded, while he was talking to Elizabeth, that the necklace was around her neck, under her high gown, or in her pocket, or in a secret drawer of her writing-desk—in any one of those strange places where women keep their valuables. Elizabeth, in truth, did not know whether the necklace was in America, Europe, Asia, Africa, or Australia.

Then Baskerville, in spite of the crisis in his own affairs, had not neglected Elizabeth. He had managed to see McBean, and had discovered that the solicitor was perfectly justified in all he had done, from the legal point of view. When Baskerville came to inquire how far Major Pelham was responsible for what was done, he was met by an icy reticence on the part of Mr. McBean, who replied that Baskerville was asking unprofessional questions, and in embarrassment Baskerville desisted. It became clear, however, and Baskerville so wrote to Elizabeth, that her concealment of the pawning of the necklace, and her inability to pay back the money she had raised on it, were very serious matters, and she should at once lay the matter before her father.

Elizabeth, however, had not been able to bring herself to that. She thought of all sorts of wild alternatives, such as asking Clavering to lend her the money; but her soul recoiled from that. She even considered writing another letter to Hugh Pelham; but at that, too, her heart cried aloud in protest. She did not know where Pelham was, but surmised that he was still in West Africa. A letter addressed to the War Office would reach him—but when?

The more she thought of this, the simplest of alternatives and the one urged by Baskerville, the more impossible it seemed. She had loved Pelham well—loved him with all her soul, her mind, her heart; and that, too, when she was a married woman, loving another than her husband, without the slightest stain of any sort upon her mind, her soul, her heart. She doubted if she would have been half so dutiful a wife, but for Pelham's love for her and her love for him. It seemed to her that his respect was as necessary to her as her self-respect. Their unfortunate attachment had been in the highest sense elevating. It had not required the soft consolation, the assurances, of weaker passions; but, lofty and austere, it was as strong and as silent as death, it seemed to be everlasting. And could a thing seem to be for ten years of storm and stress and not be?

As Heinrich Heine says, it seemed to Elizabeth as if there were no longer a great God in heaven since he had made his creatures so deceitful. What agony was Elizabeth Darrell's? To have failed in her duty as a wife would have been the surest way to lower herself in Pelham's eyes.

Clavering had reckoned upon Elizabeth's neither knowing nor appreciating the effect of the revelations about him; in this, however, he was mistaken. She had read the newspapers diligently and understood his affairs far better than Clavering dreamed. The case had made a tremendous sensation. The tragic circumstances of the catastrophe, the probable action of the Senate which was known in advance, the far-reaching scandals which would result from the making public of the findings, all combined to give the country a profound shock—a shock so profound that it was known it would seriously jeopardize for the party in power the states in which Clavering and his gang had operated.

Among public men in Washington the feeling was intense. The senators who from a combination of honesty and policy had advocated going to the bottom of the scandals and punishing everybody found guilty, were in the position of doctors who have successfully performed a hazardous operation, but are uncertain whether the patient will survive or not. There was no doubt that many criminal prosecutions would follow, but there was a general belief that Clavering was too able and resourceful a man, and had too much money, to be actually punished for the crimes he had undoubtedly committed. His real punishment was his expulsion from the Senate.

Elizabeth Darrell knew all these things, and turned them over in her mind until she was half distracted. Another thing, small to a man but large to a woman, tormented her. She must meet Clavering—but where? Not in her

- 164 -

father's house; that could only be done secretly, and she could not stoop to deceive her father. The only way she could think of was in the little park, far at the other end of the town, where their first momentous meeting had taken place. So, feeling the humiliation of what she was doing, Elizabeth replied to Clavering's letter, and named a day—the day before the one set for the final proceedings in the Senate—when she would see him; and she named six o'clock in the afternoon, in the little out-of-the-way park.

It was March then of a forward spring. The day had been one of those sudden warm and balmy days which come upon Washington at the most unlikely seasons. Already the grass was green and the miles upon miles of shade trees were full of sap and the buds were near to bursting. Six o'clock was not quite dusk, but it was as late as Elizabeth dared to make her appointment. Her heart was heavy as she walked along the quiet, unfamiliar streets toward the park—as heavy as on that day, only a few months before, when she had returned to Washington after her widowhood. Then she had been oppressed with the thought that life was over for her, nothing interesting would ever again happen to her. And what had not happened to her!

When Elizabeth reached the park she found Clavering awaiting her. He could not but note the grace of her walk and the beauty of her figure as she approached him. She was one of those women who become more interesting, if less handsome, under the stress of feeling. Her dark eyes were appealing, and she sank rather than sat upon the park bench to which Clavering escorted her.

"You seem to have taken my troubles to heart," he said with the air and manner of an accepted lover.

Elizabeth made no reply. She had not been able to discover, in the chaos of her emotions, how far Clavering's troubles really touched her.

"However," said Clavering, "the worst will be over to-morrow. I wish you could be in the Senate gallery, to see how I bear it. The vote on expulsion takes place to-morrow, directly after the morning hour, and I know precisely the majority against me—it will be quite enough to do the work." Then he added with a cool smile: "I believe if you could be present, you would realize what a pack of rascals have sacrificed me to political expediency! Unluckily I can't offer you a seat in the Senators' Gallery, as I might have done a short while ago. The fools think I will stay away, but I shall be in my seat, and from it I shall make my defence and my promise to return to the Senate by the mandate of my state. It will sound well, but to tell you the truth I have no more wish to return than the legislature has the intention of returning me. I have something pleasanter in view—it is life with you."

Elizabeth, beguiled in spite of herself, as women are by courage, glanced at Clavering. Yes, he was not afraid of any man or of anything, while she was consumed with terror over a paltry five hundred pounds and the loss of a necklace worth only a trifle in Clavering's eyes. She longed that he would break through her prohibition and speak about the necklace. But Clavering did not, and he never intended to do so. He knew very well that Elizabeth's necessities were his best advocates, and he did not purpose silencing any of them.

Elizabeth's reply, after a pause, to Clavering's remark was: "I shouldn't like to see you to-morrow. It will be too tragic."

"It's a pity that I'm not divorced instead of being so recent a widower," Clavering replied. "Then you could marry me at the moment of misfortune, as Richard Baskerville proposes to marry my daughter Anne. It would be a great help to me now, if it were possible. As it is, we shall have to postpone our marriage until the autumn."

"No," replied Elizabeth, decisively, "it cannot be until next year."

Clavering's eyes flashed. It was the first time that she had ever fully admitted that she meant to marry him, although he had from the beginning assumed it. He had very little doubt that he could induce her to shorten the time of waiting.

"We will talk about that later. Meanwhile I suppose you will stay here with your father. We can't enjoy the London house this season, but I shall go abroad in June. I shall have straightened things out by that time, and I can select a house. It will be as fine a one as that which I have lived in here. I can ship all the furnishings, pictures, and plate, with the horses and carriages, to London in advance, and have your establishment ready for you when you arrive. Perhaps it would be better for us to be married in London."

Elizabeth Darrell was not what is called a mercenary woman. She had hesitated when offered vast wealth, and had even declined it on the terms first offered to her; nor did she believe that she would ever have agreed to marry Clavering, in the event of his divorce, but for the removal of her scruples of conscience on finding that his first marriage was illegal. But these words of Clavering's about the London establishment brought to mind her former life there. She made a rapid mental comparison of Clavering with poor, honest, brave, stupid dead Jack Darrell; with Pelham as he had been; with her father; and the comparison staggered and revolted her. If it were written, however, in the book of destiny that she should marry Clavering, it were better that they should be married in London, as he suggested. She would rather escape her father's eye when that transaction took place, and nobody else in the world cared how or when she was married or what might become of her.

Clavering spent the time of their interview in planning their future life together. He offered her luxury in every form, but he was too astute a man to make his purchase of her too obvious. He by no means left out his love for her, which was in truth the master passion of his life just then. But he did not force it upon Elizabeth, seeing that she was as yet restless and but half tamed to his hand. Elizabeth listened to him, with the conviction growing in her mind that she must marry this man.

Their conversation lasted barely half an hour. Clavering urged Elizabeth to meet him again before he left Washington, which would be the next night, at midnight; but to this Elizabeth would not agree. Clavering saw that he must wait at least six months before she would tolerate any attentions from him, and he quickly made up his mind that it was best not to urge her too much now. He had practically received her promise to marry him at the end of a year, and considering the obstacles he had to contend with he felt pretty well satisfied. As on the former occasion when they had met in the little park, Clavering went after a cab for Elizabeth, put her in it, and they separated.

Elizabeth spent a solitary evening. The calm which reigned in Clavering's breast was by no means her portion. She felt that she had finally committed herself to marry him, and the prospect frightened her. She recalled Baskerville's words—the "dreadful possibilities" which might await a woman married to Clavering. Their contemplation frightened her more than ever. She was so absorbed in her own troubles that she scarcely gave a thought to Clavering's impending fate on the morrow. She remained up late, and the clock had struck midnight before her light was out.

Once in bed, Elizabeth was seized with a maddening restlessness, against which she fought for four hours. When the sky of night was wan and pale with the coming dawn, she rose and, going to her writing-table, began to write steadily. Her letter was to Hugh Pelham. She told him everything, without concealment—the story of the need that made her pawn the necklace, the story of Clavering, the story of her life in Washington, of her grief and amazement at what seemed to be Pelham's persecution of her, and it closed with a torrent of reproaches that came from the depths of her heart.

She sealed the letter and addressed it to Pelham in the care of the War Office at London. She had no idea where Pelham was or when the letter would reach him; but some time or other he would get it, and then he would know how cruel his conduct was and how far-reaching was the effect of his ill-treatment of her. She had glossed over nothing about Clavering, she had painted him in his true colors; and she had told Pelham that but for him there would have been no temptation for her to have married such a man as Clavering.

When she had finished and sealed and stamped her letter, Elizabeth went to the window and drew the curtain. The flush that precedes the dawn was over the opaline sky; it was the beginning of an exquisite spring day. The city lay still and quiet; only one footfall was heard, that of the postman collecting the letters from the mail-box at the corner. As he passed briskly along the street under Elizabeth's window, a letter softly fluttered down and fell at his feet. He glanced up and saw a window high above him being closed. The postman picked up the letter, put it in his bag, and went on, whistling.

Elizabeth, up in her bedroom, threw herself upon her bed and sank into a heavy and dreamless sleep that lasted until Serena knocked at her door at nine o'clock. Elizabeth rose, dressed, and breakfasted like a person in a dream. She remembered her letter instantly, and the recollection of it made her uneasy. Gradually her uneasiness turned to an agony of regret. She would have made almost any sacrifice to recall the letter, but she supposed it was now impossible.

Her great concern made her forget all about Clavering's impending doom that day, until quite noon. As she began to consider it, the spirit of restlessness which seemed to possess her impelled her to wish that she could witness the scene in the Senate chamber. It might take her mind from her letter, which burned in her memory and was eating her heart out with shame and unavailing repentance. She knew there would be vast crowds at the Capitol, but she felt sure that not one of her few acquaintances in Washington would be there.

About one o'clock she suddenly resolved to go to the Capitol. Covering her face, as well as her hat, with a thick black veil, she started for the white-domed building on the hill. When she reached the plaza, she found a great crowd surrounding the north wing. Not in the memory of man had such an event as the expulsion of a senator occurred, and it was the very thing to stimulate the unhealthy curiosity of thousands. A steady stream poured into the doorways and jammed the corridors. Elizabeth doubted whether she would ever get nearer than the Senate corridor, much less be able to get into the small public gallery. She noticed, however, that the multitude was pouring into the ground-floor entrance; so she determined to mount the long, wide flight of steps on the east front and enter the rotunda through the great bronze doors.

It was a beautiful spring day, and the crowd was a well-dressed and cheerful one. Nobody would have dreamed that they were about to attend a great public tragedy. As Elizabeth reached the top of the flight, she turned involuntarily to look at the beautiful panorama outspread before her in the

Southern sunshine. Fair and faintly green lay the park-like gardens around the Capitol, while the golden dome of the National Library flashed and gleamed in the noonday radiance. Never before had she thought Washington a joyous-looking city, but to-day, with sunshine and life and motion, with its animated throng of persons, this continual passing to and fro, it reminded her of Paris on a fête day.

While Elizabeth was looking upon the charming scene outspread before her, she heard the sound of trampling hoofs and the roll of a carriage below. Clavering, in his handsomest brougham, with a superb pair of horses, had just driven up. The coachman and footman wore the newest, smartest, and blackest of mourning liveries for the mistress they had seen ignored, when not insulted, during the whole term of their service. Forth from the carriage, a cynosure for the staring, curious crowd, stepped Clavering. He, too, was dressed in new and immaculate mourning, with a crape-covered hat.

Elizabeth shrank behind one of the huge pillars, but from it she saw Clavering's dignified and ever graceful air as he braved the glances of the multitude. The lower entrance being jammed with people, he leisurely mounted the great flight of steps, a thing he had never before done in all his senatorial service. The crowd watched him with admiration and gratitude—it gave them the more time and the better opportunity of seeing him. He passed close enough to Elizabeth to have touched her, as she stood quaking with shame and fear; but, looking neither to the right nor to the left, he walked on, calm, courageous, and apparently at ease with himself and all the world.

Elizabeth, still moved by an impulse stronger than her will, pressed forward through the rotunda into the corridors. They were packed, and the doors to the public galleries had long been closed. Elizabeth found herself in the midst of a surging crowd, in the corridor leading to the reserved gallery, the place to which Clavering had told her he could no longer admit her. While she was standing there, crushed on either side, a pathway was opened, and a party of senators' wives approached the door. At the same moment it was opened and some people came out. In the slight confusion several tried to get in; the doorkeepers, trying to separate the sheep from the goats, pushed the intruders back and pushed Elizabeth in with the senatorial party.

"But I have no right in here," she said hurriedly to the doorkeeper who shoved her into the gallery.

"Just go in, madam, and let me shut these people out," replied the doorkeeper, seeing the necessity for closing the door at once. So Elizabeth found herself in the last place either she or Clavering expected her to be, the gallery set apart for the senatorial families.

It was then almost two o'clock, when the morning hour expired, and the first business to be taken up was the resolution of expulsion against Senator Clavering. There was a subdued tremor over the whole scene; the senators who were to do a great act of public justice upon one of their own number were deeply moved over it. Not one of them had ever before taken part in such proceedings, and the species of civil death they were about to inflict on a man once counted worthy to sit among them was in some respects worse than the death of the body. The seriousness of the occasion affected every one present; a psychic wave of shame, regret, and solemnity swept over the whole assemblage, and a strange stillness reigned among the people who filled the galleries. Nearly every senator was in his seat, and the space back of them was crowded with members of the other house and persons who had the privileges of the floor.

Clavering sat in his accustomed place, a cool and apparently disinterested observer of the proceedings. His presence was highly disconcerting to the committee which had prepared the report, and indeed to every senator present. It had been hoped that Clavering would absent himself; there were no precedents in the present generation for such proceedings, and it would have been altogether easier if Clavering had chosen to remain away. But as he was a senator up to the moment the vote was taken, no one could say him nay.

Elizabeth found no trouble in concealing herself behind the large hats and feathers of the ladies in the reserved gallery, and she could observe Clavering closely. She thought she had never seen him look so handsome and even distinguished in appearance. Had he only been honest! Some thoughts like these raced through Clavering's brain. He recalled Baskerville's remark, "There is no real substitute for honesty," and he remembered several occasions when he could have afforded to be honest and had not been, and he regretted it. Most of all he regretted not having taken greater precautions when he was dishonest.

At last, the morning hour having expired, the next business on the calendar was the reading of the report of the committee of investigation on the affairs of the K. F. R. land grants and the corporations connected therewith. The Vice-President, looking pale and worried, recognized the chairman of the committee, who looked paler and more worried. The stillness resolved itself into a deathlike silence, broken only by the resonant tones of the reading clerk. It was not a long report—the reading of it lasted scarcely three-quarters of an hour; but it was a terrible one. As the charges were named, and declared proved, a kind of horror appeared to settle down upon the Senate chamber. The senators who had been lukewarm in the matter were shamed for themselves; those who had been charged with the execution of justice were shamed for the cause of popular government. If such things were possible in a government by the people and for the people and of the people, it was an indictment against the whole people.

During it all Clavering sat with unshaken calmness. Not by a glance out of his handsome, stern eyes nor the least variation of color in his clear and ruddy complexion did he indicate the smallest agitation. Not even the last clause, which recommended his expulsion from the Senate of the United States, and which every member of the committee signed, without a dissenting voice, had the power to move him from his cool composure.

When the reading was concluded, the chairman of the committee rose and made a few explanations of the report. He spoke in an agitated and broken voice. Before introducing the resolution of expulsion, he hesitated and looked toward Clavering. Clavering rose, and on being recognized by the chair, asked to be heard in a brief defence.

Although he had always been a hard worker in his committee-room, Clavering had not often got upon his feet to speak in the Senate chamber. As he had told Elizabeth months before, he always knew his limitations as a debater. Having been used to lording over men for many years, the courteous assumption that every senator is a wise man had never sat well on him. When he spoke he had always been listened to, because he always had something to say; but he had shown his usual good sense and judgment by not measuring himself with the giants of debate. To-day, however, he had nothing more to hope or fear from those grave men, whose scorn of him was swallowed up in the execution of justice upon him.

As he rose to speak, to many minds came back that old Homeric line, "As the passing leaves, so is the passing of men;" and this man was passing from life into civil death before their eyes. Clavering, in his beautifully clear and well-modulated voice, began his defence, if defence it could be called. He told briefly but impressively of his youthful struggles, of his lack of education, of the wild life of the West into which he was inducted early, of the disregard of written laws in the administration of the justice with which he was familiar, how the strong men ruled by virtue of their strength, how great enterprises were carried through by forces not understood or even known in old and settled communities. His story was like a book out of the "Odyssey." He described the effect of his operations in large sections of country, which made him hosts of friends and hosts of enemies. He subtly called attention by indirection to that unwritten law, noted by a British general in India, that there were in all partly civilized countries certain necessary and salutary rascalities, to be carried through by the strong and wise against the weak and foolish. Coming down to his own case, he made no appeal for mercy, and offered no plea in abatement. On the contrary, he became distinctly aggressive, and heaped ridicule upon the committee of elderly gentlemen sitting in their luxurious committee-room, passing judgment on the storm and stress of men and things as unknown to them as the inhabitants of another planet. His conclusion was a ringing defiance of his enemies, a promise of vengeance upon them, and a solemn declaration that he would return, rehabilitated, to the Senate of the United States, and every man who believed him guilty might count himself the everlasting enemy of James Clavering from that day forth.

When he sat down there was from the public galleries an involuntary burst of applause, which was instantly suppressed. Two or three women wept aloud; an aged senator attempted to rise from his seat, fell back, and was carried out half-fainting. There were a few minutes of nervous quiet and whispering, and then the final proceedings began. They were short and exquisitely painful. The resolution of expulsion was put, and received a three-fourths vote in its favor. Half a dozen senators in a group voted against the resolution, and a few others were absent or refrained from voting. Of the half-dozen senators who voted in Clavering's favor, some voted in a spirit of sheer perversity, and the rest by absolute stupidity. When the result was declared amid a deathlike silence, Clavering rose and, making a low bow toward the senators who had voted for him, left his seat and went toward the aisle. As he reached it he turned to the chair and made another bow, full of dignity and respect; and then, without the least flurry or discomposure, retired from the Senate chamber which it had been the summit of his lifelong ambition to enter and of which he was never again to cross the threshold. He was to see no more service of the great Demos. But not Alcibiades, when he called the Athenians a pack of dogs, looked more sincerely contemptuous than did James Clavering of the United States Senate when, a disgraced and branded man, he walked out of the Senate chamber.

Chapter Eighteen

In the first week of April Richard Baskerville and Anne Clavering were married, in the little Iowa town where Mrs. Clavering's family lived and where Anne had remained since her mother's death. The wedding took place at Mr. Joshua Hicks's house, one of the best in the town.

Mr. Hicks was Anne's uncle by marriage, a leading merchant in the place; and a better man or a better citizen could not be found in the state of Iowa. He wore ready-made clothes, weighed out sugar and tea and sold calico by the yard, was a person of considerable wit and intelligence, and had a lofty self-respect which put him at ease in every society. His wife was a younger, better-looking, and better-educated woman than Mrs. Clavering, and as good as that poor woman had been. Their sons and daughters were ornaments of the high school, had mapped out careers for themselves, but meantime treated their parents with affectionate deference. In their drawing-room, called a front parlor, furnished in red plush and with chromos on the walls, Anne Clavering was made the wife of Richard Baskerville, the descendant of the oldest landed aristocracy in Maryland and Virginia. Clavering himself had said he would be present, but at the last minute telegraphed that he would be unable to come, having been suddenly called to Washington. He sent Anne a handsome cheque as a wedding gift. Élise and Lydia, who had spent the intervening time between their mother's funeral and their sister's marriage in shopping in Chicago and preparing for a precipitate trip to Europe, returned to the little town and remained over a train in order to be present at the wedding. Baskerville would have been glad if they had decided to stay away. Reginald Clavering gave his sister away.

It was the plainest and simplest wedding imaginable. The bride wore a white muslin, made by the village dressmaker. The bridegroom arrived on foot from the village tavern, where he had been staying. They began their wedding tour by driving away in the Hicks family surrey to another little country village seven miles off. It was a golden April afternoon, with an aroma of spring in the air; and the fields and orchards echoed with songs of birds—it was their mating-time. Mr. Hicks's hired man, who drove the married lovers to their destination, where they spent their honeymoon, declared he had never seen a bride and bridegroom so little spoony. He had in truth, although he knew it not, never seen a bride and bridegroom who loved each other so much.

Clavering's call to Washington, which prevented him from attending his daughter's wedding, in reality consisted of a few lines from Elizabeth Darrell. After that March day in the Senate chamber, Elizabeth fell into a settled listlessness. She felt herself obliged to marry Clavering eventually, as the only way out of an intolerable position; and this listlessness from which she suffered always falls upon those who succumb to what is reckoned as irrevocable fate. The spring was in its full splendor, and the town was beautiful in all its glory of green trees and emerald grass, and great clumps of flowering shrubs and sweet-scented hyacinths and crocuses and tulips. No city in the world has in it so much sylvan beauty as Washington, and in the spring it is a place of enchanting verdure. All this awakening of the spring made Elizabeth Darrell only the more sad, the more dispirited. The old, old feeling came upon her of the dissonance of nature and man—the world beautiful, and man despairing.

Reading, her sole resource, no longer amused her. It was a solace she had tried, and it had failed her; so she read no more, nor thought, nor worked, nor did anything but quietly endure. She affected cheerfulness when she met her father in the afternoons, and General Brandon, whom a child could deceive, thought how improved in spirits she had grown since the autumn. The General's confidence in Clavering continued quite unshaken, and he proclaimed solemnly that no man in public life, since the foundation of the government, had been so hounded and persecuted as "that high-toned gentleman, sir, ex-Senator Clavering."

Next to the thought of marrying Clavering, the most heart-breaking thing to Elizabeth was the memory of the rash letter she had written to Hugh Pelham. The only mitigation of this was that he would not get it for many months, perhaps never. Her cheeks burned at every recollection of it. The month had passed away at the end of which McBean had promised to appear, but so far she had heard and seen nothing more of him. She felt sure, however, that McBean had not forgotten her, and she looked for him daily. Then she must ask Clavering for money, and that would settle her fate.

One soft spring night she sat at the open window of the drawing-room, looking out on the quiet street, where the great Clavering house loomed dark and silent and deserted. There was no light in the drawing-room where Elizabeth sat, but a gas-jet in the hall cast a flame of yellow radiance in at the doorway. Elizabeth sat in the shadow and the silence. Suddenly a peremptory ring was heard at the bell, and in a minute or two Serena entered the room and handed Elizabeth a white envelope with a telegram in it.

Elizabeth had more than the usual feminine dread of a telegraphic despatch, and she held the envelope in her hand for ten minutes before she could summon courage to open it. Only Clavering or McBean could be telegraphing her, and to hear from either meant a stab. At last she forced herself to tear the envelope open. It was a cablegram from London, and read:—

"Your letter just received. Am sailing for America next Saturday. You must not, shall not, marry Clavering. Why did you not write me before?

HUGH PELHAM."

Serena, who dreaded telegrams, went back to her own regions. Presently she returned and looked in the drawing-room door at Elizabeth. She was still sitting by the open window in the half darkness, in the same position in which she had been half an hour before. The colored woman, who knew and had known all the time that Elizabeth was unhappy, went away and was troubled in mind. Half an hour later she returned. Elizabeth had changed her position slightly. She was resting her elbows on the window-sill, and her face was buried in her hands.

"Miss 'Liz'beth," said Serena, in her soft voice, and laying a hard, honest, sympathetic black hand on Elizabeth's shoulder, "fur de Lord's sake, doan' 'stress yo'sef so. Doan' yo' marry dat Clavering man, nor any 'urr man, ef you doan' want to. Me and de Gin'l will teck keer on you. Doan' yo' trouble 'bout nothin' 't all, honey."

"Oh, Serena," cried Elizabeth, raising a pale, glorified, serene face and throwing her arms around Serena's black neck, "I am the happiest person in the world! He is coming! He will start day after to-morrow. Oh, Serena, I am not distressed, I am not frightened any more!"

"'Tain' dat Clavering man!" answered Serena. She alone of the whole world had suspected Clavering's intentions.

"No, no, no! It is another man—the man I—" Elizabeth, without finishing the sentence, slipped out of Serena's arms, upstairs to her own room, to be alone with her happiness.

Although she had heard Clavering's name spoken, it was near midnight before she really gave him a thought. Then she wrote him a few lines, very humble, very apologetic; but no man of sense on earth could fail to know, on reading them, that the woman who wrote them was fixed in her resolution not to marry him. And as in the case of the former letter, she watched for the passing postman in the early morning and dropped the letter at his feet.

She summoned up courage to tell her father next day that Pelham was coming. "And I am sure," she said, blushing and faltering, "all will be right between us, and he will explain all that seemed unkind in his conduct to me."

General Brandon was sure of it, too, just as he was sure everybody meant to do right on all occasions, and was as pleased at the notion of rehabilitating Pelham as if somebody had left him a block of stock in the Standard Oil Company.

Elizabeth scarcely knew how the next week passed, so great was her exaltation. It is said that the highest form of pleasure is release from pain. She had that, and other joys besides. It was to her as if the earth had at last recovered its balance, with Pelham once more her friend. She did not dare to whisper anything more, even to herself. And every day brought her nearer to that hour—that poignant hour—when she should see Pelham once more as he had always been to her. She scanned the newspapers, and found what steamers sailed on the Saturday. She guessed by which one Pelham would sail. She watched out eagerly when they should be reported, and the morning and afternoon papers were in her hands by the time they were left at the door.

On the Saturday afternoon, which was warm and summer-like, Elizabeth was watching at the window for the afternoon newspaper—the morning newspaper had not chronicled the arrival of any of the Saturday steamers. When the negro newsboy threw it on the doorway, she ran out, and in her eagerness stood bareheaded on the steps, looking for the names of the incoming steamers. She found them—all the Saturday steamers had arrived to the day, and at an early hour. And Hugh Pelham might come at any moment! The thought brought the red blood to her cheeks and a quivering smile to her lips.

She looked down the street, under an archway of green, where played a fountain in a little open space, with brilliant tulip beds. The avenue into which the street debouched was gay with carriages and autos and merry, well-dressed girls and men, tripping along by twos and threes. As she gazed toward it, a hansom clattered up and in it sat Clavering. His arrival was so sudden that he could not but note the change in Elizabeth. He had thought on his first glance that he had never seen her look so youthful and so handsome. She had in truth regained much of her lost beauty, and when she saw him and recognized him, the pallor, the shame, the repulsion, in her face were eloquent. She drew back from him involuntarily, and her greeting, although gentle, did not conceal her feelings in the least.

As usual, Clavering appeared to be in the pink of condition. The crisis through which he had lately passed, the shock of the disappointment contained in Elizabeth's letter, his four days of hard travel, had left no mark upon him. He was a strong man in physique as well as in will. Elizabeth showed great embarrassment, but Clavering met her without the least awkwardness. As soon as they were alone in the drawing-room, cool and darkened from the too ardent sun, Clavering came to the point.

"I was, of course, astounded to receive your letter," he said. "I was on my ranch. I had just arrived, and was sitting down to supper when the mail was brought from the post-office twenty miles away. I found if I left at once I could make the midnight train, and that would give me fast connections all the way through. So, when I had finished my supper—it took me just twenty minutes—you know a ranchman's supper isn't a function, so to speak—I got on horseback and rode nearly thirty miles in four hours and a half. I had been riding all day, too. So you see I'm a very determined lover. This is my first love, you know,—the first like this, I mean,—and I couldn't afford to throw it away."

He was smiling now. The idea that the slim woman, dressed in black, sitting before him, with the red and white coming and going in her cheeks, could seriously resist him really seemed preposterous to him. Elizabeth remained silent, and Clavering knew that silence in a woman is momentous. As she made no reply he said, after a long pause, "And how about that other man?"

Elizabeth had said no word in her letter about any one else, and started at Clavering's words. "I—I—" She could get no farther. It was in the beginning only a shrewd surmise of Clavering's, but Elizabeth's faltering words and shrinking manner had confirmed it.

"I knew, of course, another man had turned up; that's why I came post-haste," coolly remarked Clavering. "Now tell me all about him."

Elizabeth was forced to answer. "It is—there was—my husband's cousin, Major Pelham."

"Oh, yes; the fellow that persecuted you after your husband's death. He, however, is hardly the man to interfere with me."

"I—I don't understand it quite. I thought he knew all that was being done. But I had a cablegram from him."

"You must have written to him."

"Yes."

"Before or after you wrote me?"

"Before. And when I got his reply by cable I wrote you."

"I see. You prefer to marry him?"

"Major Pelham has not asked me to marry him," replied Elizabeth, with dignity.

"But he will. Elizabeth, you are promised to me. I told you I loved you—not in the flowery style of a young loon, but of a man who has worked and thought and fought and seen enough to make him know his own mind. Of course I can't coerce you, but the man who gets you away from me may look out for himself. See, the habits of a man's early life and thought never leave him. My first instinct has always been to take care of my own, and I was bred and made my mark in a country where neither wife-stealing nor sweetheart-stealing is permitted. Sometimes wives and sweethearts were stolen, but it was a dangerous business. Oh, I don't mean to use a gun; that went out twenty-five years ago. But there are many ways of ruining a man—and a woman, too."

He spoke quite pleasantly, sitting close to Elizabeth and holding his crape-covered hat in his hand. There was nothing to indicate vengeance in Clavering's easy, graceful manner and charming voice, but Elizabeth shuddered at the truth of what his speech might mean.

"Now tell me how you feel toward this man Pelham?"

"Major Pelham was my best friend during all my married life. I could not understand his conduct to me after my husband's death. One night lately I felt the impulse to write to him—shall I tell you everything?"

"Yes." Clavering was all calm attention then.

"It was the night after our last interview. It come over me that—that I would rather die than marry you. Yes, I mean what I say. I didn't mean to kill myself. Oh, no! But I would rather have been killed than married to you."

Clavering's ruddy face grew pale. He got up, walked about the room, and sat down again, still close to Elizabeth. He saw she did not mean to be intentionally cruel, but was striving earnestly to tell him the whole truth.

"I have often heard of your power over other men, and I am sure you have great power over women too; for I felt in some way obliged to marry you unless some one came in to help me. And then I thought of Hugh Pelham, and I thought it would be at least two or three months before he got my letter; but he was evidently in London, and he cabled back. I feel sure he reached New York early this morning."

"And did that money you owed have anything to do with it?"

"Yes. It troubled me dreadfully."

"And for a paltry thousand or two you have broken your word to me, broken it when I needed most of all your faith in me?"

"It was not the money wholly."

"It was also that I had lost my seat in the Senate of the United States?"

"Not altogether that; but I knew—I knew—I was at the Capitol that day."

"Pardon me, but you don't know. What does a woman know about such things? How do you know what it is for a man as strong as I am, as mature as I am, and with such a history as I have, to love? Yes, by God, to love for the first time. What does a woman's pale reflection of passion know of the love of a man like me? I know all about life and death too. I have been a half-dozen times within six inches of a bullet that was extremely likely to be shot into my brain. I have felt the whir of a knife, that sometimes got planted in me, but never quite far enough to kill me. I have signed my name fifty times to things that meant either millions of dollars to me or state's prison. These are only a few of the things that I know all about, but I tell you, Elizabeth Darrell, that they all seem like milk and water compared with what I feel for you. Do you know that the first time I saw you, when you were a mere slip of a girl, that night I crushed your little pearl heart under my foot, I felt a strange, even a superstitious interest in you? I never forgot you; and the first moment I saw you that Sunday afternoon, last November, something came over me which made everything in the world seem small, beside the thought of winning you. I have gone through a good deal since, but nothing has really mattered to me except you." Clavering stopped. His voice, always earnest, had remained calm and even low.

Elizabeth was trembling from head to foot. Her resolution never to marry Clavering was not shaken in the least, or even touched, but like a child who has heedlessly set the torch to a powder magazine, she was appalled at her own work. She remained silent—what was there for her to say? And then she saw a figure pass the bowed shutters, making a shadow flit across the floor; and it was the shadow of Hugh Pelham. She sprang to her feet, a new light in her eyes which Clavering had never seen before. Clavering was for an instant as completely forgotten as if he had never been. He saw his fate in that look, that action. He rose, too, and the next moment Hugh Pelham walked into the room. He was visibly older, more weather-beaten, than he had been two years before, and, although ten years Clavering's junior, he looked quite the same age. Evil-doing is very often good for the physical man and well-doing bad for the physical man. The two men instinctively recognized each other at the first glance, and hated each other instantly with a mortal hatred. Elizabeth stood next Pelham. She had given him her hand without a word, and he held it firmly.

Clavering turned to Elizabeth and said: "When can I see you again? Pray make it as soon as possible. That much I can ask, after what has passed between us."

"Excuse me," said Pelham, politely, "but I don't think Mrs. Darrell can see you again."

A dull red showed under Clavering's skin, and a slight tremor shook his massive figure. It was a situation hard for any man to bear, and almost intolerable to James Clavering. He said the only thing possible under the circumstances. "I must decline to accept your decision. It rests with Mrs. Darrell."

Elizabeth turned to Major Pelham. "Will you kindly leave me with Mr. Clavering for a moment? It is his right, and later I will explain all to you."

Pelham, with a bow, walked out of the drawing-room, and, opening the street door, gazed upon the great pile of stone which the Claverings had lately inhabited. Clavering, when he and Elizabeth were alone, said at once:—

"I know how it is; I saw it in your face and eyes when the other man came. I am not one likely to ask for quarter or give quarter. I accept my fate as I accepted my expulsion from the Senate and the loss of many millions of dollars. There are in the world compensations to me for the other things. For the loss of you there is no compensation. It is my first and my last chance of leading a better life, for I swear to you, Elizabeth, I meant to lead a better life if you had married me. But now—it doesn't matter in the least. I was born a hundred years too late; then I should have married you by force. I would have given my seat in the Senate to have seen such a look in your eyes when I came in as I saw when the other man came. Good-by, Elizabeth."

Elizabeth gave him her hand. In all their acquaintance this was the first glimpse, the first suspicion, she had had that anything like a noble and uplifting love existed in Clavering; but he, this man, smirched all over, a bad husband, a bad father, who knew no truth nor honesty in his dealings with men or other women, loved once, truly, and at the moment of losing everything else he lost the only thing worthy the name of love which he had ever known in his whole life. He held Elizabeth's hand in his; he had never so much as kissed it. He raised it to his lips, but Elizabeth drawing back with a violent and undisguised repulsion, he at once dropped it again. He looked at her for a full minute, compelling her against her will to meet his gaze, and then, turning, walked out of the house. On the steps outside he passed Pelham. Neither man spoke.

Pelham went into the drawing-room, where Elizabeth stood, pale and trembling. As he closed the door after him she said in an indescribable voice, "He never kissed me—he never so much as kissed my hand."

"I don't think you would ever have married him in any event, Elizabeth," replied Pelham, gently. "But let us not speak of him. I came home as soon as I could—I had not had any news from England after I was well in the interior of Africa. I knew nothing of what had been done until I got your letter. I was coming to you, anyway—your year of widowhood was over. Oh, Elizabeth, how could you misjudge me as you did?"

Clavering found himself in the largest room of the large suite of rooms he occupied at the most expensive hotel in Washington. The April sun was just setting, and it flamed upon a huge mirror directly opposite the luxurious chair in which he sat. He looked at his own image reflected full length in the glass. It seemed to be moving, to be surrounded by other figures. He saw them well—painted and bedizened women, some of them loaded with jewels and with coronets on their heads. Their faces were beautiful and engaging and made his pulses leap, and then suddenly these faces changed into those of vultures with bloody beaks and hungry eyes. Then there were men, some in court dress and with orders sparkling on their breasts. All of them had a foreign look, they spoke a language he only half understood; and they too changed into hungry, distorted figures which he knew were the shapes of vampires and harpies. They smiled upon him and fawned upon him, and he saw himself smiling back, rather pleased, it appeared. Sometimes he and this crowd were moving through splendid rooms; there were balls and dinners going on, and he could hear the clash and rhythm of orchestras. Again, they were in dismal business offices, or in raging crowds upon Continental bourses. At first he was always surrounded, and it seemed as if he were losing something all the time.

Gradually the men and women about him no longer fawned upon him. They were familiar with him; then they jeered him; and presently they menaced him. They tried to strangle him, to rob him, and he had lost something— money or power or capacity, or perhaps all three, and he could not defend himself. And they grew more and more foreign to him, he could not understand their language at all. They talked among themselves, and he did not know what they were saying. And after a while he grew helpless, and did not know where he was; and then he saw himself standing on a bridge at night, in a foreign city. There were many lights upon the bridge, which were reflected in the black and rushing river. He was about to throw himself into the river, when it suddenly came to him that it was cold and he was thinly clad and hungry. And then he knew that he was in a strange country, and it came to him that he would return to his own land, to a place where there was warmth and comfort and the strange thing he had lost would be awaiting him. But then he heard wolfish voices shrieking at him out of the darkness that he had no home, no country—that he would never again be warmed and fed, and invisible hands like lions' claws were clutching him and thrusting him into the dark waters, and he could only feebly resist them. There was a great mocking, reddish moon in the wild night sky and it reeled about and fell into an abyss of black clouds and then dropped into the blacker river.

And the stars were going out one by one, so that the heavens and the earth had a blackness of the blackest night.

This produced a kind of horror in him, which made him cry out—a loud cry, he thought it. But it was really low and half smothered. And to his amazement he was not in his room at the hotel, but standing in the doorway of his own house. It was night, and he heard a great clock inside his own house strike the hour—nine o'clock. He could not remember how or why he had got from his hotel to his deserted house. He saw the caretaker, an old hobgoblin of a negro, peer at him from a basement window, and he shrank behind the great stone pillars of the doorway. It was a warm, soft spring night, without a moon, but the purple floor of heaven glittered with palpitating stars. The street was always a quiet one; to-night it was so strangely still that he feared to move lest his footfall should sound too loud. And while he stood, dazed and hesitating within his doorway, he saw two figures come together down the street and stop at Elizabeth's house. One was Elizabeth, the other was the man she loved. The night was so warm that the house door was left open. Clavering watched the two figures mount the steps and go into the house. The man touched Elizabeth's arm in helping her up the steps. It was a simple, conventional thing, but Clavering saw revealed in it a love so deep, so constant, so passionately tender, that he thought he had never seen real love before. He turned away, to enter upon the fate that had been laid bare to him.

THE END

Milton Keynes UK
Ingram Content Group UK Ltd.
UKHW010708240424
441619UK00004B/374